THE DE

THE SLEER LED the ... snapping branches a... Langley and Lania ... Carew brought up the rear, picking his way with care and occasionally shuffling along on his backside when the drop became almost sheer.

He'd slipped the laser into his belt, to free his right hand, when something shot past his left ear and slapped into a tree trunk directly before him. He saw the trunk dissolve before his eyes, the whole process taking perhaps two seconds. He fell onto his back and rolled. In an instant his laser was in his right hand and he was firing up the incline. Whatever was following them had vanished. He yelled to the others, glanced over his shoulder down the hillside. There was no sign of Lania, Langley, Villic or the Sleer. Then he caught a glimpse of Lania as she took cover behind a tree and drew her weapon.

He saw a boulder to his right and rolled into its shelter. He scanned the vegetation cloaking the incline above him. All was still, quiet. Only his heart sounded, deafening in his ears. He peered over the rock, willing whatever it was to show itself. A Sleer, he guessed. Armed with an acid weapon? He glanced at the unfortunate tree. It was stripped down to its inner rings, the wood steaming. An acid weapon of some kind, then. Which, in the hands of a Sleer, was a combination to be feared.

Also by Eric Brown

NOVELS
Xenopath
Necropath
Cosmopath
Kéthani
Helix
New York Dreams
New York Blues
New York Nights
Penumbra
Engineman
Meridian Days
Guardians of the Phoenix

NOVELLAS
Starship Fall
Starship Summer
Revenge
The Extraordinary Voyage of Jules Verne
Approaching Omega
A Writer's Life

COLLECTIONS
Threshold Shift
The Fall of Tartarus
Deep Future
Parallax View (with Keith Brooke)
Blue Shifting
The Time-Lapsed Man

AS EDITOR
The Mammoth Book of New Jules Verne Adventures
(with Mike Ashley)

Eric
Brown

WEIRD SPACE
THE DEVIL'S NEBULA

ABADDON
BOOKS

W W W . A B A D D O N B O O K S . C O M

An Abaddon Books™ Publication
www.abaddonbooks.com
abaddon@rebellion.co.uk

First published in 2012 by Abaddon Books™,
Rebellion Intellectual Property Limited,
Riverside House, Osney Mead, Oxford, OX2 0ES, UK.

10 9 8 7 6 5 4 3 2

Editors: Jonathan Oliver & David Moore
Cover Art: Adam Tredowski
Design: Simon Parr & Luke Preece
Marketing and PR: Michael Molcher
Creative Director and CEO: Jason Kingsley
Chief Technical Officer: Chris Kingsley
Weird Space™ created by Eric Brown

ISBN: 978-1-78108-023-8

Printed in the US

For Josh, Bella and Esther

CHAPTER ONE

SHE KILLED THE creature on the third attempt.

Her first shot singed its hackles and fizzed off into the jungle canopy. Her second ploughed a bloody furrow through the meat of its shoulder, succeeding only in enraging the beast. The six-legged kreesh howled and slunk off into the undergrowth.

"Oh, very well done," Ed Carew said.

They crouched behind a spur of rock, Lania Takiomar cocking her head to follow the sound of trampled vegetation as the kreesh made a detour and came in from behind.

On her haunches, she swivelled. She was like some kind of primitive wild beast herself; a jaguar, perhaps, her small, compact body injection-moulded into the curved confines of her jet-black smartsuit.

She snapped, "If you could do any better..."

Carew smiled. That's what he liked about his pilot: she spoke her mind.

The third member of their party, Jed Neffard, cowered behind his captain. For an ex-convict who had sampled the hospitality of half a dozen prison planets in his thirty-odd years, he exhibited a surprising, and endearing, lack of courage.

They turned slowly as one, tracking the sound of the kreesh as it circled through the vegetation.

"I thought you said," Jed whined, "that Hesperides had no wild animals."

"It didn't," Carew said under his breath, "fifty years ago, when it was evacuated."

"So what happened?"

"My guess is that the kreesh escaped from a menagerie. Lania?"

Her smartsuit wasn't called a smartsuit for nothing. Carew liked to garner his information the old way, from screens – and preferably in a quiet library on some idyllic backwater world – but he had to admit that there was no beating a smartsuit for getting information on the fly.

It was Lania who, ten minutes ago on first sighting the creature, had accessed her suit's memory cache and identified it as a kreesh. Now she said, "You're right. Kreesh aren't native to Hesperides. There was a zoo on the outskirts of Valderido. Probably got out of there."

"Is there anything else you aren't telling us about this place?" Jed asked.

Carew smiled, to mask his guilt. There was one other piece of information he'd thought it prudent not to tell his crew, but now was not the right time to come clean.

"We'll be fine, Jed," Carew reassured the engineer. "Trust in Lania's markswomanship."

Staring intently ahead, Lania hissed between gritted teeth, "If that's supposed to be funny, Ed, stow it."

"Not funny, Lania. Merely ironic."

He glanced at Jed, who was ogling the way Lania's curves moved beneath the figure-hugging smartsuit. Lania crouched, laser rifle solid against her right shoulder, a study in concentration.

A rustle sounded directly in front of the cowering trio, and a moment later the beast leapt at them from the jungle. Lania fired. Jed yelled. Carew felt his heart leap. Before he knew it, half a tonne of dead meat slammed to the ground before them. The stink of part-cooked flesh and gamey body odour wafted their way in a sickening miasma.

Lania stood up, blew across the muzzle of her weapon with a hollow piping note, and lodged a foot on the haunch of the carcass. "One for the album, Ed?"

Carew stood and examined the animal, working to maintain his characteristic reserve. "Well done, Lania. My word, but it certainly is an ugly beast."

Evolution had primed the kreesh well in the dental department. Its face was all teeth, a circle of sickle barbs below two eyestalks.

Lania frowned as she accessed her suit's memory. "A native of Deneb III. Used by the natives there as a hunting animal. It was listed as an endangered species twenty years ago and its captivity proscribed by the Terran Zoological Organisation."

Carew said, "There must be others in the area. What say we round them up and transport them to the nearest breeding centre? They must be worth millions."

Lania gave him an uncertain look.

Carew smiled. "I'm joking. We came here to locate an *objet d' art*, not wild animals."

Jed gave a relieved laugh. "For a second, there…"

"How long have you known me, both of you? Five years, Jed? Ten, Lania? When will you come to realise that I *do* have a sense of humour?"

"That's the thing, Ed. You really don't."

"I'm offended, Lania. Now, if you've finished posing, shall we continue?"

He stepped gingerly over the corpse of the kreesh and led the way through the jungle.

ONE HOUR LATER, Jed said, "How far are we from Valderido?"

"As the cyber-assisted crow flies," Lania said, "about an hour. Through this salad, it's going to take us about two."

The haywire tangle of ferns and lianas was proving no barrier to their progress. Carew simply adjusted the setting of his laser and burned a path through the undergrowth. The terrain was a little uneven, taxing muscles accustomed to light exercise aboard his ship, *The Paradoxical Poet*, but he kept the pace at a little above a leisurely stroll. Days were long on Hesperides – the planet turned slowly on its axis, so that a day lasted over seventy standard hours – and they had landed just after dawn.

He had wanted to come down closer to the capital city, but after consultation with his crew had elected to land ten kilometres south of Valderido. On the way to Hesperides, Lania had reported picking up the ion trail of another ship; she'd had no idea how old the trail was, and even though there was no visual sign of a Vetch ship in the area, they'd decided to play it safe. The Vetch were vigilant in their patrols of their territory, and the capital city of the once-thriving human colony would be the obvious place for a salvage vessel to make landfall. Carew suspected that the ship was long gone, but he was taking no chances.

He led the way through a steaming tunnel of his own making, breathing shallowly so as not to inhale the smoke from the burning vegetation. Jed followed, trotting at his heels, and Lania brought up the rear, ever ready to repel the next attack.

The haunting calls of unseen wildlife bassooned through the sultry air, counterpointed by the piccolo notes of tiny birds darting through the slanting sunlight in riotous profusion. Hesperides was a world returned to bounteous nature, now that humankind had fled.

"Thirty thousand?" Jed asked.

Carew blasted a clear cone through the jungle. "Approximately."

"Thirty thousand for *each* of us?"

"That's the agreement."

"If," Jed went on, "the dealer is as good as his word."

Carew stepped over a charred log. "I've no reason to doubt his honesty, Jed. I have worked with him before."

"And if," Lania called from the rear, as pessimistic as ever, "*if* we find the thing."

Carew said, "We will. Of that I have no doubt. The museum was cleared of all that was considered valuable in the hours before the start of the evacuation."

"And the statuette wasn't considered valuable?" Lania asked.

"They had limited time in which to make their choices. According to the dealer, the museum's director and his staff tore through the place and crated up only about half their holdings."

And the tiny alien statuette, made by the race native to Hesperides but extinct for millions of years, had been left. The dealer, a colonist on Hesperides at the time of the forced evacuation, had spent many a childhood weekend staring at the figurine, his imagination fired by its alien makers, who had long since ceased to exist.

And now he was prepared to pay Carew and his crew a total of one hundred thousand units if they could secure the statuette and bring it to him.

He had assessed the dangers, considered the rewards, and bargained the dealer up from fifty thousand units to a hundred thousand. The stretch of space demarcating Vetch space from human space was long indeed – some thirty light years, in total – and the Vetch had only so many ships with which to patrol the border.

In his thirty years of space-roving, Carew had undertaken more dangerous missions.

Jed had taken some cajoling, though. Thirty thousand units had proved persuasive enough, in the end.

"I'll spend a month on the pleasure planet of Darby's Landfall," Jed said now. "I'll eat the finest food and make love to the most expensive courtesans."

Lania sneered. "The most expensive courtesans wouldn't touch you with remote somaforms, Jed."

"Then I'll make do with the not quite as expensive," the engineer replied, "and save money."

"You'll end up with the cheapest, most diseased whores on the planet and consider yourself lucky," Lania laughed.

"Or even," Jed mused, "I'll pleasure myself in the virtual palaces. I've heard the sex is just as lifelike."

"You're a sad, sad man, Jed Neffard," Lania sighed.

Carew smirked as he listened to his faithful crew. He was delighted they rubbed along so well.

"And you, Captain?" Jed asked.

He had promised his crew a month's leave on the successful completion of the mission. He imagined he'd be in need of a retreat after Hesperides, somewhere quiet and restful after the memories the evacuated planet would no doubt provoke.

"I'll be going to the phrontistery at Yann," he said.

"Never heard of the place," Jed admitted. "What's a phron... phron – ?"

Lania said, "Phrontistery. The area in a monastery used for contemplation. What do you intend to contemplate?" she mocked.

Ed smiled. "Life, death, existence, non-existence. The arbitrary nature of the universe; the chaos, the order..."

Jed grunted.

Lania said, "Why bother, Ed? I mean, that way lies madness. Why not just live for the minute and leave the thinking to the philosophers?"

Because to live for the minute, he thought, does not bring me the remotest satisfaction. He said, "Each to his own, Lania. Each to his own."

He pressed the stud of his laser and the tangle of vegetation before him disintegrated. This time, instead of the blast revealing a further expanse of packed undergrowth, he found himself staring at a vast panoramic view.

Cautiously, he picked his way over the charred ground and halted. Jed was beside him, then Lania. She whistled.

They were standing on the edge of an escarpment, which dropped precipitously for a hundred metres. Beside them, the boles of trees thrust up into the sunlight. He imagined that the three of them would look like ants on the edge of the drop, between the rocky precipice and the sprouting trees.

He stared out and his breath caught. There, perhaps a kilometre distant, was what once had been the planet's proud capital city. Now it resembled an architect's scale model of a city, but one which had been left in a great Petri dish and overrun by fungus.

Lania pointed. "Look," she said.

She was not pointing to the city, but the far horizon and what lay above it.

The sun was still rising slowly behind them, and ahead the sky was a twilit indigo expanse, scattered with a million tight-packed stars. Jed laughed. "It's beautiful."

"But how can something so beautiful," Lania said, "harbour a race so evil?"

"The Vetch aren't evil," Carew said. "They're just acting out a hardwired biological imperative, one we don't understand." He wondered, even as he spoke the words, if he really believed them.

Lania turned to him, her expression harshly incredulous. "Not evil? Was what they did on Palladine not evil? What they did on Tourmaline and Santiago? They razed those planets. They killed millions of innocent men, women and children. And that wasn't evil? I didn't have you down as a Vetch-lover, Ed."

He turned away from her, staring at the array of far stars, and let his anger flare and subside. Now was not the time or place – if there ever would be a time and a place – to lecture Lania on the Vetch and what the alien race had done, fifty years ago. She was mouthing cheap prejudice and ignorance common across the human Expansion; it would be hard to correct that prejudice with a lecture now. They had more pressing matters to hand.

But she said, "Well?"

He turned to her. "Was the kreesh that attacked us evil, Lania?"

She blinked. "What?" She laughed. "It was an *animal*, Ed. A beast. It didn't know the difference between right and wrong. It was acting out of primitive drives, to attack, to defend its territory, to eat. The Vetch are a civilised race. They should have known better."

"They're aliens. How can you judge aliens by our own standards? Our concepts of right and wrong, good and evil, are arbitrary when applied to alien races. We should not judge."

She rattled a noise in her throat, a disgusted *achh* and strode off to stare down the precipice.

The problem was that Carew knew exactly what she meant, how she felt. He often felt the same himself. In his case, however, he was entitled to these feelings. He alone among them was entitled to pass such judgements. Even if the rationalist in him knew them to be wrong.

Jed hopped about beside Carew, playing the fool. He disliked it when Lania and Carew had their frequent spats. He was like a child whose certainties were undercut by the arguments of his parents.

He said now, "I don't know about good or evil, Captain, but I know they certainly look damned ugly."

Carew smiled and refrained from saying that even beauty was arbitrary. "Have you seen one, Jed?"

"Only in virt-houses. Ugly creatures! Like dogs, but with mashed-up faces. And they stink!"

Carew said, "Oh, they have olfactory virt-houses now, do they?"

Jed's round pudding of a face looked blank. "What?"

"You smelled a Vetch in a virt-house?"

"No, but this guy in a bar on Hollister told me so. Like meat gone rotten, he said."

Not like meat gone rotten, Carew thought, but like the sickly sweet smell of a flower in bloom, cut and left to die in the sun. A stench that, once smelled, seemed to live in one's senses for ever.

Lania returned from along the precipice. "Well," she said, "*aren't* they ugly? I've always thought they looked pretty damned ugly."

Carew said, "And you, with your scraped back hair and flawless coffee complexion, your soft curves; you'd seem pretty hideous to a Vetch, Lania."

She stared at him. He stared her down and she gave in and turned, muttering something to herself.

"So," Jed said, "how the hell are we going to get down this cliff-face?"

Lania bowed her head and sub-vocalised something to her suit. She stared at her forearm, where a map suddenly appeared on the material.

She pointed. "A couple of hundred metres west... there's a track cut into the precipice."

Carew brushed past her and released a cone of destruction into the foliage at the edge of the escarpment. He led the way through the smouldering corridor until they came to a dip in the land, then blasted away the cover of undergrowth to reveal a track sloping down the cliff-face.

He burned the blockage of undergrowth and they moved forward.

It took thirty minutes to reach the foot of the escarpment, where Carew called a halt. He looked up. The sheer façade of the escarpment seemed to go on for ever, terminating in a fringe of shaggy jungle which was incandescent now with the light of the rising sun.

He stared at the far horizon. The sky was paling, the stars of Vetch space fading as he watched.

The outskirts of the deserted city of Valderido stood perhaps two kilometres distant. The jungle down here was not as dense as that on the plateau above: the going from now on would be considerably easier.

They had left the ship three hours ago and Carew was hungry and thirsty. He called a break and they sat side by side in the shade of a leaning tree and broke out their water canteens.

Lania said at last, "Sorry if I touched a nerve back there."

He smiled; even her apologies were confrontations. "Apology accepted." He took a long swallow of ice-cold water.

"Why so touchy, though?"

He shrugged the question off. "You know me. Always playing Devil's advocate."

Lania grunted, "You intellectual types. Give me lunks like Jed, any day."

The engineer wiped his thick lips on his sleeve. "That a promise, Lania?"

"In your dreams, dwarf," Lania said.

Jed shrugged and tipped more water onto his face.

Lania commanded her smartsuit to project a map of the city into the air before them. She plucked a stalk of grass from the ground and indicated the centre of the map. "The museum's here, in this square. It's pretty central. We simply follow the main highway into the city and turn off here. Another hour and we'll be there."

Carew stared through the map at the silhouette of the city itself, or rather what remained of it: a cluster of low buildings furred by overgrowth, like a block graph denoting the rise and fall of some notional fortune. He wondered what feelings might hijack him on the journey into the city, what reminders of a once-thriving community might stir his own memories of the planet where he'd spent his childhood.

He unsealed a tray of food and ate slowly, savouring the salad and protein slabs. Lania watched him as she chewed on her biltong. She'd been incredulous a decade ago when she discovered he was vegetarian: another philosophy, he thought, beyond the limited remit of her experience.

They rested up for a further hour, then stowed their water bottles and litter in their backpacks and set off again towards the city.

There was only limited canopy cover here, and for long stretches they were forced to walk in the full glare of the rising sun. The temperature climbed steadily, reaching thirty-five Celsius as they came to the first vine-entombed building on the outskirts of the city.

They found a highway overgrown with low bindweed and trudged along in the shadows of buildings to their right.

There was something beautiful, he had to admit, in the way nature had reclaimed the city, softening the harsh angles and embroidering the hidden façades with alien blooms. The flowers ranged from the tiny to the vast, from blooms the size of coins to others as huge as the blast-cones of a starship engine. A warm wind blew and the scent of the flowers wafted over them in heady, pollen-laden waves.

They passed down a narrow street between buildings like children's blocks covered in vines. A muffled silence filled the canyons. There was no birdsong or calls from other wildlife. It was as if nature itself were aware of the atrocity committed here, and the resulting silence was its eloquent comment.

Lania pointed to an intersection up ahead and they approached the corner and turned into the square where the museum was situated.

And, as one, they stopped in their tracks.

Later, Carew would look back at his reaction and wonder what had prevented him from moving in a bid to save himself. Shock, obviously: the sheer, unexpected shock of seeing there, in front of him, the very last thing he had expected to see in the square of a long-deserted city.

A Vetch patrol vessel.

CHAPTER TWO

CAREW FELT A strong hand grip his arm as Lania yanked him back around the corner. Even then, they weren't safe – they needed to put more distance between themselves and the alien ship. They scuttled frantically into the opening of an old store, clawing away at vines to gain entry.

In the cool, dark interior, he collapsed to the ground, gasping to catch his breath.

He expected a Vetch warrior to appear at any second.

Lania whispered, "Do you think they saw us?"

"No... no. They'd have sent someone." Even to his own ears, he sounded pathetically panicked, his voice tremulous.

"What do we do?" Jed whispered.

It was enough, at that moment, that they were still alive. He had no thought for the future, only for how disastrously events could have played out.

He gathered his wits and tried to consider Jed's very relevant question. "We sit tight. We don't move."

Lania and Jed nodded. The silence stretched.

At last Lania said, "It's as if they knew where we were heading."

In the half-light of the room, Carew stared at her shadowed face. She looked shocked. He said, "You mean, the museum?"

She nodded.

"No way," he said. "There's no way they could know that." He thought about it, rationalised the presence of the ship there. "It's one of the biggest squares in the city. The natural place a ship would come down." He considered the ion trail Lania had detected in orbit. "So they were up there, and recently. The chances are they detected us and waited 'til we landed."

Jed said, "Why? Why not just blast us to bits up there?"

Carew shrugged. "They wanted our ship?" He paused, something even more unpleasant occurring to him. They wanted *us*? But he didn't voice the thought out loud.

"The fact remains, they're out there and the chances are that they know we're here."

She sub-vocced, contacted the ship and nodded. "It's AOK. They haven't located the *Poet*."

Carew let out a relieved breath. "Thank fate we decided to come down in the jungle."

"Good thinking, boss," Jed laughed nervously.

"So what do we do," Lania asked. "Sit tight 'til they leave?"

Carew nodded. "That'd be safest."

Lania looked around the room. "Okay. But I'd be happier if I was somewhere with a vantage point. I'd like to see all the approaches to this place, in case the bastards come close. Can I take a look around?"

Carew thought about it. She knew how to look after herself. He had no idea where she'd gained military training – he'd never felt the need to enquire too closely – but she could handle herself as well as any combat soldier he'd met. He nodded.

She pointed across the room to a staircase. "I'll see where that leads."

"We'll sit tight here," Carew said. "No radio communications, okay?"

Lania smiled and punched his shoulder. "No need to tell me that, fool."

She took off like a cat and disappeared silently into the shadows.

Carew looked at Jed. His big face was drenched in sweat. "Try not to worry, Jed. We've been in tough situations before now."

"But we've never had Vetch warriors breathing down our necks," Jed said. He paused, then went on, "What will they do to us, if they find us?"

Summary execution and confiscation of all hardware... But Carew wasn't about to tell his engineer that. He shook his head. "Not applicable. They won't find us."

Jed looked up at his captain, something almost puppy-like in his expression of trust.

"Remember Altair?" Jed laughed.

Carew smiled at the recollection. That had been almost five years ago, just after Jed had signed aboard the *Poet*. They'd had word that a liner travelling from Mars to Betelgeuse II, a hundred years earlier, had fallen foul of a meteor storm just off Altair; the wreck was still there, awaiting salvage. Carew had taken the *Poet* in for a swift reconnaissance and found the spavined ship becalmed. They'd also discovered, on boarding the ship, that it had been taken over by a ferocious race of crab-like aliens who took exception to their domicile being invaded.

Carew had learned something about his crew then, as they beat a retreat back to their ship limpeted onto the skin of the liner.

One, that Jed Neffard, despite being an ex-small-time-crook, and although he was a fine engineer, was not to be relied on in a skirmish. In a flight or fight situation, Jed had self-preservation down to a fine art: he always ran.

Two, that Lania Takiomar, despite standing five feet nothing and being as slim as a wand, was a tenacious fighter who never let a situation, no matter how tough, get her down. Although Carew himself had been far from useless in the fire-fight, it had been Lania who had laid down covering fire and picked off the advancing crabs, one by one, before hauling the men back to the safety of the *Poet*.

Jed laughed. "Lania saved us then, boss," he said, something like hero-worship in his voice.

"As I recall," Carew said, "you redeemed yourself a little later."

Jed shrugged modestly.

Lania had been all for pushing off back into the void and leaving the ship to languish among the asteroids, but Jed had had an idea.

If they could get rid of the hostile crabs, then they'd be able to attach grapples to the wreck and haul it through the void to the scrap-station at Antares VII.

Lania had grunted, "So you're going to volunteer to go back in there and flush the crabs out single-handedly, Jed?"

"No need," he'd replied. "The crabs are in the cargo hold, right? And the hold is pressurised. So all we have to do is blow a hole right through the hold and the crabs'll be sucked out into space."

Carew had baulked at the idea of annihilating the extraterrestrial crabs, but Lania was ahead of him. She accessed her suit's memory and said, "Don't worry your conscience on that score, Ed. The Karyx are vacuum dwellers. They live in space. We'll just be dispossessing them of a temporary home."

So they had taken Jed's suggestion and blown two holes in the carapace of the hold and watched as a thousand tumbling crabs were sucked, cart-wheeling, into the star-lit vacuum.

Then they'd towed the wreck back to Antares, and Carew's confidence in his unlikely-looking crew of two had grown appreciably, not to mention his bank-balance.

"What's she doing up there?" Jed said now.

"Don't worry. She can handle herself."

"But it's been ten minutes, at least."

"I think we might have heard something if the Vetch had caught sight of her. Ah, speak of the Devil."

A sable shadow detached itself from the darkness at the rear of the room and padded across to them. "Okay," Lania whispered. "Come and look at this."

Jed followed her, Carew bringing up the rear. They climbed a flight of concrete stairs to an upper-storey room, lit by errant shafts of sunlight filtering through a vine-shrouded window.

Lania indicated a door leading to to another flight of steps. They climbed and emerged a few moments later onto the flat rooftop, then crept through the vegetation and paused, side by side, at the edge of the building, concealed by the lolling leaves of a giant fern. Lania hunkered down and carefully back-handed a leaf aside. "There," she whispered.

They had a perfect view of the square and the Vetch patrol vessel squatting before the jungle-covered triangle of the museum building. The ship looked like a bloated black-and-yellow wasp, twice the size of the *Poet*.

And then Carew saw a Vetch warrior for only the second time in his life and, in spite of himself, he experienced a sudden flare of hatred.

The alien emerged from the entrance of the museum and crossed to the ship. The Vetch was perhaps eight feet tall, its legs disproportionately long, its body compacted. But it was its head that marked it as grotesquely alien. Hairless and mottled pink, it had the wattled appearance of something haemorrhoidal: a more charitable comparison, Carew thought, was to an albino hound-dog after a bloody collision with a brick wall.

Either way, it was hideous.

The sight of it brought back a slew of unwanted memories, and Carew fought to suppress them.

Jed said, "What are they doing?"

"They've been at it ever since I got up here," Lania said.

Only then did Carew see that the first Vetch was merely the vanguard: it was leading other aliens from the museum. A dozen Vetch carried boxes and cases across the square and filed aboard their ship.

"What the hell?" he said.

"Raiding the place for artefacts," Lania murmured.

"I didn't have the Vetch down as aficionados of human history. Can you make out what's in those cases?"

Lania pulled something from the material of her suit, a transparent strip which she placed across her eyes. She tapped the end of the strip over her temple.

"It's hard to see. They're... I don't recognise anything... Weird, they seem to be scraps of metal, burnt and twisted. Not artefacts, as such. They're all the same, in every box and case; just scraps of wreckage."

"Wreckage?" Carew repeated, his interest aroused.

Lania shrugged. "That's what it looks like to me."

Carew wondered. The other reason he had brought his ship to Hesperides, quite apart from the retrieval of the alien statuette, was to investigate a story he'd heard from a reliable source not that long ago.

And now the Vetch were taking what might be starship wreckage from the museum.

Jed whispered, "Perhaps they don't know anything about us being here, boss. Perhaps they just came for that stuff."

"That would certainly let us off the hook," murmured Carew.

They watched for the next hour as the Vetch transferred their haul from the museum to the ship. Carew kept a lid on his revulsion, but it wasn't easy. Even the way the Vetch *moved* caused his flesh to crawl. Their legs were long and muscular and gave at the knee with a peculiar snap and fall: he could almost hear the cartilaginous grind as they bobbed along.

A little later Lania touched his arm and whispered, "I think they're leaving."

The last alien had climbed the ramp into the ship and the hatch dropped shut behind it. A second later the ship powered up with a crescendo of engines, lifted and turned on its axis. It seemed to hang for a second before climbing slowly from the square, clearing the triangular apex of the museum and heading north and out of sight.

Carew sat back and let out a long breath.

"So they don't know we're here!" Jed laughed.

"Perhaps," Carew said, "hard though I find it to believe."

Jed wiped a slick of sweat from his grinning face and said, "So what now?"

"Now we wait a while," Carew said. "We don't want the Vetch realising they've forgotten something, coming back, and finding us." He pulled the canteen from his backpack and drank.

Lania was watching him. She said, "Hell of a coincidence, hm?"

"Their being here just as we land?"

"And their raiding the museum like that," she said. "I don't like it."

He stared at her. "What's not to like? It's just a coincidence, nothing more."

She shook her head, clearly bothered by something she was unable to articulate. "I don't know. But... things like that don't just happen. I mean, what are the chances?"

"What else can it be?"

He consulted his chronometer, then gazed into the sky, aluminium-white with the glare of the giant sun. There was no sight or sound of the alien vessel.

"You ready to move on?"

Jed nodded and Lania pushed herself to her feet. They retraced their steps to the staircase and descended, then paused in the cover of the hanging vine and scanned the square.

Carew glanced at Lania. "I don't detect anything out there, Ed."

"Okay, we keep to the shadows and make for the museum. After me."

He led the way from the building, turning left and skirting the square. The Vetch ship had burned a great patch of vegetation in the centre of the square, but around its edges the undergrowth was a dense tangle. Carew was loathe to use his laser to clear a way, even though common sense told him the Vetch were long gone. Instead he high-stepped through the undergrowth, barbs and brambles catching at his leggings. He was thankful they were in the shade for much of the time: according to the gauge on his chronometer, the temperature was touching forty Celsius.

They had almost reached the museum when they saw the figure, standing before the building's triangular entrance. A moment later, a hundred metres across the square and partially concealed by vegetation, he made out a second Vetch vessel, a one-man scoutship.

Lania was the first to react. She grabbed Carew and Jed and dragged them into a mews between the museum and the next building.

The corridor was haywire with jungle, but plants had no thorns and were not too tangled, allowing the three relatively easy passage. By the time Carew's shocked senses had processed the image of the

Vetch – the alien had seen them and had hesitated between drawing its firearm and giving chase – they were a hundred metres from the front of the museum. They tumbled from the undergrowth and found themselves in a clearing behind the museum, a scorched area that suggested Vetch ships had landed there recently.

"Split!" Lania hissed. She pushed Carew across the clearing. "There was only one Vetch. Jed, that way. Find a hiding place and lie low. I'll find you. Okay, go!"

Lania turned left and dived back into the jungle, while Jed drew his laser and turned right. The pair soon disappeared. Carew took off, sprinting across the burned vegetation to the jungle on the far side. As he ran, he wondered at the Vetch's sudden interest in the museum. Had they happened upon the same information as he had himself?

He came to the cover of the jungle and fled into its shade with sudden relief. The temperature dropped appreciably, out of the direct sunlight. He turned and looked across the clearing.

The Vetch stumbled from the jungle on the far side and looked left and right. There were no tell-tale signs of where Lania and Jed had fled to, but Carew's own passage was clearly marked in the ash. The alien saw the trail and gave chase.

Heart hammering, Carew turned and struggled through the riotous growth: the vegetation was not as benign here and every bramble seemed to grab him and hold him back like hands intent on impeding his progress. He gave a shout of frustration and resorted to firing his laser straight ahead, burning a path through the growth. He knew, even as he fired, that he would lead the Vetch to his position, but his immediate concern was to put as much distance as possible between himself and the alien.

The jungle vegetation gave way to something a little more tamed and ordered, and he realised that he had strayed into what once had been a municipal park. He made out an orderly plantation of trees to his right, and to his left a pavilion of some kind.

His earpiece bleeped and Lania's voice sounded. "Ed!"

He panted, "I thought I said no radio communication?"

"Desperate measures, Ed. I saw the Vetch follow you. Just to say, I'm right behind it, okay? As soon as I get a clear shot, I'll take it." She cut the connection.

A palpable wave of relief swept over him. He came to the vine-cloaked wall of the pavilion and scrambled through an open window. He was panting hard and his right ankle throbbed painfully. He dropped to his haunches and leaned against the brickwork. With luck he had lost the alien, and Lania would account for it in short order.

He controlled his breathing, calmed himself and decided to take a look. He turned slowly, lifted his head and peered cautiously through the window.

The alien had emerged from the plantation of trees and was looking out across the waist-high tangle of undergrowth.

Carew would have fired on the Vetch there and then, but he was shaking so badly that he stopped himself for fear of missing and giving away his position. He could see the alien as it stepped cautiously from the line of trees, concealed himself by the shrubbery growing around the window frame.

He was much closer to the Vetch than earlier, when he had viewed the aliens from the top of the building in the square. At close quarters, he saw how monstrously tall the creature was, and how broad. Atop the pink mess of its face was a mane of ginger hair that gave it, despite its black uniform, an animalistic aspect.

Its appearance was painfully familiar to Carew; he fought back the urge to vomit.

As he watched, the Vetch touched something at its throat. Then it spoke.

"Human, I know you are nearby." It made a noise, which the translator did not reproduce: a sound like a growl, which Carew guessed was laughter. "I can smell you. Humans stink, did you know that? You reek of the stench of your mother's blood!" Again the growl of alien laughter.

It stepped forward, towards the pavilion, its large, flattened fish-eyes raking the building's façade. Then it was staring directly at where Carew crouched.

"I see you, human." The transistorised voice was loud, filling the area. Carew tried to move, to duck, but he found himself frozen, immobilised by fear.

He saw movement behind the tall figure of the Vetch and glimpsed a patch of Lania's black one-piece suit between nodding leaves. *Fire*, he thought, *before the bastard shoots me.*

Then the alien turned with a speed belied by its size, brought its rifle to bear and fired, once. Its pulse-beam belched like a klaxon. Lania was punched backwards by the impact and lay unmoving on her back, cushioned by a hammock of brambles.

Something pulsed in Carew's vision, a mist of blood, and he had to force himself not to cry out loud.

"Human," the Vetch went on, "answer me this: what brings you to Akaria?"

Akaria: presumably the Vetch name for Hesperides.

He gripped the butt of his laser, determined now to avenge Lania's death – even at the risk of his own life.

The Vetch answered its own question. "Greed, as ever. Is there any other motivation that drives your kind, but greed?" The alien paused, as if awaiting Carew's response. When none came, it said, "You plan to sack the museum, am I correct? Or... Or is there something else on Akaria that brings you here?"

The alien paused, swung its great ugly head back and forth, ever vigilant. It resumed, "We were told that you were on your way, human."

His pulse loud in his ears, Carew closed his eyes. So his secondary reason for coming here was why the Vetch were here, too, and his source had been compromised.

The growl again, the alien analogue of mocking laughter. "But you were too late, human. Far too late. We, too, knew of the starship. You will find nothing in the museum."

His earpiece bleeped, alarmingly. He suspected Jed had heard the Vetch's pulse-beam. He would tell his engineer to lie low, on no account approach the old park.

"Ed..." The voice was weak, almost undetectable. "Ed, it didn't kill me. Just stunned. I'm..." He heard her attempt at laughter, and joy overwhelmed him. "I'm paralysed, but I'll be okay. Don't panic. Maybe..." Another spurt of laughter, "maybe the bastards aren't as evil as I first thought, hm?"

"Lie still," he hissed. "Don't move. We might get out of this alive."

"AOK, Ed." She laughed and cut the connection.

But why, he asked himself, had the Vetch spared Lania's life, when it would have been just as easy, and more practical, to have killed her?

The Vetch stepped forward, its knees giving that terrible flex and bob. It seemed to be directing its vast eyes straight at him.

"Will you show yourself," it said, "so that we can discuss this like... like civilised beings? Or will you cower there for ever, like a coward?"

Carew was in two minds. The alien had spared Lania when it could just as easily have fried her alive. And now it wanted to talk. If he showed himself and spoke to the alien about the crashed starship, then would it spare him to leave the planet with his life?

Or was the Vetch playing a game? Would it keep the humans alive in order to find out how much they knew, and then slaughter him and Lania dispassionately?

He saw movement to the alien's left and his first assumption was that Jed had taken it upon himself to play the unlikely hero.

Then he caught the flash of golden fur as the animal leapt towards the Vetch.

He had no idea what moved him to stand and fire at the kreesh.

His first shot – unlike Lania's earlier that day – connected squarely with the beast's head, and it dropped to the ground a metre from the stunned Vetch.

Carew was in full view of the Vetch, and the alien was an easy target.

Seconds stretched and the representatives of two very different races regarded each other under the glare of an alien sun.

At last the alien spoke, "I owe you my life, human."

Carew said, "You did not kill my colleague."

It took a few seconds for the alien's translator to relay Carew's words, then it responded, "We are not barbarians, human. Despite your stories, despite the actions of a few of my kind in the past, we do not kill indiscriminately."

Carew inclined his head, "Humans, too, or many of us, are loath to take life, save that which threatens us."

Carew stepped from the pavilion and approached the giant alien. He felt fear clutch his gut and a pounding in his head which told him to fight, or flee. He was twelve again and he was on his homeplanet of Temeredes, attempting to look after his ten year-old sister.

He staunched those memories, fearful of where they might lead, of what they might impel him to do here, today; actions which he knew might prove fatal.

He faced the Vetch, something he had never expected he would do, and he did not flinch as he beheld its ugliness. "I was told of the starship, how it crash-landed here a hundred years ago. My source didn't know where it came from, though he did say it was not Vetch."

"It was not our ship, but we too heard rumours."

"Rumours?" Carew echoed. His source, an elderly Hesperidian politician, had mentioned no rumours.

The Vetch blinked, once, its pink eyelids nictitating from the bottom up and cupping the bulging eyes grotesquely. It seemed to be assessing how much to tell him, and decided to keep its own counsel.

It said, "If you are ignorant of the rumours, then it would be unwise of me to enlighten you. Suffice to say that the alien ship was not Vetch – it came from beyond what you know as Vetch space."

The Vetch raised a hand to its misshapen lips and spoke into a handset.

Carew said, "You will allow us to leave, unharmed?"

"As I said, human, we are not barbarians. Your colleague will return to full fitness in due course. My ship is coming for me. I suggest that you leave Akaria and do not return." He paused, staring down at the sprawled carcass of the kreesh. "For your actions here today, human, I thank you."

And so saying, the Vetch turned on its heels and stepped into the cover of the jungle.

Carew moved across to where Lania lay, face up on a bed of brambles. He lifted her with some difficulty, eased her to the ground and placed his water bottle to her lips. She drank, watching him all the while with an unreadable expression in her eyes.

He guessed he would soon have much explaining to do.

CHAPTER THREE

Lania wondered what hurt the most: the stunning impact of the Vetch's pulse-beam, or the fact that Ed had lied to her about the reason for coming to Hesperides.

Her immediate reaction, on seeing the alien turn and fire its weapon before she could do the same, was despair at dying in such a stupid fashion. She could only imagine the disgust of her military teachers at the manner of her end. She had been silent in tracking the Vetch, but she had not taken into account the direction of the breeze: it was her scent, she realised, that had alerted the alien.

Then the pulse-beam hit her and flung her backwards and she truly thought she was dying. Pain tore like fire through every muscle of her body. Then the agony abated little by little and she came to the amazing realisation that she was still alive. That, for whatever reasons, rather than kill her, the Vetch had chosen merely to stun.

She had heard voices: the oddly inhuman transistorised words of the Vetch and Ed's cautious replies. And then she forgot the physical pain as she learned that Ed Carew had come here, had endangered his life and those of his crew, for reasons other than the retrieval of the precious statuette.

Now he knelt and lifted her from the bed of thorns and lay her on the ground. Despite her anger, she felt safe in his arms; she hated herself for it, but it was as if she were a child again, cradled in her father's safe embrace.

When she'd marshalled all her strength and had control of her limbs, she dashed the bottle from her lips and glared at him.

Patiently he picked up the bottle, snapped the lid shut and said, "I can understand how you feel, but I saw no reason to inform you and Jed about the starship."

She struggled upright, wincing as pain lanced through the muscles of her back. "You lied!" she said. "You lied to us!"

He shook his head. "I was merely economical with the truth. I said we were coming here for the statuette, which was true."

"You said nothing about the starship, or that the bastard Vetch would be here too!"

He stared at her. "I didn't know that the Vetch would be investigating the ship. Do you think I would have brought us here if that were so?"

"But why didn't you tell us about the starship? Why didn't you want us to know?"

He gestured with an upturned palm, one of his unflappable gestures which infuriated Lania. "It wasn't that I didn't want you to know. I would have told you when we had the statuette. It was merely that I didn't want you and Jed – Jed, principally – objecting to spending any more time here than was absolutely necessary." He smiled at her. "You don't know what a pain you two can be when you decide to gang up on me."

She could not help but smile, but resented the impulse. She struggled to her feet, batting away Ed's attempt to assist her. She grabbed the water bottle from him and hobbled into the centre of the clearing, as much to give herself time to think as to get away from him.

The city of Valderido was in a basin, enclosed to the north, east and west by the mountains known as the Three Sisters. She thought it must have been a wonderful place to live, before the enforced evacuation.

She took a long drink of water and said, "You two seemed pretty pally."

Ed stared at her across the clearing. He was a tall, slim man, unnaturally pale, his lean face thin and hawk-like. He disdained any kind of uniform, wearing instead a casual two-piece outfit comprising straight-cut trousers and bodice, the kind of attire worn by millions across the Expansion.

Lania had known Ed Carew for ten years, ever since he had recruited her at a time of her life she would rather forget about: and yet, she thought, she had never got to know him. He was guarded about his past and just as reticent about his feelings.

The odd thing was that she trusted this man, this lone starship captain who was, to all intents and purposes, still a stranger.

Lania had tried to talk about her past to him, yet whenever she began, he found some way to divert the conversation to other, inconsequential things. It was as if he didn't want to know her, and at first that had hurt.

Over the years she had come to realise that this was just who Ed Carew was, a loner. He had no emotional attachments of any kind, and no wish to form them.

He said, "I saved its life."

"Do you think it might have killed us, otherwise?"

He hesitated. "I honestly don't know. It would have been within its rights. After all, we are trespassers on Vetch territory."

"But it didn't kill me," she pointed out.

"As it said, it and its kind are not barbarians – despite what we've been led to believe."

She stared at him. She detected conflict in his voice: it was as if he, too, found it hard to believe the alien's... humanity.

"Why the interest in the crashed starship, anyway?" she asked.

His reply was interrupted by a roar of jet engines. Instinctively she ducked and ran towards Ed on the edge of the clearing. They took cover in the undergrowth, Ed's arm protectively around her shoulders, and looked up as the Vetch scoutship swept overhead, flew in a great loop over the capital, then angled upwards and vanished into the stratosphere.

A great weight seemed to lift from Lania's shoulders.

"Well?" she said, staring at her captain.

"I'll contact Jed, and then I'll explain."

They stood in the shadow of the jungle and Ed opened up radio communications. "Jed?"

"Captain..." The engineer's voice sounded, tremulous with fear, in Lania's earpiece.

"Where are you?" Ed asked.

"I... I don't know. In the jungle. I heard firing."

Lania instructed her smartsuit to locate Jed's position, then projected a map on the air. A tiny red light blinked, half a kay north of the museum.

"Follow me," she said.

"We're coming for you, Jed," Ed said.

Lania led the way through the jungle, following the map that hung in the air a metre before her.

They came across the engineer ten minutes later.

He was still cowering in the undergrowth, for all the world like some animal gone to ground in fear of its life. Which he was, Lania thought as she stood above him and prodded his ample backside with the toe of her boot – an overweight, cowardly animal burying its head in the sand.

Ed helped him to his feet and he looked sheepishly at Lania. "I thought you were dead. I heard firing. What happened?"

She told him what had occurred in the clearing. "But Ed has a confession to make."

Jed looked confused, an expression which rather suited his doughy face.

They followed the blasted tunnel back through the undergrowth towards the museum. Ed said, "Not a confession, Lania. More an admission."

Jed shook his head. "Will someone please tell me what you're both on about?"

They emerged into the sunlit square and moved into the shade of the museum's entrance. A plinth of steps rose towards a triangular glass door, shattered to opacity now but still intact.

They sat on the top step and drank from their water bottles.

"A month ago I heard a story about a crashed ship on Hesperides," Ed began. "I was on Terpsichore, while you two were on leave."

Lania looked away. She'd told Ed she was going to her homeplanet of Xaria, to visit her family. Instead she'd spent her time in a gymnasium on one of the moons of Terpsichore.

Ed was saying, "You know I have an interest in the evacuated worlds. In my research I came across the story of an alien ship that'd come down a hundred years ago, here on Hesperides. I tracked down a politician in office at the time and he told me a little more about it. All very hush-hush. The ship had crash-landed almost fifty years before the Vetch ordered the evacuation, but it wasn't a Vetch ship, nor did it belong to any of the other known star-faring races. The odd thing was that the authorities who investigated the wreck found no signs of life aboard the ship, and it couldn't have been running on auto as it didn't posses the technology to do so. The authorities feared that whoever had landed were abroad on the planet, which opened up all sort of security problems."

Jed said, "Were aliens ever traced?"

Ed shook his head. "No, which makes it all the more mysterious. And now we find that the Vetch are curious about it, too. So that's why I wanted to come here, quite apart from the fact that we could make a little money by retrieving the statuette."

Lania said, "Presumably the crash-site has been well and truly scoured by now?"

"I still wanted to see for myself," Ed said. "Also, the politician said that items from the ship were stored in the vaults of the Valderido museum."

Lania tapped his knee. "That's before our ugly friends took them away, Ed."

He moved his leg from her reach and nodded, conceding the point.

She said, "I still wish you'd told us about it, Ed."

He stood quickly and regarded the shot-glass doors of the museum. "You forget yourself, Lania. I'm the Captain of the *Poet*, I need tell you nothing."

He strode off, pushed open the swing door and disappeared inside.

Open-mouthed, Jed watched him go. "What's eating him, Lania?"

"Oh, he's just being his usual old, cold self," she said.

They stood and hurried after their captain.

LANIA HAD ALWAYS found museums rather sad places, the termini of relics from cultures long dead and almost forgotten. As a child on the old colony world of Xaria, she'd spent hours in the cultural history museum of the capital city, staring solemnly at the artefacts of races, both alien and human, who had had their day and died.

It was a poignant reminder that the spread of her own people through this sector of the galaxy was but a passing show across the vast face of the universe.

Now, as they walked reverently through dusty halls with half-emptied cases to their left and right, she knew that even sadder than the museums of her childhood were museums like this one: museums whose exhibits stood in mute testimony, not only to long dead civilisations, but to a present and future bereft of citizens to gaze upon the wonders of ages past.

A terrible melancholy seemed to fill the echoing halls, an atmosphere which demanded silence from the trio as if they were treading the sacred precincts of a cathedral.

Lania found herself whispering, "Do you know where the statuette was kept?"

If Ed was still upset with her, he didn't show it. "The dealer said it was in a hall given over to the remains of the Hhar civilisation, the race which became extinct here a million years ago."

Ed gestured along the length of the vast central hall, indicating an opening to his right. They came to the archway and paused on the threshold.

"It's almost untouched," Ed said. "I don't know whether to be sad about that, or glad."

Jed looked at him. "Because the statue'll be easier to find?"

Ed smiled. "Something like that, Jed."

Lania watched Ed as he stepped into the chamber containing rows of cases of Hhar artefacts. There were times, she thought, when he exhibited more compassion towards things and ideas than towards real, living people.

A row of glass cabinets lined the walls and ran down the centre of the room. Ed said, "A small statue of an alien figure, about as long as my hand, carved from grey stone."

He moved to the left-most series of cases, while Jed checked the central aisle and Lania began peering into the cabinets to the right.

She wondered why none of the Hhar artefacts had been salvaged, either by staff or the looters who came afterwards. Were these pieces worth nothing, these exquisitely carved representations of wild Hesperidian animals, admittedly primitive but nevertheless carved with care and a knowledge of the subject? Like their creators, they were destined to be lost in the mists of time.

In the third case was a small carving of what looked like a scaled lion. She worked out how to open the case, reached inside and picked up the cold, heavy object.

She turned the carving, admiring the intricacy of the detail, the fidelity the ancient artisan had brought to the leaping musculature and the ferocious head.

"Lania?" Ed called. "Found it?"

"No – just this." She held it up. "To remember Hesperides by, Ed."

She slipped the carving into her pouch and moved to the next case. Five minutes later she came to the last one and admitted defeat. Ed was still peering into a cabinet across the chamber, a gangly, professorial figure absorbed in antiquities, when Jed called out, "Here, boss. I think I've found it!"

Lania moved to his side and Ed joined them. The statuette occupied a cabinet of its own, standing on a black velvet plinth. It was as Ed had described it, perhaps ten centimetres tall and iron-grey, an attenuated alien figure with long legs and short arms and a long, thin head.

Jed was fumbling in an attempt to open the case. Lania eased him aside and showed him how.

Ed reached into the case and took custody of the figure.

He examined the alien carving, then passed it to Jed who hefted it in his right hand. "A hundred thousand units," he said in wonder.

Lania took the figure and examined it, wondering what made this example of Hhar culture so valuable.

As if reading her thoughts, Ed said, "The dealer wants it for his private collection. He collects carvings of alien races, ancient and modern."

She looked at him. "Is it worth what we went through, Ed?"

He smiled. "He'll certainly think so, Lania."

She wondered if it had been worth the fear and tension she'd experienced during the past few hours and decided that, on balance, it was. She would put the thirty thousand in her savings, towards the villa on Xaria by the ocean where her father had lost his life.

"Lania," Ed said, interrupting her thoughts, "summon the *Poet* and have it land in the square immediately."

"We're leaving?" Jed asked.

"We're heading north to the crash-site," Ed told him, "just as soon as I've checked if the Vetch left anything of the wreckage."

They followed him from the Hhar chamber and turned right along the atrium, following the scuffed trail in the dust left by the Vetch. It led down a flight of stairs to the basement and along a dim corridor. An open door gave onto a long room full of metal racks, most of which were empty. Only half a dozen plastic containers remained, and these had been emptied.

Ed found a scrawled ticket, which might once have been attached to an artefact. He passed it to Lania. "Miramar," she read.

"The place where the wreckage of the starship was discovered," Ed explained.

"Well, the Vetch have been pretty thorough here," she said.

"Let us hope that they have been less conscientious at the site itself."

Some hope, Lania said to herself as she followed him from the basement room, but thought it best not to voice the opinion.

THE PARADOXICAL POET squatted on its ramjet haunches, in the full glare of the sun, as they emerged from the museum. For a fifty year-old ex-navy survey vessel, superannuated when Ed purchased it twenty years ago, it looked pretty good, and performed even better. Even though Lania was just its pilot, she always felt a surge of pride at the sight of the old junkpile. Its bodywork was excoriated by the void, its armour plating blasted by a million micro-meteorite hits – and dented by a hundred larger impacts – but it retained its dignity despite its manifest hard living, like a veteran soldier who had survived numerous campaigns, bloody but unbowed.

Lania climbed to the flight-deck – the ship was so old that it still had ladders in place of elevators – slipped into the pilot's sling and commanded her suit to meld with the ship's smartcore nexus. Jed took the sling beside her and powered up the auxiliary drive.

Ed took his seat to the rear of the flight-deck, lounging on a couch he'd bought at a mansion-clearance on Deneb IV. It was farcically old-fashioned and matched nothing on the flight-deck, even though he'd personalised the space with Lyran wall-hangings and artwork from across the Expansion.

Ed gave her the co-ordinates of the crash-site and she relayed them to her smartsuit. She closed her eyes and became one with the *Poet*, no longer aware of herself as a separate entity with human cares and worries. Flying the ship was a soul-soothing drug that allowed her release from the more disturbing recollections of her past. Flying, she was truly happy.

She opened her eyes as the ship lifted slowly, the surrounding jungle-covered buildings obscured by churning smoke and blasted debris. She turned the *Poet* north and eased it forward, and they moved slowly from the city.

Soon, all evidence below them that humanity had once inhabited this planet was lost beneath the brilliant green cover of the jungle. Here and there, towering stalks erupted from the canopy, ending in heliotropic blooms like inverted marquees which gave the scene a touch of the bizarre. Straight ahead, two moons sat above the horizon, lacy and insubstantial.

Ed pointed to a distant scar in the jungle on the slopes of a rearing mountain. She brought the *Poet* down with the delicacy of a balloon kissing the ground, and gave Jed the command to power down the drive. Through the screen she had a perfect view along the length of the furrow as it rose in a die-straight line towards the distant mountain-top.

"The politician told me," Ed said, "that for some reason nothing would grow at the site of the crash-landing. He said it wasn't radiation, or anything else that their scientists could detect."

Jed exchanged a fearful glance with Lania, who smiled to reassure him. "Some alien bacteria," she said. "It won't be harmful now, Jed."

He peered through the screen. "There's still nothing growing down there."

Lania looked at Ed. "Perhaps we should wear breathing masks?" she suggested.

He nodded, then pointed up the kilometre-long furrow. "Magnify the screen. Zoom in on the very end of the trench."

She did as commanded and the shell of a starship, very alien and rococo, sprang into view. It appeared burned out, with its upper half sheared off and its length broken in about three places.

"Okay, let's take a closer look," Ed said.

Jed powered up the drive and Lania took the *Poet* on a short kilometre hop up the furrow. She settled the ship beside the wreck and ordered her suit to break the link with the smartcore.

They equipped themselves with face-masks and boarded the dropchute. Even in the shadow of the *Poet*, the heat was staggering. Lania kicked at the ground, wondering if this was the first time she had seen bare soil since landing on the planet. Nothing grew. She turned and stared down the length of the furrow, a stark black exclamation mark cut through the verdant jungle. The starship must have come in at some speed, which no doubt accounted for its broken-backed state now.

She left the shadow of the *Poet*, wincing as the sunlight smote her unprotected head, and approached the alien vessel.

It was, she saw now, a leviathan. Perhaps three hundred metres long and thirty high – though its height was hard to assess, since its upper superstructure was missing – it dominated the landscape, dwarfing the trees that rose on either side. She stepped into the welcome shade and stared up at its underside. A complex pattern of scrolls and curlicues flowed across the bodywork, and a dozen fins and balancers, curved like scimitars, told her that this ship was nothing that any human had designed.

Keeping in the lee of the ship, she walked its length until she came to a great vertical rent in the flank. She hesitated, then stepped inside. Now she saw why the ship appeared to have lost its upper sections: they had collapsed on impact and fallen into the belly of the ship, and from the evidence of the blackened interior, fire appeared to have consumed the wreck.

She told her suit to scan for radiation; a few seconds later, its soft feminine contralto spoke in her earpiece. "No radiation detected beyond background levels."

Ed was beside her. They climbed onto the fallen superstructure and strolled up the length of the ship, for all the world like holiday-makers taking the air on the pier on a pleasure planet.

"It's... magnificent," she said.

"It's quite something, certainly," Ed said, his voice muffled by the mask. "I was told it came down during the night, and it wasn't until hours later that the first colonists were on the scene. They found no sign of whoever had crewed the ship."

She looked at him.

"That's what intrigues me, Lania. What happened to the beings who flew the ship? Where did they go? Why did they come here – and from where?" He paused, then went on, "And why are the Vetch so interested?"

Jed joined them. "You know something, boss? This is familiar."

Lania stared at the engineer. "It is?"

Jed frowned, recalling something. "I was on a planet called... Tamalkin, that's it. About twenty years ago. And I saw a crash-landed ship just like this one, same fins, same patterns."

Ed said, "Exactly the same?"

The engineer nodded. "Identical, I'd say. It was a tourist attraction." He shook his head. "I can't recall much more about it."

Ed nodded and moved off towards the front of the ship. Lania followed, curious to examine the flight-deck; perhaps the accoutrements there – the slings, couches or harnesses – might give some clue as to the physical makeup of the ship's elusive crew.

They stopped when they came to a break in the deck, where the nose cone had sheared off from the rest of the ship. Lania glanced to her left, through a fracture in the flank. She froze at what she saw there and dropped to her knees.

She opened a comm channel to Ed and Jed. "Stop what you're doing and come here."

She saw Ed turn and stare at her, then hurry back. She pulled him into the cover of the curving wall and pointed through the sheared metalwork at the Vetch ship squatting on the far side of the alien vessel.

Jed joined them. "I thought the bastards had gone," he hissed.

"It's not the same ship as the one we saw earlier," Ed murmured.

Although daubed in the same black and yellow livery of the first Vetch ship, this one was smaller, chunkier, a faceted polyhedron standing on crab-like legs.

Jed said, "Back to the ship, before they find us?"

Ed said, musingly, "But why didn't they hear our engines when we landed?"

Lania imagined the crew of the vessel on the other side of the metal wall, squatting out of sight as they were, debating how to go about attacking the humans.

The Vetch ship stood on the very edge of the jungle, and only when Lania examined its six short legs did she notice that they were enwrapped with vines and creepers.

She nudged Ed. "Look at its stanchions."

Ed nodded. "I've noticed." He stood up and peered through the gap. "It's my guess that it's been here for some time." He jumped through the gap and walked across to the Vetch ship.

Jed looked alarmed. "Boss!"

Lania lay a hand on his forearm. "It's okay, Jed. The ship's empty. It's been there for decades, at least."

They jumped down and followed Ed.

Despite her words and her conviction that the craft was old and long vacated, she found her hand straying towards her laser as she stood in the shadow of the vessel and gazed up at its bulbous form.

"Curiouser and curiouser," Ed said to himself.

Seen at close quarters, the ship showed further signs of having stood *in situ* for a long time: a mantle of lichen coated the back of the vessel, and stray vines had worked their way up the stanchions and wound themselves around fins and microwave antennae.

Ed gestured up a short flight of steps to an open hatch.

"Should we take a look?"

"Be very careful, Ed," Lania counselled.

"As if I'm ever anything but," he said as he drew his laser and climbed cautiously up the ladder.

She looked at Jed, and the engineer followed Ed. Lania looked around, the security-conscious part of her mind suspicious of a potential trap. She dismissed the idea as paranoid and climbed in after her colleagues.

The hexagonal flight-deck was perhaps five metres across. Four big swivel couches faced a strip viewscreen and a wraparound control panel, and three of the couches were occupied. The fourth couch was empty – but its erstwhile occupant was nearby, sprawled across the deck.

Jed stepped forward and touched the back of the closest couch, turning it to face him. He stepped back with a small cry of revulsion as the corpse swung into view.

The Vetch was mummified, and if the aliens were ugly in life, then they were even more grotesque in death. Its pink wattles and flaps, the tentacular proboscis and labial flanges, had dried and darkened in the heat, tightened and shrivelled so that the blackened flesh shrink-wrapped the bulbous skull in a hideous death mask.

Lania kicked at the second couch and it swung to reveal another mummified body. She examined the third and only then noticed the scorched hole in the chest of its jet-black uniform. She returned her attention to the other corpses, which bore similar wounds.

Ed was kneeling by the prostrate Vetch. "Look at this."

The alien lay on its side. Its blackened hand gripped a pistol, the end of which was inserted into its mouth: the top of its skull was missing, though at first glance the shredded mess blended with the rest of its alien grotesqueness.

"I'm no expert," Ed said, "but it looks to me as if our friend here accounted for his colleagues, then turned the pistol on himself."

Lania looked around. "Any guess how long ago this happened?"

"None whatsoever. Some time in the last fifty years, obviously."

"Mutiny?" Jed asked.

Ed thought about it. "What I don't understand is why the Vetch haven't removed the ship and the bodies? They've been here recently, so why leave the ship?"

Lania's imagination ran riot. She thought of the furrow and the lack of vegetation.

"Perhaps..." she began. "Perhaps they were fearful of infection? Some viral plague carried from the ship out there, which is why nothing is growing in the furrow?" She looked at the dead Vetch. "Perhaps that might explain this? They found out they were infected and..." She gestured towards the bodies.

She asked her suit to scan for signs of harmful viruses and bacteria, and received the answer she'd been expecting: her suit did not possess the requisite facilities with which to make such an assessment. She smiled to herself. She really should have taken a little more time and stolen a higher-spec smartsuit, all those years ago.

Jed said, "Or maybe they just disagreed over a card game?"

She laughed. Trust Jed to crack a joke.

She looked at Ed. "What now?"

"Now," he said, "we say a fond farewell to Hesperides."

They left the Vetch vessel and emerged into the full glare of the noon-time sun. She looked around, at the aluminium white-hot sky, half expecting to see a swooping Vetch ship. They climbed up and crossed the wreck, then jumped down and walked in its shadow along the furrow towards the *Poet*. Its squat bulk had never seemed so welcoming.

Lania slipped into her sling, and five minutes later they were rising slowly from the surface of the planet. She watched the furrow recede, becoming a brown brushstroke in the vastness of the jungle. Valderido came into view, a dead city choked by rampant vegetation.

As they climbed, the continent resolved itself beneath them, a great curving landmass hard up against the lapis lazuli of the sparkling ocean. Then the planet fell away, became a sphere corded with cloud, brilliant against the sable backdrop of deep space. Lania never left a planet without feeling an involuntary surge of nostalgia; she was fourteen again and leaving Xaria.

She glanced at Ed, ensconced in his couch. "Captain?"

"I have an engagement with a certain dealer on Egremont," he said. "Jed, lay in co-ordinates for Duba IX."

"And then?" Lania asked.

Ed considered, then said, "I'm going back to talk to the old Hesperidian politician and then I intend to investigate the alien ship a little further, if that will be at all possible."

Lania stared at him. "You're not coming back here, though?"

"Of course not. I'll do my research from a distance, Lania."

She nodded. "Egremont it is, then." They'd been to the planet a month ago, when Ed had met the dealer. A world famed for its patronage of the arts, a centre for artists and artisans, it was liberal and bohemian, and Lania thought a week or two in its mountain-top capital city, spending just a little of the thirty thousand she was due, might be pleasant.

She melded her smartsuit with the ship's core and was about to initiate the phase into void-space when her suit signalled an alert. "We're being followed, Lania," it trilled dispassionately in her earpiece.

She felt her pulse quicken and accessed the data. A vast ship was one astronomical unit away and closing.

"Ah," she said. "I don't want to alarm you, gentlemen, but we have company."

Ed sat forward. "Put it on the screen, Lania," he said calmly.

Beside her, Jed swore.

She instructed the smartcore to patch the image to the screen and a second later a great sprawling starship resolved before them.

"It's an Expansion patrol vessel," Ed said.

Lania said, "A Mantis. That's the Judiciary." Her stomach tightened sickeningly. Their only hope was to phase into the void, and trust in her skills as a pilot, and the *Poet's* speed, to escape the pursuit of the patrol ship.

"I'm phasing, Ed," she said.

"Do it," he snapped.

She complied gladly: contravening Expansion law and landing on an evacuated planet was bad enough, but they had all accrued sufficient misdemeanours over the years to warrant a protracted term in a high-security penitentiary.

She steeled herself for the chase.

A second before they gained the refuge of the void, a jarring shudder shook the *Poet*. Ed spilled from his couch and Lania and Jed rocked violently in their slings.

The smartcore reported that it was aborting the phase manoeuvre.

"Explanation?" Lania snapped.

"We're inoperable, Lania, immobilised in traction stasis."

She glanced across at Ed, whose usual pallor had taken on a deathly shade. Beside her, Jed was chewing his knuckles.

Within a few seconds, a communication channel opened between the ships and the smartcore relayed a smug communiqué from the captain of the judiciary vessel.

"You are in the custody of Expansion Security. Once in the holding compound of *Macready's Revenge*, come out unarmed with your hands in the air."

The lights on the flight-deck stuttered and the overridden main drive powered down. On the screen, the hapless crew of the *Poet* watched the Expansion vessel grow ever larger as they were drawn inexorably into its cavernous maw.

The last thing Lania saw, before the viewscreen flickered and died, was a platoon of heavily-armed combat drones moving into position on the open deck.

CHAPTER FOUR

MAATJA CAME AWAKE with the big red sun driving dazzling spikes of light through the weave of the hut. Her mother, father and sister were still asleep, so she rose quietly and eased herself through the door.

Two hundred huts lined the deserted clearing. Halfway down the row was the long-house where her people held many of their gatherings. At the far western end was the second long-house, where the Harvester dwelled.

Across from the dwellings was the edge of the fissure and the long, long drop to the river.

Quickly she left the hut, hurried across the clearing to the fissure, and peered down. The sides fell away steeply, cloaked in jungle vegetation. The sun had not yet risen high enough to illuminate very far into the chasm, and the lower reaches were swathed in darkness.

A little way down the incline, beside the broad flight of steps which her people used on ceremonial occasions, Maatja had a favourite tree where she liked to sit and watch the stars come out. Many years ago her father's father and thousands of other humans had ventured across space in a vast starship and settled on World, and she still found the idea amazing.

When Maatja had asked why her people had come here, her father merely smiled and said, "We were called, Maatja. We were called."

She had asked who had done the calling and he had replied, "Who do you think, Maatja? Who gives us life? Who sustains us? Who do were serve?"

She peered into the fissure, wanting to climb down to her tree and rest in its shade. But she knew that, if she did this now, her mother and father would be angry. Today was phar day and the ceremony was due to start an hour after dawn.

Across the clearing, she heard the door of a hut scrape open. She looked back to see the small shape of her sister, Hahta, squeeze through the gap and hurry across to her.

"Phar day!" Hahta cried with excitement.

Maatja smiled with feigned pleasure: it would not do to let anyone, not even her trusted little sister, know that she was not as overjoyed at the prospect of phar day as were the rest of her people.

They sat side by side, cross-legged, in the warming light of the sun.

"Are you hungry, Maatja?"

"Of course," she lied.

Yesterday her people had run out of dried phar, so today the Harvester excreted fresh phar – a thick, milky fluid that, over the course of a few hours, would set solid in the heat of the day. This was what her people ate, the staple that sustained their life in the jungle here on World.

All the people, that was, with the exception of Maatja.

"I can't wait!" Hahta was excited. "Isn't phar day the best of all?"

Maatja smiled. "It is."

Over the years she had worked hard at concealing the fact that she did not eat the phar – or, more correctly, that she ate the phar and then later, in the jungle, vomited it back up.

Thanks to the Outcast she had met, many years ago, she was unlike the other people of the fissure.

Hahta said, "I heard mummy and daddy talking, last night."

Maatja looked across at her sister, a smaller, thinner version of herself; brown limbs, a small, pointed face and, long sun-bleached hair. "Talking about what?"

Hahta beamed. "Daddy might be going away," she said.

Maatja's heart leapt with alarm. "What exactly did they say?"

Hahta shrugged. "Just that mummy must prepare herself and that daddy was doing his duty."

"But was daddy a Chosen?" Maatja asked, desperate to know.

From time to time, adults left the fissure people. They left the huts and trekked into the jungle, looking further afield for berry bushes and fruit trees. Always these people returned, after days or weeks. However, the Chosen made their way down river and never returned.

Maatja felt sickness grip her stomach as Hahta replied with a shrug, "I don't know."

"But what did they say!"

"I didn't hear everything, Maatja! Just that daddy was going away and that mummy had to prepare herself. Then I was so tired I went to sleep."

Anger or fear must have shown on Maatja's face, as Hahta peered at her and said, "But wouldn't you be happy, Maatja, if father was one of the Chosen?"

She fashioned a smile. "Of course. It's just that... I would have liked them to tell me, that's all."

Hahta beamed. "They will tell us, if he is a Chosen! Oh..." she clapped her hands together in delight, "oh, wouldn't that be wonderful?"

It was at times like this that Maatja felt very much apart from all the other fissure people.

"Wonderful," she echoed, without enthusiasm.

Sometimes the Weird came to the clearing and pronounced: they would be taking this man or that woman – and these people would be the Chosen and, on the appointed day, they would descend into the fissure and take the raft downriver to join the Weird in their lair.

And they would never be seen again.

To her people, this was a thing to be celebrated.

Maatja appeared to be alone in thinking that it was a thing of horror which, soon, might be happening to her own father.

Behind them, across the clearing, hut doors were opening and her people were stirring, leaving their huts and stretching in the red light of the sun.

Their mother called across the clearing, "Maatja! Hahta! Here at once!"

They rose and hurried across to their hut. Outside every other hut, families were gathering. A murmur of expectation filled the clearing.

Leah and Rahn, the Elders – even though they were only a little older than Maatja's parents – stepped from their hut and smiled around the gathering. This was the signal. A cheer went up from the people. Leah and Rahn moved to the head of the crowd and strode down the clearing towards where the Harvester was penned. The people fell into step behind the Elders and followed them, silent now.

Hahta found Maatja's hand and squeezed excitedly.

All Maatja's friends, and the adults she had heard talking about the Harvester, thought that the creature was beautiful – as were all the Weird. But Maatja didn't agree. She thought it was a monster.

They came to the long-house where the creature lived.

The long-house was just a thatched roof, perhaps twenty metres long, supported by a dozen pillars. The Harvester occupied the space under the roof, a vast bloated grey mound of fat, so big that its body bulged between the timber pillars. At one end were a dozen tentacles, and at the other end a single, thicker trunk from which the beast excreted phar.

Now the people lined up and walked past the Harvester, brushing its bulging flank with fingers and murmuring their gratitude. Maatja heard her mother say, "We give thanks for your munificence..."

Maatja followed, her fingers touching the hard grey hide. She muttered under her breath, "You're a fat ugly thing and phar tastes like poo."

It was the only verbal form of dissent she allowed herself.

Her father carried a small pail he'd fashioned painstakingly from woven branches and dried mud. They stood in line while the other families received their ration of phar. When her family arrived at the back end of the Harvester, her father knelt before the dangling trunk. He placed the pail beneath the rheumy sphincter and Maatja watched with revulsion as the pink orifice opened and a litre of pale fluid spurted from the beast and filled the receptacle.

Her mother and father murmured their thanks, rose from their kneeling positions and led the way from the long-house. The next family moved forward, knelt and placed their bucket beneath the trunk.

She sat outside their hut and her father passed her and Hahta a small ladle. First Hahta dipped it into the thick fluid, lifted it to her lips and drank. She swallowed, then sighed and smiled, and a look of relief crossed her face.

And now it was Maatja's turn to simulate delight without spewing up the noxious liquid.

With rising nausea, she dipped her ladle into the pail, feeling the initial resistance of the fluid and then the give as the ladle broke the surface and filled up quickly. She lifted the ladle, heavy now, and brought it slowly to her mouth. She closed her eyes, felt the rubbery moisture touch her lips, and opened her mouth and drank. The phar seemed to expand in her mouth, filling it completely with its oddly chalky, sour mass, and it was all she could do not to gag and spit out the food.

She forced herself to swallow, tip the ladle again and take a second gulp.

Then it was down and it was her father's turn to drink.

Maatja smiled in feigned happiness and looked at the fiery circumference of the sun, a great dome now over the jungle canopy.

Phar day was over for another week. Now the stuff would dry and in its dried form was much easier to eat.

After the phar meal, Maatja joined her foraging group and moved off into the jungle. If she hated phar day with a vengeance, she loved the foraging that followed.

She slung her gathering basket over her shoulder and followed Jaar, a boy a little older than herself, and a couple of adults, along the jungle path. Perhaps five hundred paces from the clearing, she looked around. The other foragers, men, women and children, had spread into the jungle in threes and fours, and were hidden from sight. The rule was that you must always remain within sight of your group, for deeper in the jungle rogue Sleer and Outcasts roamed.

Maatja had taken great delight in disobeying this edict from an early age.

Now, when she was sure that the adults had gone on well ahead and Jaar's attention was fixed on the path, Maatja slipped from the worn track and ducked into the surrounding undergrowth.

She ran, exhilarated by the sudden sense of freedom.

She moved ever deeper into the jungle, away from where the foragers worked, towards the territory of the Outcasts.

She came to the clearing and the lakka bush. She sat beneath it, in the dappled sunlight that fell through the canopy a kilometre above her head, and plucked the small red berries from the bush. She ate them one by one and when she had swallowed a dozen she felt her stomach heave.

She squatted, leaned forward and retched.

A great torrent of pink-white fluid sprayed from her mouth, the phar and the berries, and she felt suddenly shaky with relief at expelling the alien mass. It lay on the jungle floor, already attracting insects and bugs.

This done, she proceeded to gorge herself on the fruit and berries that grew prodigiously around the clearing. The phar filled her people's stomachs, and they consequently required far less sustenance than did Maatja. For every fruit she threw over her shoulder into her basket, she popped two into her mouth. In this way, she would not draw attention to herself by gorging at the evening meal, though it did mean she had to work with speed.

When she reckoned she had her daily quota, she moved from the clearing, deeper into the jungle, and sought out the meeting place. This was a smaller clearing, marked by a ghala tree, where sometimes Maatja met the Outcast boy, Kavan.

It was Kavan who, years ago, had told her what the phar was doing to her people and what she could do about it. Maatja had never liked phar – unlike most other people she knew – and to sick it up every day was a welcome relief.

And, after a week of doing this, she came to think more about the Weird and what they were doing to her people.

And came to realise – thanks in large part to Kavan's words – that her people were enslaved to the alien race.

At first she had thought the wild jungle boy one of her own people. She was young then and had not met everyone in her tribe. But after a few meetings Kavan told her the truth: that he was an Outcast, a member of the tribe who lived in the treetops far away from the clearing, who were not addicted to phar and were not the slaves of the Weird.

Kavan had often exhorted her to come to live with his people, but always she had resisted. She loved her mother and father and her sister, and she could not envisage life without them. Her repudiation of the phar was the extent of her rebellion.

She came to the clearing and searched for Kavan's sign: a complex pattern of woven leaves, skewered by a twig, which told her, depending on its position in the clearing, when Kavan would meet her.

Today, however, there was no symbol awaiting her. This happened from time to time, when Kavan was unable to get away from his work duties, or when the Weird had instigated another purge to rid the jungle of the Outcasts and he had to be especially careful in his movements.

Now she made her way back through the dense undergrowth, at once dejected that she would not be meeting Kavan and worried for his safety.

Fifteen minutes later she saw one of her people through the trees and casually moved to join them as if she had never been away. She noted, with satisfaction, that she had collected more berries than anyone else: her father would be proud.

When they returned to the clearing later that afternoon, a great excitement gripped her people.

Jaar came running from his family hut and told a group of children that the Weird had communicated with the Elders while they had been foraging. In two days, he said, a Weird Flyer would arrive at the clearing, with 'great news.'

All that afternoon, the children speculated what the great news might be.

"Perhaps we'll *all* be Chosen!" a girl shouted, "and we'll all go to the lair of the Weird!"

"Or the Weird have found more humans on other planets and they're bringing them to live with us!"

Maatja drifted away from her friends. She had no idea what the Weird wanted with her people – not even Kavan could tell her that – so she thought that her playmates' wild guesses were a waste of time.

That night she slipped into the fissure and climbed her tree. As the bloated sun sank over the horizon, the sky slowly darkened and the stars came out. To the north, over the jungle, the night sky was resplendent with the gaseous pale red cloud that her father had told her was the Devil's Nebula. To the south was a mass of brilliant stars: the swathe of Vetch space, and, beyond, the hazy sweep of stars that was the human Expansion, from where her people had originally ventured.

She stared for a while at the distinctive horned shape of the nebula, then transferred her attention to the stars of the Expansion. She wondered how many populated planets existed out there, and not for the first time found herself wishing that one day she might be able to leave World and explore them all.

CHAPTER FIVE

THE REGIME THAT governed the human Expansion represented everything that was anathema to Ed Carew's philosophy of life. They were draconian where he was liberal; authoritarian where he was anarchic; and conservative where he was bohemian. He had spent his life in open – and not so open – defiance of their ideals. As a child, raised on the planet of Temeredes on the edge of Vetch space, he had dreamed of free travel among the stars, adventuring with a ship of his own. When the Vetch had declared their ultimatum and the Expansion had stood by, too weak to intervene, while his planet was evacuated, Ed Carew's hatred of the Expansion government had been born.

Later, as a young man travelling the length and breadth of the Expansion, teaching and learning and soaking up as many of the diverse philosophies – human and alien – as it was possible for his intellect to comprehend, his disgust at the ruling regime was compounded: again and again he came up against repressive laws and codes, illiberal and totalitarian regimes that held entire planets in thrall. Somewhere along the way, his defiance of the rules crossed the line into lawlessness – though where the authorities might have called him a criminal, Carew preferred to think of himself as a free-thinker bound not by the laws of planetary governments but by his own morality. It had begun, he supposed, when he purloined a small starship from someone he considered a true criminal, and for almost thirty years he had managed to keep one step ahead of the law, mixing legitimate salvaging operations with shadier deals. Now, it would appear, his run of good fortune and freedom had come to an abrupt end.

His one regret was that Lania and Jed had been brought down with him. They were good people, despite what the authorities might claim about their respective misdemeanours, and over the years they had been with him he had come to see himself as their protector.

Well, no longer.

They had left the *Poet* as instructed, unarmed and arms aloft, attended by an overkill of armed guards, and had been rapidly and silently processed into the custody of a convict shuttle. Here four guards had inserted him into a narrow metal tube like a coffin. As cold as a corpse, garbed only in a prison shift, he'd experienced the subtle nausea of void transition and wondered where in the galaxy they were sending him.

Now he rolled and rattled inside the torpedo. No matter how hard he braced his arms against the curving walls of the tube, he could not prevent his head and shoulders connecting painfully with the cold, hard steel. The journey seemed to last an age.

It was yet another example of the regime's inhumanity, meant to cow a criminal, physically as well as mentally, before he or she came to trial.

Then the rattling stopped, and a period of blessed calm followed; blessed to begin with, that was, after the discomfort of transit. As time passed, and the temperature within the tube grew even colder, he realised it was yet another ploy of the authorities: give the criminal time in which to dwell on what travails might be awaiting him.

He wondered where Lania and Jed might be, and if he would ever see them again. He thought not, as the judiciary was not a service designed to keep old friends connected: they would no doubt serve their time separated by light years, linked only by common memories.

The prolonged darkness within the tube fostered images he would rather not have experienced. He tried to dwell on happier times, on the wrecks he had salvaged and the people he had helped to throw off the shackles of oppression, but always images of his childhood came swimming into his mind's eye. He was twelve again and the Vetch – making an example of Temeredes, lest any other human colony exhibit such tardiness in evacuating their citizens – were landing on the planet in wave after wave of assault ships. Then their shock troops were razing his hometown and killing his parents.

The tube rattled jarringly, but he found the physical pain of being shaken like a rat in a pipe a welcome respite from the nightmare images.

Abruptly, the tube was tipped vertically and he slid until his feet made contact with the flat base of his prison. Faint light illuminated the tube. He looked down to see a circle of white light encompass his bare legs like a fallen halo as the shell of the tube lifted and released him.

He was in a small white room which boasted, surprisingly, a screen through which he could see limitless deep space, specked with stars. He stepped from the base of the container, his legs cramped after so long a confinement, and hobbled over to the viewscreen.

He peered down, then up. He was in a holding cell in the face of a colossal star station, the like of which the Expansion maintained all along the length of the disputed territory with the Vetch. The stations were vast floating cities inhabited by soldiers and spacers, who flew face-saving missions along the disputed territory, a futile rattling of sabres, more a sop to human public opinion than any real threat to the truculent Vetch.

He wondered why he was being held here, instead of in one of the many judicial holding centres where criminals were more normally incarcerated while awaiting trial.

A sudden din sounded above him. He cowered instinctively, covering his head with his hands, and watched as first one sleek grey torpedo dropped from the ceiling, and then a second.

As he stared, the case of the first tube lifted to reveal a pair of dark, shapely legs and then an ill-fitting shift identical to his own.

Lania blinked, and a second later she was in his arms.

He eased her away, kissed her forehead like a father, and together they turned and watched as the case of the second tube lifted and Jed stared at him in amazement. He stepped off the disc into Lania's embrace. Then Carew held the small man by the shoulders, staring into his eyes.

"I can safely say, my friends, that I thought I would never see your smiling faces again."

Lania laughed. "I never thought I'd admit to missing you, Ed."

Jed turned and stared through the viewscreen. "Where are we?" the engineer asked.

"A star station on the edge of disputed territory," Carew said. "But precisely which one, I don't know,"

Jed stared at him. "Not a judiciary holding station?"

"No. Very strange."

"But stranger still, Ed," Lania said, "is that we're together. Why? I mean, I never expected to see you two reprobates again."

Carew smiled. "A processing error? Or perhaps it's another sadistic ploy, to make us think we'll be allowed to stay together." But he thought not. He shook his head. "No, this isn't going by the book at all, my friends."

Jed said, "Perhaps they have nothing on us, boss? They might not have seen us lift-off from Hesperides."

Lania grunted. "Use your head, Jed. We were caught red-handed. And they have the *Poet*, remember? They'll ream the smartcore and find out exactly where we've been every minute of the past ten years."

Jed looked stricken. "Do you think they'll know that I...?"

Carew said, "We'd better face the fact that they have enough on us to send us down for a few lifetimes."

"If they don't decide to execute us, one by one," Lania put in helpfully. "Which is probably why we're still together."

"Sometimes, my dear, your pessimism is as welcome as a dose of Lyran bowel worms."

Lania tipped an imaginary hat.

Carew looked out at the stars. In the distance, a salty scatter of far suns towards galactic north, he made out the territory of the Vetch.

"I'm sorry I dragged you into this," he murmured.

Lania waved away the very idea and Jed said, "Where would I be if you hadn't hired me, boss? I'll tell you where – dead or clapped up in some stinking jail."

"Jed's right," Lania said. "We're with you because we chose to be." She stopped there, though Carew had the impression that she wanted to say more.

Lania sat cross-legged in the centre of the room, and Jed slid down the wall with his legs outstretched before him. Carew remained before the viewscreen.

Jed looked across at Lania. "I don't know whether I like you best in that," he said, "or in your smartsuit. At least now I can see what your legs look like."

Lania scowled at him. "I feel naked without the suit. You don't know what it's like." She wrapped the hem of the shift tightly around her thighs, covering herself.

Carew smiled. He wondered why it was only now, *in extremis*, that he truly appreciated the company of his crew.

He was about to lighten the mood with a story about a tight spot he'd been in on Acrab V, fifteen years ago, when the hatch in the far wall irised open and an armed guard waved them out of the cell.

CAREW HAD A ploy he used when faced with minions in positions of authority, such as armed guards, police officers and the like. He would obey their commands, but at his own pace, and he would never establish eye contact. If he was accompanied, he would keep up a running commentary under his breath. It destabilised the power dynamic between captor and captive; it helped him retain dignity, and gave the impression that he was in some measure of control, and it often unsettled those in charge.

"Perhaps," he murmured to Lania and Jed, "we'd better take up their kind offer of relocation. I found these quarters rather cramped, didn't you?"

Lania smiled. "You're right. Let's go."

Carew led the way out at a stroll. The six guards who escorted them from the cell and along a maze of white corridors were the usual bull-like drones, oiled body-armour clamped around bulky torsos. Only their heads showed, comically tiny between their hulking shoulder slabs. They carried enough fire-power to bring down a starship and were the ubiquitous face of Expansion authority. Carew had seen their like on every planet he'd visited, and their constant presence had filled him with despair.

"Lania, is the word *overkill* sufficient to describe our escort?"

She managed a laugh. "They obviously respect your prowess at unarmed combat."

"Or Jed's ability to evade the tightest security," Carew said.

"Cut it out..." muttered Jed, spoiling the effect somewhat.

Ahead, a triangular door in a blank wall slid aside and they were marched into a great circular chamber like an amphitheatre.

One of the guards gestured.

"I think that means, in goon-speak," Carew interpreted, "that we ought to install ourselves in the dock."

They moved across to a rectangular holding pen, situated in the well of the amphitheatre, and seated themselves on a hard banquette. The guards manipulated controls on the side of the waist-high holding pen. Carew felt something hard and cold encircle his midriff, a metal band that pinioned him to the bench.

Lania grimaced down at the band at her waist, tugging at it futilely.

"And now we wait for the show to start," Carew murmured.

She looked at him. "I've never seen you this light-hearted before. I'm worried."

"I have a saying which I use in times of stress," Carew said. "It's this: reality is never as bad as you expect it to be."

Jed stared at him. "Great. What if they execute us?"

Carew smiled. "They won't, Jed."

The guards had retreated out of sight. Carew suspected they were not far away. The chamber was perhaps fifty metres wide, banked with seats, and directly ahead of them a long viewscreen looked out into space. Below the screen was a raised platform on which were five chairs – more like thrones – and a long table.

Five minutes passed, then ten.

"Why are they making us wait like this?" Jed complained.

"Part of the softening-up process," Carew said.

Jed looked at him. "We've had it, haven't we? Be honest, boss. This is it, isn't it?"

Carew thought about it, then said to Jed and Lania, "I'm not at all sure. There's an old saying: I smell a rat."

"A rat?" Jed said.

"A verminous rodent, once popular on Earth. To smell one was to suspect that all was not as it seemed."

"How can smelling a verminous rodent," Jed objected, "mean that you think that all is not what it seems?"

Lania snorted. "Jed, for pity's sake." She looked at Carew. "What do you mean?"

Carew held up his fingers. "One, the authorities didn't separate us – they've kept us together. Two, we haven't been summarily executed, which is how trespassers on Vetch-held worlds are often dealt with. Three, all this... If you've failed to notice, this isn't your usual criminal courtroom."

Lania muttered, "I'll take your word for it."

"Jed?" Carew prompted.

"Like nothing I've seen before," Jed said. "But then it's been six years or more since I was last arrested. Things might've changed."

Carew looked around the amphitheatre, considering the possibility that judicial procedure had undergone a transformation. He dismissed the idea. Something was not right with what was going on, and his inability to work out what was wrong disturbed him.

A hatch to the side of the viewscreen sighed open and five robed men and women strode onto the platform and seated themselves behind the long table.

They touched controls in the table-top and screens appeared in the air before them. They gave their attention to the screens.

Carew leaned over to Lania. "It's nice to see the faces of the opposition," he said.

"Who are they?"

"Good question. I've no idea."

But his suspicion that this was not a run-of-the-mill judicial session was heightened by the figure in the centre of the five, seated on a chair raised slightly above the others, who wore a military uniform beneath his silver cloak. He was a tall man – attenuated, as if hailing from a low-gravity colony world – whose skull appeared almost inhumanly narrow; it gave him the appearance of the creature Carew had mentioned earlier – a rat.

"For the record," he said, "this session convenes at nine hundred hours on the thirty-second of St Jude's, 1745, New Reckoning. Present are magistrates Dar, Matteo, Shor, Simmons, and myself, Commander Gorley."

The rodent-faced Gorley stared at Carew. "Session convened to try the following citizens: Edward Tracey Carew, fifty-five Terran standard years, formerly of the colony Temeredes; Lania Tara Takiomar, twenty-eight, formerly of the colony world Xaria; Jedley Neffard, thirty-five, formerly of the Pederson trading station, Perseus Sector. The charge is wilful transgression of Vetch space, unlawful landfall on Hesperides, Vetch legal territory."

The woman to the right of Commander Gorley leaned forward. "Further charges to be considered, pending."

Commander Gorley inclined his head. "These will be considered following the initial charge." He reached out and touched the screen before him, and all five turned in their seats and stared up at the viewscreen.

Carew shifted uneasily, as much as the constricting metal band would allow, and transferred his attention to the screen.

The scene of deep space flickered and was replaced by a view of their ship, *The Paradoxical Poet*, as it phased from void-space in orbit around Hesperides and began its spiraldown.

Jed hissed, "How the hell?"

"A drone, obviously," Carew said.

He wondered if drones circled all Vetch-territory worlds now, waiting for the appearance of trespassing vessels, or if they had been betrayed and followed.

The viewscreen showed the *Poet* as it landed in the jungle south of Valderido. The viewpoint of the drone remained elevated, speeding through shots of the jungle canopy until the trio emerged in the city.

Commander Gorley waved at his screen and the image stilled. He stared at Carew. "The charge: transgression of Vetch space, unlawful landfall on Hesperides. How do you plead?"

Carew had another ploy he used, this time with dignitaries in command: far from refusing eye contact, he would attempt to out-stare them, holding their gazes until they relented and looked away.

He stared at Gorley and said, "How do I plead? I make no plea. I refuse to acknowledge the legitimacy of any court upholding the aggressive annexation of Expansion territory by the Vetch." His eyes bored into Gorley's abnormally thin visage. The Commander held his gaze.

A small woman at the end of the table leaned forward and murmured at her screen. "Plea inadmissible."

Commander Gorley said, "Lania Takiomar? How do you plead?"

Lania licked her lips. "I, too, refuse to acknowledge the charge."

"Jedley Neffard?"

The engineer looked terrified. "Me too."

Carew smiled across at Gorley, who looked away to consult his screen. He had scored a small victory.

The viewscreen flickered and the scene of deep space beyond the station resumed.

The woman beside Gorley began reading from her screen.

"The further charges, pending, on each individual run thus: Edward Tracey Carew charged with the transportation of one renegade telepath to the colony world of Xaranxa, Deneb III, in the year 1731; such transportation deemed illegal and likely to destabilise the political situation on Xaranxa. How do you plead?"

Carew said. "I refuse to acknowledge the right of this session to judge the lawfulness of my actions."

The woman went on, "Lania Tara Takiomar, you are charged with, on the fourth of Jeremy, 1735, absconding from military custody on Blanchard's World, Altair II and illegally obtaining a Jenson-Meers smartsuit from military stores. How do you plead?"

Carew saw Lania's hands form into tight fists as she said, "Fuck you all."

He smiled to himself. She had never mentioned her past, or rather had given him a sanitised version of how she had come to own the smartsuit, and he found himself wanting to know more.

He was overwhelmed by the notion that he might never now have the chance.

"Jedley Neffard, you are charged with, on the seventh Sacristian, 1739, absconding from police custody on High's World, seriously injuring an officer of the law, and stealing an air-car. How do you plead?"

Jed stared defiantly at the woman. "Not guilty," he said.

Commander Gorley was saying, "These are specimen charges, of more than twenty-five in total, with which the Expansion may try Carew, Takiomar and Neffard."

The official to his right spoke in modulated tones. Gorley listened, nodded, then leaned forward, his hands clasped before his chin as he stared across at Carew. He spoke, and for the first time Carew received the impression that the man was not following a prepared script.

"For almost thirty years, Edward Carew, you have roamed the Expansion aboard your ships, first *The Grayling* and then *The Paradoxical Poet*, no doubt playing out, in your own imagination, the role of agitator, *agent provocateur*, champion of the oppressed. In reality, your actions have proved deleterious to the smooth running of the ordered, civilised society which the Expansion judiciary attempts to maintain. The list of your misdemeanours alone, without taking into account those of your accomplices Takiomar and Neffard over the course of the past ten and five years respectively, warrant the severest penalties. The crimes of Takiomar and Neffard, likewise, are such that only the most extreme sentences will serve in order to deter likeminded individuals from replicating your exploits."

Gorley turned and inclined his head, ever so slightly, to the man seated at the end of the table.

This official, who had yet to speak, cleared his throat and said, "Edward Tracey Carew, formerly of the colony world Temeredes, for your crimes against the Expansion, you are hereby sentenced to death."

Beside him, Lania gasped. Jed made a whimpering sound, quickly suppressed. Carew felt himself grow hot, but he stared straight ahead into the dark eyes of Commander Gorley, determined not to show the slightest reaction to the death sentence.

"Lania Tara Takiomar, formerly of the colony world Xaria, for your crimes against the Expansion, you are hereby sentenced to death."

A quick, indrawn breath was Lania's only reaction. Carew wanted to reach out and take her hand, but his innate reserve stopped him.

"Jedley Neffard, formerly of the Pederson trading station, Perseus Sector, for your crimes against the Expansion, you are hereby sentenced to death."

Carew turned to look at Jed, to offer a word of consolation, but the small engineer was staring straight ahead, a heartening expression of defiance on his stolid face. Carew felt pride rise in his chest.

Commander Gorley was saying, "...sentences to be carried out at noon, station time. Session adjourned."

The five men and women rose as one and, without a further word, strode from the platform and passed through the triangular exit.

The guards released the prisoners and escorted them back to the cell.

THREE TRAYS OF food awaited them on a ledge protruding from the cell's wall.

"The condemned's last meal," Lania said.

Jed moved to the corner of the room and curled into a tight ball on the floor, his eyes closed. Lania picked up a tray, then sat down against the wall and stared at the food.

Carew still retained the odd feeling, somewhere deep within him, that something was not right. He wondered if he were deluding himself – the walking dead man, dreaming of a last-minute reprieve. The entire session in the amphitheatre had about it the feeling of something staged, a theatrical event intended to maximise the terror of the accused.

So why did he refuse to believe in the death sentences handed down? Was it merely some psychological survival mechanism, a deep-seated optimism that life was assured and death a far-off thing? But what he'd said earlier to Lania and Jed – the fact that they were still together and had been tried in a session like no other to his knowledge. Surely these facts must count for something? Or maybe he was deluding himself.

He picked up a tray, sat down beside Lania and began eating.

She pushed a fork through limp salad and looked at him. "For some reason, Ed, I have no appetite." She smiled wanly.

He said, "You were in the military, Lania? Went AWOL and stole one of their smartsuits?"

She shrugged. "It's a long story," she said. "Remind me to tell you all about it when we have a little more time."

"We have a little time now," he said.

She grunted, "How long have we got? I've lost all track. It's strange, being without my 'suit. I feel as if I've had a few vital senses removed, senses I relied on without really thinking about them." She screwed her eyes shut and Ed watched as tears squeezed out and tracked down her brown cheeks. "Not the only senses I'll be without, soon," she whispered.

He patted her knee, a wholly inadequate gesture in the circumstances.

Jed said, "The session began at nine, didn't it? And the bastard said we'd die at noon. We were in there about an hour or so?"

Lania looked up and dried her eyes on the material of her shift. "So we have a couple of hours left, a little less?"

Jed stared at her. "I never thought it'd end like this," he said.

Carew smiled at him. "How did you think it'd end?"

The engineer shrugged. "Dunno. In a chase, with the cops after me. Me in a flyer, with a haul on the passenger seat. Speeding through towerpiles on some rich core world. I'd go out in a blaze of glory... I never thought the bastards'd get me."

A silence stretched. Carew finished the meal and set aside the tray. He found, to his surprise, that he was still hungry. He looked at Lania's discarded tray and she gestured at him to help himself.

He picked up the tray and began eating.

At last, she said, "I'm young. I'm twenty-eight. I always thought I'd live 'til I was two hundred and die in my villa on the coast on Xaria." She smiled sadly at her hands knotted on her lap. "Did I tell you that I had a grandma? She lived to be two hundred and two. I remember seeing her a few months before she died. I would've been about twelve at the time – she was a hundred and ninety years older than me. And do you know something? She was fit and alert right to the end. She looked about eighty, not a day over." She fell silent, then said, "And I'll die at twenty-eight."

Jed said, "How do you think they'll do it, boss? Injection? Firing-squad?"

"Those armoured goons," Lania said, "they'll take us to some specially prepared chamber and zap us one by one, then flush our bodies out into space."

Jed looked at Carew. "Reckon that's what they'll do, boss?"

Carew found himself shaking his head. He had meant to keep quiet about his suspicion, for fear of raising their hopes only to have them dashed.

But now he said, "No. No, I don't. I don't think they'll kill us at all."

Lania and Jed stared at him. "You don't?" Jed said. "But that bastard back there, he..."

Carew finished the second tray of food and set it aside. He looked from Jed to Lania. "I know what he said. I know it sounded convincing. Too convincing."

Lania laughed at that. "What do you mean, *too* convincing?"

"Just that. It was as if they were trying to frighten us, to convince us that we were going to die." He gained conviction from his own words as he spoke. "I mean, in the normal course of events, three run-of-the-mill small-time chancers like us? Believe me, they wouldn't go to the trouble of staging such an elaborate set up. They'd have a single-magistrate session and execute us straight away, with none of this five-man charade and back and forth between cell and court and cell and execution chamber. It's ludicrous! And why the hell keep us together like this? That'd never happen, normally."

Lania was staring at him, something in her expression suggesting that she wanted more than anything to believe him. "You really think so, Ed? You're not just saying that to make us feel better?"

He reached out and tapped her bare knee. "That," he said, "would be cruel."

Jed was on his feet, pacing the cell. "But why? Why the hell would they sentence us to death if they weren't going to carry it out?"

Carew nodded, considering his words. He said, "To frighten us, Jed."

"Then they've succeeded," Lania murmured to herself.

"But why the hell would they want to frighten us, boss?"

"As for their motives..." Something had occurred to him, as he'd held forth, but he was loath to air his supposition. It sounded too unlikely, even to himself. And if he were wrong, then he'd never forgive himself for furnishing Lania and Jed with false hope.

Lania grunted. "I don't buy it. They want to frighten us, slap our hands and tell us to be good? Then what? Let us go, so we'll behave like normal citizens in future?" She shook her head. "You're putting a positive spin on a bad situation, Ed. We're dead and you know it."

Jed looked across at him, like a dog kicked in the balls by its owner. "That what you're trying to do, boss?"

Carew stood up and strode to the viewscreen. He stared out, marvelling at the beauty of the massed stars, the far nebula he would like to explore, one day. He turned and saw that they were both staring at him, something like nascent hope on their faces.

He said, "You can believe what you like, both of you. But I'll tell you one thing – I'll tell you what I believe: I believe that we'll leave this station, together and alive."

Lania looked up at him, smiling sadly. Jed shuttled a look between Carew and Lania, smiling like a child wanting to believe in fairies despite all the evidence.

Seconds later the door sighed open and a guard in hulking armour waved with his pulse-gun.

Carew led the way, casually, his heart thundering in his ears. They passed down the same labyrinthine corridors and paused before the same triangular sliding door. It slid open and, despite all his fine words back in the cell, a part of him expected to be prodded into a laser-blackened cell where they would be lined up against the wall and shot in the head.

He was surprised to see the familiar expanse of the amphitheatre, and as he stepped into the chamber, he thought that perhaps his optimism had been well-founded.

The guards ushered them to the rectangular holding pen, and again they were held securely by the metal bands around their waists.

Through the viewscreen the immensity of deep space, bedecked by a million stars, promised liberation.

But what if he were wrong? What if this was how the judicial system worked now, even for petty criminals like themselves? What if the prior session had been convened by five sadists who liked to watch people squirm?

The hatch beside the screen opened suddenly, and three men stepped through and seated themselves at the table. Carew was heartened to see that Commander Gorley was not among their number: the bastard would have come to gloat, surely, if the death sentence were to be upheld.

A silver-haired patriarch took the central chair; to his right was a small, thin man in his fifties, of Indian origin. To his left sat a bald-headed albino, whose thin arms and lined face spoke of great age.

The patriarch leaned forward slightly, his fingers laced before him, and spoke quietly in cultivated tones. "For twenty years, Edward Carew, you have utilised *The Paradoxical Poet* in your nefarious errands throughout the Expansion. Be aware that, whatever else happens, the *Poet* will never again know such usage."

He gestured. The screen flickered and the stars were replaced by a close-up shot of his ship. The very sight of it made his heart leap, despite the patriarch's ominous words.

As he watched, the view pulled out to show another vessel – a small fighter frigate of the Expansion navy.

Lania said under her breath, "No..."

Carew clenched his fists, knowing what was about to happen but powerless to prevent it.

The frigate fired a prolonged, concerted beam, and before them *The Paradoxical Poet*, his home for twenty years, first became a floating ball of slag, and then violently exploded. In moments, nothing remained to mark where the *Poet* had been, other than scraps of floating debris like metallic confetti. The frigate banked, its terrible duty done, and returned to the station.

Carew was overcome by contradictory emotions. The first was instinctive and wholly understandable – a terrible sadness and regret that the *Poet* had been so wilfully destroyed. The second, following quickly, was a sudden kick of hope: why would the powers-that-be on the station want to show three condemned criminals the destruction of their own ship?

The action did not make sense, in the normal run of events. There had to be some ulterior motive, surely?

He thought of the statuette, which he'd left in his haste on the flight-deck. Gone now, along with the rest of his belongings.

Lania turned to him. "Why?" she whispered. "Why destroy the *Poet* if they're going to kill us?"

He held her gaze. "Exactly."

The patriarch and his colleagues turned from the viewscreen and looked down on the condemned.

"In your earlier session," the patriarch said, "Commander Gorley passed upon you a death sentence, the only sentence available for him in the circumstances. The law by which the judgement was passed was that of the Expansion judiciary, the ultimate arbiter of law and order in the Human Expansion. However, in extraordinary circumstances, decisions arrived at by that law can be overturned. It remains to be seen, in the course of the next hour, whether you will accede to the commutation of your sentences."

Carew fought not to smile as relief flooded through him.

Jed turned to him and said, "What the hell does *that* mean, boss?"

"I think he's saying that, if we agree to... to *something*... then we might escape with our lives."

Lania whispered, "But what the hell do they want, Ed?"

Carew sat up with as much dignity as he could muster and said, "What do you want from us, Mr...?"

"I am Director Yan Nordquist, head of External Operations. My colleagues here" – he gestured first to the albino and then the Indian – "are Dr Galve Aldo, of our psychiatry department, and Anish Choudri, my deputy at External Operations."

Carew nodded and sat back. "I take it that it isn't every day you commute the death sentence of three criminals."

Director Nordquist smiled. He had the easy gestures and mild manner of a seasoned diplomat. "To be honest, this is the first time in living memory that the ruling council has overturned a sentence passed by the Expansion judiciary. We are not in the habit of making exceptions to our rules."

"But the fact that you've done so in this instance suggests... extraordinary circumstances?"

Nordquist paused, then said. "I was informed that I would find you an educated, articulate individual, Captain."

Carew smiled, without humour. "Not all criminals, as you call us, are uneducated, Director."

"What surprises me, Captain, is that an educated man would chose to lead the life of a criminal."

Carew gestured. "If we were to waste time debating the matter," he said, "then I would first demand a definition of terms: I would demur at being labelled a criminal, to begin with; and more, I would contend that a life opposing what I see as a totalitarian regime chose me, rather than the other way around."

Nordquist smiled; Carew was upset by the thought that, in other circumstances, he might have allowed himself to like the Director.

"Quite," Nordquist said. "But as you suggest, we have no time in which to debate the finer points of the matter."

Beside him, Lania cleared her throat impatiently. "Could you tell us, Director, just what it is you want from us?"

Carew felt a surge of pride in his pilot.

Director Nordquist nodded slightly to the man on his right, and the slim, dapper Indian leaned forward and smiled.

"That is simple, my friends," he said. "We would like to give you a starship."

CHAPTER SIX

CAREW STARED AT the Director.

Lania was the first to recover from the surprise. "Give us a starship?"

Jed swore, succinctly, and Carew found himself laughing out loud. The entire situation was just getting all the more mysterious.

He said, "We are being given a starship, Director – but not, I take it, our freedom?"

Nordquist smiled. "Your freedom, at this juncture, is not negotiable."

"Then what is?"

"Whether or not you will take up the offer of the starship."

"And the strings that are attached, no doubt?" Carew said.

The albino to the Director's left, Dr Galve Aldo, leaned towards Nordquist and whispered something to him. The Director nodded and said, "Perhaps, before we come to the finer points of our negotiations, you might like to see the starship itself?"

He gestured to the viewscreen and the scene of deep space changed instantly. Carew stared into a hangar occupied by a sleek golden ship perhaps twice the size of the *Poet*. It was, he thought, the most beautiful space-going vessel he'd ever seen, lean and arching with sweeping delta wings and what looked like four big void drives.

Lania said, "I've never seen anything like it."

"Those engines..." Jed said.

Carew said, "It looks pristine. Has it ever flown?"

"Only in test flights," Choudri replied. "It's the latest model void-liner from the Volk manufactory on Mars. Its engines are state-of-the-art, faster than anything in production across the Expansion. Several of its sub-routines have not yet been fitted in our regular space-fleet vessels."

"And you're giving it to us?" Lania said, more than a note of scepticism in her voice.

Choudri smiled. "A temporary loan, for the duration of the mission," he said.

"Ah," Carew said. "Now we're getting to the heart of the matter."

"Details later," Director Nordquist said, moving to a hatch set in the wall beside the viewscreen. "Would you care for a conducted tour of the *Hawk*?" He gestured to the guards, who released the prisoners from the dock.

They followed Nordquist through a hatch and down a flight of stairs into the well of the hangar. The *Hawk* loomed above them as they strolled across the deck; it was, Carew thought, a thing of grace and beauty, pleasing to the senses above and beyond its cutting-edge engineering. It was also, he thought, well-named: sleek and predatory, its nose-cone narrowing like a vicious beak. Its swept-back wings made it look like it was about to launch itself into space.

The officials climbed a ramp that led into the lavish fuselage and escorted Carew and his team to the flight-deck.

Lania stared around her in wonder. "May I?" she asked, gesturing towards the primary sling.

"Be my guest," Nordquist said.

She slipped into the sling, glanced up at Carew and grinned.

Jed was moving around the flight-deck, caressing surfaces, marvelling at fittings and fixtures like a child on Christmas day.

Lania opened her eyes and smiled at Carew. "It makes the *Poet* seem antique, Ed."

Carew nodded, piqued that the Expansion authorities thought their heads could be turned by having this bauble dangled before them. No – he thought – what piqued him was the fact that they *were* being bought by the promise of the bauble.

Nordquist had them where he wanted them, of course; the alternative was unthinkable.

"I'd like to take it on a test flight," Lania said.

"Of course. All that will be sorted out in time," Nordquist said.

Carew interrupted, "Naturally, we first need to know the nature of the mission."

Nordquist smiled. "Naturally, Captain Carew. You will be taking the *Hawk* – if, that is, you agree to the specifics of the mission – into Vetch space."

Carew exchanged startled looks with Jed and Lania as Nordquist gestured and they were escorted from the *Hawk*. They left the hangar and returned to the amphitheatre, the irony of the situation not lost on him. They had been handed down a death penalty for transgressing Vetch space, but the sentence would be commuted if they agreed to do the very same in the state-of-the-art *Hawk*.

Carew could not help smirking as he stepped into the chamber.

The sliding door at the far end of the room opened and Commander Gorley stepped through brusquely. He consulted with the officials, then gestured to Carew, Lania and Jed to be seated on a foam-form.

The three officials sat opposite, while Gorley remained standing, in the manner of someone about to give a briefing.

Carew regarded the man and confirmed to himself that his earlier assessment of the Commander was unchanged: he did not like Gorley. Everything about the Expansion man, from the authoritarian cut of his black uniform to the cruel glint in his dark eyes, spoke of the repressive regime he detested.

Commander Gorley cleared his throat and said, "You have seen the ship and you are aware of the choice before you. Stated simply, it is the choice between death by lethal injection, or the opportunity to undertake a mission of utmost importance to the Expansion."

Carew interrupted. "Which is also," he said, "a suicide mission."

Gorley turned his dark gaze towards him and, although he wanted to look away, Carew stared at the Commander. "Well?" he said.

"As you are in ignorance of the nature of the mission," Gorley responded, "you are mistaken to deem it a suicide mission."

Lania spoke up, "And you think a flight into Vetch space isn't?"

"I have every faith in the *Hawk*," Gorley said, "and in its crew. I am sure that a mission into – or rather *through* – Vetch space will prove a resounding success."

Choudri spoke, "I must concur. I certainly would not volunteer for the mission if I thought it was going to be suicidal."

Carew stared at the Indian. "You're going too?"

The little man inclined his head. "Why, of course. I wouldn't miss it for the world."

"Likewise," Gorley said, "I will be accompanying you through Vetch space as part of the military component of the mission."

Carew tried not to show his displeasure at this. He said, "Of course, that presumes our agreement to undertake the flight."

Beside him, he felt Jed stiffen in his seat.

Gorley rose and stood before the viewscreen. He gestured, and the view through to the cavernous hangar darkened. On the screen appeared the still image of a starship.

Jed murmured, "An old colony vessel, boss. Out of the Aldebaran yards. I'd say it's more than a hundred years old. Look at those ancient slow-boosters."

The ship was a chunky collection of lashed-together modules and tanks. To think, Carew mused, that in the early days of the Expansion, hundreds and thousands of desperate colonists entrusted their lives to this kind of vessel. It was thanks to this early workhorse and others like it that humankind was spread across the length of the spiral arm.

"Almost one hundred years ago," Gorley was saying, "*The Pride of Procyon* set off from the colony world of Vercors, Procyon V. It carried a complement of five thousand colonists in cold sleep, and a skeleton crew of twenty-five technicians who would cycle in and out of suspension over the course of the voyage."

Jed said, incredulously, "And they headed into Vetch space?"

Gorley ignored the interruption and went on. "They were part of a little-known sect or cult, persecuted by the authorities on their planet. They wanted a new world on which to live by their own ideals –"

"Which were?" Carew enquired.

This time Gorley scowled at the interruption, but replied, "Unfortunately, little is known of their beliefs."

"Don't tell me, Commander," Carew said, "you wish to track down these cultists and eliminate them?"

Gorley ignored Carew's jibe. "They set off on a course which would take them through Vetch space, looking for a suitable world on which to start a colony."

"In Vetch space?" Lania said.

Gorley shook his head. "Their idea, insofar as we can tell – this was nearly a hundred years ago, remember – was to go *beyond* Vetch space, to a sector of stars on the very edge of the Devil's Nebula, so called because of the 'horns' projecting from the nebula itself." He gestured to the screen and the ship vanished, to be replaced by the image of a gaseous nebula, a bright swirl of orange and mauve. Its resemblance to a devil's head, Carew admitted, was striking.

Jed said, "They must have been insane! Why not try further along the arm, out of reach of the Vetch?"

"As you no doubt can appreciate, I am not privy to the motives of the colonists at the time. Supposition is that they did not want the inexorable expansion of the human race to catch up with them, to infect their ideals with notions they abhorred. So they took a chance and ventured through Vetch space, in search of El Dorado."

Lania was shaking her head. "But they'd never have made it, would they? I mean, a slow ship like that, against the Vetch?"

Gorley said, "One would suppose that the chances of their success in evading the Vetch would be minimal. Perhaps it was a measure of their desperation, or their desire to found a virgin colony, that motivated them to take the risk. At any rate, the fact is that succeed they did."

Carew stared at the Commander. "What?"

"They succeeded in crossing through Vetch territory undetected – or, if not undetected, at least unmolested – and making landfall on the planet of a star on the edge of the Devil's Nebula."

"How can you be sure?" Jed asked.

"A little over a year ago, technicians working on this station detected faint void-space signals, obviously human in origin, issuing from the nebula. It was not a message as such, but a repeated code which, when deciphered, proved to be the mayday signal of an old colony-class vessel. The signal was coded such as to inform receivers that the ship had landed, but had subsequently suffered some form of... distress, let's say. There were follow up signals, but these proved too faint to decipher."

In the silence that followed Gorley's words, Carew pondered their implications. "So now the Expansion, in their altruism, is sending a vessel to rescue these poor benighted cultists?" he asked with a healthy dose of scepticism.

"Call it a scientific follow-up mission," Gorley said. "A mission with a two-fold purpose: to locate and possibly aid the surviving colonists – they are human, after all – and to explore the so-far uncharted territory of the Devil's Nebula."

And to claim it in the name of the Expansion, Carew thought.

Lania said, "And you'll be coming along yourself, and Director Choudri, despite the dangers of transgressing Vetch space?"

"We are more than confident that with the *Hawk*, and with your expert assistance, we can evade the attention of any Vetch intercept vessels. I would not be embarking on this venture if I thought otherwise."

He looked from Carew to Lania and Jed. "Any further questions?"

Carew nodded. "Just this: why us? Why not draw a crew from the thousands of pilots, engineers and captains you have working for the Expansion?"

Gorley looked at Director Choudri, who said, "We have been watching you and your ship for some time, Captain Carew. You have been, as the old saying goes, on our radar."

Jed said, "You wanted the best?"

"And you have proved yourselves to be that," Gorley said. He hesitated, then went on, "Well, do I have your agreement to fly the mission?"

Carew looked from Lania to Jed. He turned to Gorley. "We'd like to discus the matter amongst ourselves, if it's all the same to you." He smiled at the Commander; their decision, he knew, was a foregone conclusion, but he didn't want to give Commander Gorley the satisfaction of seeing them eat out of his hand.

Gorley nodded. "You have two hours. That should allow you sufficient time to see sense and agree to the offer."

"If we do decide to help you out," Carew said as they stood, "when will the voyage commence?"

"The *Hawk* is scheduled to leave the station in three days," Gorley said.

Carew nodded. "And when and if we survive, will we be allowed to keep the *Hawk*, in recompense for the *Poet*?"

Gorley barely hid his smile. "I am afraid that would be impossible. When you return, you will be granted your freedom. You should be thankful for that, Captain Carew."

Director Choudri looked at his watch. "Gentlemen, Pilot Takiomar, I look forward to our next meeting."

The guards were summoned and the trio were marched from the chamber.

This time they were not returned to the spartan cell on the upper levels of the station, but escorted to a suite of rooms on the lower levels overlooking the access port, through which all manner of starships came and went like bees at a hive.

Carew saw the smartsuit first, occupying the floor in the corner of the room like an oil slick. Only then did he see his own clothes, and those of Jed, neatly folded on a foam-form.

"Cleaned and neatly pressed," Carew observed as the door slid shut behind them. He pulled off the regulation prison shift and quickly dressed.

Lania exclaimed under her breath. "Hell... Ed, this isn't my smartsuit."

He turned to find her holding it up, a flimsy jet-black garment like the skin of some fabulous animal. "You're sure?"

"I lived in the thing for over ten years. It grew with me. This one..." She shook her head. "It's the latest model, far more advanced than my old one."

She turned her back on them, pulled her prison garb over her shoulders, and stepped into the smartsuit. It seemed to flow up and over her nakedness like something alive, coating her contours as if made to measure.

"Ed," she said in amazement, "they've downloaded my old suit's memory core and settings. This one is exactly like the old one, but..." She closed her eyes and murmured something, communicating with the suit. "It's faster. It knows more – its memory cache is far larger than the old suit's." She shook her head, laughing.

Carew reached into his trouser pocket and found the old coin which he'd carried with him since the age of ten. He felt for the statuette, thinking that the authorities might have seen their way to supplying him with that too – but such largesse was too much to hope for.

Jed found a mini-bar and broke out three ice-cold beers in celebration. He passed them round and hoisted his own. "To life," he toasted.

"If not liberty," Lania rejoined.

"That supposes," Carew said, slaking his thirst with a mouthful of beer, "we agree to undertake the mission."

"As much as you detest the Expansion elite," Lania said, "I can't see you not agreeing to their offer. Or would you rather die by lethal injection?"

Carew smiled. "As much as I detest the bastards..." He paused. "You're right. I'll agree. Jed?"

"What do *you* think, boss?"

"And Lania?"

"I'd choose life over death any day. And to tell the truth, the idea of speeding through Vetch space on the *Hawk* is rather exciting. Call me shallow, but I'd do this even if my life didn't depend on it."

Carew nodded. "That's settled then. We accept the offer."

"Does that mean we're going?" Jed said.

"Yes, Jed," Carew said, clapping the engineer on the back, "that means we're risking our necks on a harebrained mission through Vetch space on a spurious errand after long-lost colonists."

Lania cocked her head at him. "You don't believe what Gorley said?"

Carew thought about it. "Let's say that I'll treat his explanation with a healthy dose of scepticism, until we find out the real reason – if we ever do."

She nodded. "I must admit, when he claimed it was a scientific mission, as well as a rescue mission, I began to wonder."

"And yet," Carew began, "what else can it be? I'd like to know a little more about these cultists from Procyon, if possible."

Lania spoke to her smartsuit, but shook her head. "Nothing in the cache," she said.

"I wonder if the information was intentionally excised?"

Jed pointed to a terminal and screen in the corner of the room. "How about trying the station's net?"

"I'll give it a go," Lania said, striding over to the screen and running expert fingers across the touchpad. The Expansion flag, a florid capital E bounded by a dozen stars, rotated on the screen.

She smiled up at Carew and said, "Limited access only. But" – she nipped her bottom lip between white teeth – "I'm pretty certain I can get around that."

Carew drained his beer and opened another one. He moved to the viewscreen and stared out. A dozen starships, varying in size from two-person exploration vessels to vast void liners, moved slowly to and from the station, scintillating in the starlight.

Lania said, "That's strange."

"What?" He joined her at the terminal. Jed stood beside Lania, staring at the scrolling text.

"There's absolutely no information at all on the cultists from Procyon." She looked up at him. "It's obviously been removed."

"Procyon cultists," Jed said to himself.

Carew looked at him.

"It's just..." The chunky engineer hesitated. "When I was on Tamalkin, twenty years ago and I came across that crashed starship I told you about – well, I remember this group who didn't exactly worship it, but it was the centre of their beliefs in some way."

"In what way?" Lania asked.

Jed shook his head. "That's just it... I can't remember. But I do recall they called themselves the Sons of Procyon."

Carew said to Lania, "Trawl for crashed starships and see what we come up with."

Lania nodded and her long fingers danced across the touchpad.

Seconds later the results came up and she shook her head. "Same again. Absolutely nothing."

Carew took a long swallow of ice-cold beer and nodded. "That's interesting in itself. So we know that the authorities want no-one to know anything at all about Procyon cultists or crashed starships."

Jed said, "What do you think they're hiding?"

"I wish I knew," Carew said. "But it must relate to the mission. They want to trace the colonists for some reason known only to themselves, and all this talk about 'scientific exploration' is so much hot air."

For the next hour they drank and chatted amongst themselves, Carew impatient – now that they knew the mission was imminent – to give their decision to the officials and get under way. There would be the *Hawk* to test-fly, the flight-path through the void to program into the ship's smartcore.

Lania lay on a foam-form, miles away, as she played with her new smartsuit. For his part, Jed drank a great many beers – suggesting at one point that he regale his friends with a series of bawdy poems he had learned from a bar-keeper on Mintaka III. Carew managed to dissuade him, nursing his beer and contemplating what the future might hold.

Lania resurfaced from her communion with the smartsuit and smiled across at him. "What are you thinking, Ed?"

He grunted a humourless laugh. "Looking ahead, Lania. Wondering what we'll do when we get back."

"Tough they won't let us keep the *Hawk*."

Carew smiled. "I never really thought they would, in all honesty."

"So we'll be bankrupt, without a ship – and who'd employ three known ex-criminals?" She gave him an odd look. "And what about the statuette the dealer wanted?"

"Destroyed with the *Poet*," he said. "I left it on the flight-deck when they dragged us out."

She looked at him, smiling her *I-know-something-you-don't-know* smile. "You sure about that, Ed?"

"Sure I'm sure. How was I to know the bastards would slag the *Poet*?"

She said, "You left it on the recess beside your lounger, hm?"

Carew laughed. "You picked it up, didn't you? But they searched us."

"They just stripped us to ensure we weren't carrying weapons, Ed. But I *was* carrying the statuette and the animal figure I liberated from the museum."

Jed looked across at her drunkenly. "How could you be carrying them if they strip-searched you?" He stopped. "Oh."

"Didn't you wonder why I was fidgeting on the couch, Ed?" She shuffled uncomfortably. "I'll retrieve them just as soon as we're installed aboard the *Hawk*."

Carew laughed. "Does your talent know no limits, Lania Takiomar?"

"So when we do get back from the far side of Vetch territory," she said, "you think a hundred thousand units will buy us a new ship?"

"Something at the bottom end of the market, perhaps."

Jed raised his bottle. "To... to L-lania Takiomar!" he slurred.

"I'll drink to that," Carew said.

The toast was interrupted by a chime from the door. It slid open, and Commander Gorley and Director Choudri strode into the room.

Gorley looked from Jed to Lania; then his contemptuous gaze alighted on Carew. "I can see you have been availing yourselves of the hospitality provided," he said. "I take it you've come to a decision?"

Carew raised his bottle. "You'll be pleased to know that the decision was unanimous," he said. "We'll fly you through Vetch space to the Devil's Nebula."

Director Choudri tempered the atmosphere with a smile. "Excellent, my friends. Now, I advise you to get some rest. The test-flight is scheduled to commence in a little under ten hours from now."

He nodded a farewell and strode from the room.

Carew stood and moved to the viewscreen. Soon, he would have liberty, of sorts. He looked beyond the starships moving around the station and stared at the sweep of stars that was Vetch space.

Way beyond, a faint smudge at the limit of his vision, was the distinctive horned shape of the Devil's Nebula.

CHAPTER SEVEN

THAT MORNING OVER breakfast Maatja tried to detect some change in her parent's manner. If her father had indeed been chosen by the Weird, then surely he would have said something. At the very least, the honour conferred by the aliens would be obvious to her. But he behaved just as he always had: calm, softly-spoken, smiling and joking with Maatja and her sister.

They sat in their cool hut and ate a meal of fruit and phar, dried now and cut into chewy strips. It was more palatable like this, but still Maatja found it hard to swallow. She wondered if this was because she knew what it was doing to her people, or simply that it didn't taste very good. Perhaps a bit of both, she thought.

"Tomorrow the Flyer comes!" Hahta said.

Maatja looked at her father. "Why is it coming?" she asked.

"It brings news," he said. "News that will be important to us."

"Did Leah and Rahn tell you this?"

"At a meeting three nights ago, they said they had been contacted by the Weird and told of the coming."

Only the Elders, Leah and Rahn, communicated directly with the aliens. Sometimes, a giant Sleer came to the clearing and sought out the Elders, and they would all go into their hut and talk for hours. Or Maatja presumed they talked, though she had never heard voices issuing from the hut.

It was not a foraging day today, but even so Maatja told her mother that she was going into the jungle for berries. While her parents repaired the thatch of their hut and Hahta played with other children her age, Maatja stepped into the undergrowth behind the hut and ran into the jungle. She took the well-worn path used by the foragers, then struck off north to the clearing of the ghala tree.

On the way she stopped at a lakka bush, sat before it and picked a dozen berries. She ate them one by one, then felt her stomach heave. She vomited her breakfast all across the jungle floor and a minute later began to feel hungry.

On the way to the clearing, she picked fruit and berries and ate a second breakfast.

She came to the ghala tree and looked about for the twig-and-leaf symbol. She found it across the clearing, stuck into the loam. Kavan, the outcast boy, had told her that the circle of the clearing denoted the time it took the sun to circle World. The left half of the clearing marked the hours of darkness and the right half daylight. The stick symbol was planted in the daylight half, a body's length from the top of the circle – which meant, Maatja calculated, that she didn't have long to wait.

She would tell Kavan about the coming of the Flyer tonight and see if he knew anything about it. Sometimes he was full of information about the Weird and the fissure people, but at others he said he knew nothing. All his information was gleaned from what he overheard at the Outcast's nightly meetings, and from what his father had told him about the fissure people.

At first, Maatja had refused to believe his stories. She had been brought up to believe in the goodness of the Weird – after all, they provided for the fissure people, didn't they? But then a few years ago Kavan had told her about the effect of phar on humans, and as an experiment she had taken lakka berries every day for a week and expelled the phar from her system, and over the next few days she had begun to notice a difference. She felt brighter, more alert; and strangely, she no longer felt in awe of the Weird. They were just another life-form, one among many, but the ones who provided the foodstuff that kept her people drugged.

"But why do they give us phar?" she had asked Kavan a long time ago. "What do they want from us?"

The lithe jungle boy had simply shrugged and said, "They want *us*, Maatja. They want humans. You know that the Harvester sometimes takes humans, and sometimes they are Chosen and go to the lair of the Weird."

"Yes," she had persisted, "but *why* do they want us?"

And Kavan had shrugged again and admitted his ignorance.

She waited in the dappled light of the jungle, alert for sounds of Kavan's approach. As an Outcast, he prided himself on his stealth. Only on time in twenty did she hear him coming; more often, he approached from behind and frightened her with a dangled vine or tossed yikka spider.

She sat up suddenly. This time, for some reason, Kavan was making no effort to soften his approach – if indeed it was Kavan crashing through the undergrowth. She leapt up and concealed herself behind a stand of ferns, her heart beating fast.

Seconds later Kavan burst into the clearing and looked around wildly, a tall gangly boy with thin limbs and a shock of almost-white hair. He saw her behind the fern and ran across to her.

He grabbed her hand and pulled her from the clearing.

"What – ?" she began as she stumbled along beside him, sprinting ever deeper into the jungle.

"Sleer!" he hissed.

The word sent a jolt of panic through her. They ran even faster, leaping over fallen trees and dodging hanging vines. From time to time Kavan darted a glance over his shoulder, then redirected their course minimally.

Then she heard it – the sound of pursuit – and her heart felt as if it might burst from her chest.

She heard a crashing in her wake, the rending of trees and undergrowth. She looked over her shoulder and caught a glimpse of something purple and blue – like a huge, animated afterbirth, in the approximate shape of a human being – following them at speed.

They darted left, beneath the purple fronds of a ghala tree. Kavan pulled her after him, jinking this way and that in a zigzag course in an effort to lose the creature.

"Lots..." – he panted – "...lots of Weird activity at the moment. Something's... happening. Don't know what."

They burst into a sunlit clearing and Kavan tugged her across it, then stopped suddenly.

Before them, hanging from the treetops, was the massive proboscis of a yeela. Twice as thick as a grown man and as tall as a tree, it hung a metre from the jungle floor, the questing snout of an animal that lived high above in the treetops.

It bulged, as if something was imprisoned within its skin.

She turned. The Sleer had emerged from the jungle and stopped dead, staring across at them with vast black eyes set in its bloody face.

She had seen Sleer in the clearing, of course, but never as close as this.

It was man-shaped, but bloody and blue, as if it had been freshly skinned. She knew the Sleer were immensely strong and did not require weapons to kill their victims. Its big, bare hands were powerful enough to crush a human skull.

It set off towards them, then stopped suddenly.

Something was protruding from its neck and a liquid – like blood, but much thicker – geysered from the wound.

Maatja turned. An Outcast knelt behind her, firing another arrow at the Sleer; behind him, a second Outcast dropped from the orifice of the yeela's trunk.

Before her, the Sleer took a step forward, reaching out for them. Another arrow hit home, this time slamming into its great chest. The creature fell to its knees.

Maatja felt a hand grab her arm. She was dragged towards the yeela's trunk, and a second later she was pulled up into the dark, fetid confines of the proboscis. It convulsed, and before she knew it she was being carried up, away from the clearing, in a great, muscular spasm.

She closed her eyes and tried not to think about what the Sleer might have done to her and Kavan.

She wondered if she would find herself inside the stomach of the yeela and wondered how they might emerge. But a minute or so later she saw daylight above her head – a circle of red light. A face appeared and hands reached out for her, pulling her from the trunk; behind her, Kavan and the two Outcasts tumbled out.

She blinked. She was high in the treetops, standing on what looked like a great fungal platform lodged between the branches. As she watched, the hole from which she'd emerged irised shut.

Kavan smiled at her. "It's how we get to the jungle floor so fast," he explained.

One of the men looked from Maatja to Kavan. "So this is your little fissure friend," he said.

Kavan said, "Maatja. She eats lakka."

"You were lucky," the Outcast said. "The Sleer swept through the jungle six hours ago, looking for us. They caught one of us, before the rest of us escaped. Then they went back to their fetid lair, apart from that one bastard."

Kavan said, "I came to warn you, Maatja. The Sleer would have taken you for an Outcast."

"What would it have done to me?" she asked in a small voice.

The man made a squashing gesture with his fist and a squelching sound with his lips.

Maatja looked around the platform. It was vast, extending for hundreds of metres through the treetops. Here and there she saw great hanging seed pods as big as huts, where Kavan's people lived. Dozens of Outcasts sat on the platform, making things with vines and leaves; others came and went from the pod-houses.

The man smiled at her amazement. "We are civilised up here," he said. "Not quite the savages your people would have you believe." He paused, then said, "You should think about coming to live with us, Maatja."

Before she could reply, the man spoke quickly to Kavan. Maatja didn't catch his words.

Kavan said, "I must take you back now. This way."

Maatja felt a moment of panic when she thought they were about to descend to the jungle floor, but Kavan took her hand and led her across the platform. The man nodded at her in silent farewell.

She tripped after Kavan; they passed families preparing fruit, and children playing. A minute later they left the populated platform and moved along a narrow, grey strip of material, slung like a bridge between the treetops.

She said, "And all this is a yeela?"

He nodded. "The yeela is nothing but a vast skin, with trunks that suck up food from the jungle floor. It absorbs insects and plants through the membrane of its trunks." He laughed. "It doesn't like humans."

"How far does it stretch, Kavan?"

"Oh, kilometres and kilometres. In some places it's wide like the platforms back there, in others thin like this."

"And it doesn't mind you living on its skin?"

The boy laughed. "Well, it's never shrugged us off," he said.

From the position of the great bloated sun hanging above their heads, Maatja could see that they were heading south, towards the fissure. They walked for an hour, stopping from time to time to stare across the canopy cover and admire the view. The jungle seemed to extend for ever, and from this vantage point, for the very first time, Maatja could see the series of fissures that split the skin of World.

Kavan stopped, touched her arm and said, "Look." He pointed through the trees.

Far below was her clearing, a long stretch of sandy earth next to the fissure. She looked down at the line of huts in the shadow of the jungle and all her people going about their daily chores.

Kavan took her hand and led her towards another grey platform slung between high branches. At its centre was a dimple, which sprung open as they approached.

"How does it know we want to go down?" she asked.

"It doesn't. It just opens in response to pressure, thinking we might be small birds or something. I'll come down with you."

He slipped into the trunk, taking her hand and helping her down after him. Maatja felt the tight skin constrict around her, then she was drawn down the trunk like a morsel of food in the throat of a giant.

As she dropped, she wondered if any of the fissure people had travelled like this before.

Minutes later Kavan was deposited on the jungle floor. He caught her as she fell from the end of the trunk.

He pointed. "Through there," he said.

"Will you be at the ghala tree tomorrow, Kavan?"

He nodded. "Same time?"

She smiled, then raised her hand in a quick wave and hurried through the undergrowth. When she looked back, Kavan had climbed back into the yeela trunk and was a small bulge travelling up its grey length.

She hurried through the jungle, picking berries as she went, and came to the clearing a few minutes later.

She moved to her hut. Her parents were finishing off the thatch and Hahta was playing with her carved wooden jeera-pig. Her mother smiled at Maatja as she sat in the shade of the hut; it was as if she had never been away.

She thought of the Sleer and the Outcasts' tree-top retreat and wondered what it might be like to live the life of an Outcast.

That night, as the sun went down, Maatja sat in her tree and watched a procession of a dozen Flyers, transiting the ruddy dome of the sun.

CHAPTER EIGHT

THE TEST-FLIGHT had gone well. Lania and Jed had taken the *Hawk* on a vast ellipse around the station, a team of armed guards on the flight-deck at all times, monitoring their every move. Lania had integrated seamlessly with the smartcore and Jed reported that the drives ran like a dream. She had emerged from the meld, hours later, in a state little short of elation. While she had loved the *Poet*, she had to admit that it had been a junk heap beside the *Hawk*.

An odd effect of melding with the *Hawk* was that, unlike her integration with the *Poet*, she lost all awareness of the passage of time. What had seemed to her like a flight of mere minutes turned out, when she emerged and consulted with Jed, to have lasted almost two hours.

Twelve hours later, she boarded the *Hawk* with Carew and Jed and was escorted by a guard to a suite of rooms adjacent to the flight-deck. Their berths were small but comfortable, and to her surprise she found all of the possessions she had assumed incinerated with the destruction of the *Poet*: her holo-cubes showing herself as a child with her father, her moving picture book of Xaria, the wardrobe of clothes which she hardly wore these days, thanks to her smartsuit.

She hurried from her berth and knocked on Ed's sliding door. "Ed, they've collected all my stuff from the *Poet*."

"Likewise," Ed said. "I thought I'd never see my books again. They've brought over everything but our weapons."

"Oh – and I thought you might like this." She held out the Hhar statuette.

He took it, smiling. "Thank you."

She shrugged. "Chances are they would have returned it anyway, but I didn't know that, then."

They were to be accompanied on the mission by six heavily-armed militia, outfitted in bulky golden armour. Lania wondered whether these hulking men and women – silent, surly types who seemed to be under orders not to speak to the flight-crew, never mind establish eye-contact – were there to monitor Carew, Jed and herself, or to provide security at journey's end. She asked Ed.

"Both, I suspect," he said as they walked onto the flight-deck.

Jed was already hammocked in his sling, going through pre-flight diagnostics. He smiled as they entered. "I could spend my life with these beauties," he murmured as they took their positions.

Lania slipped into her sling and felt the ship fitting itself around her, much as the smartsuit enveloped and cradled her. She could almost feel the power of the *Hawk,* gathered in her belly, in her head. The ship was an extension of her body; she felt energised and in control.

Commander Gorley and Director Choudri strode onto the flight-deck and took their seats at the rear. "Estimated time of departure?" Gorley snapped.

"Fifteen minutes and counting," Lania said. She went through routines checks with Jed and tried to ignore the presence of the Expansion officials.

The voyage through the void, transecting the outer edge of Vetch space, was scheduled to take a little over four days, if everything went smoothly and according to plan. The *Hawk* carried the latest weaponry, controlled of course by the complement of militia, and the Expansion officials were confident that they would outgun the aliens in any dog-fight. From the far edge of Vetch space to the fringe of the Devil's Nebula was a journey of less than a day.

Lania would not be melded for the duration of the journey, only at departure and landfall and if anything untoward occurred in between. From time to time during the journey, she might integrate herself with the smartcore in order to ensure the smooth running of the ship, but for the most part the *Hawk* would be on automatic pilot.

Now Jed powered up the main drives and counted down from ten, and Lania eased the ship away from the station, allowing the drives to kick in incrementally.

"Phasing," Jed said.

They made the transition from real space to the realm that underpinned reality, the grey non-space through which ships could travel vast distances, reaching far stars, without approaching the speed of light. Through the viewscreen, the sweep of stars that was Vetch territory disappeared, to be replaced by the swirling pewter monochrome of the void. The sight was familiar and reassuring; Lania felt herself smiling as she sank into the *Hawk*, lost all sense of self and the passage of time. She was the *Hawk* and they were arrowing through the void faster than any ship before it.

She came to her senses twelve hours later, feeling as if just an hour had elapsed. A smiling Jed, no longer in his sling, passed her a steaming mug of coffee. Ed was laid out on his couch, snoring gently. There was no sign of Gorley, Choudri, or the militia.

"Thanks." She cupped the coffee and took a welcome sip. She felt drained but elated. The ship thrummed beneath their feet.

"How was that?" she asked Jed.

"Like a dream, Lania. You?"

She laughed. "That about sums it up, Jed. Like a dream. You think we can steal the *Hawk* when the goons aren't looking?"

"I'll work on it," he said.

A little later, Ed woke up and stretched. He looked around. "How nice to be all alone," he said. "Just like old times."

Jed said, "Gorley and Choudri lasted an hour, then turned in. I slept for a few hours a while ago. We're keeping station time, so it's just about breakfast time."

Lania laughed. "You think about nothing but your stomach, Jed."

"Not quite true," he said.

"Is," she said. "I recall that time on Venson when all you wanted to do was eat the local truffles rather than go –"

"Well, they were rather good, Lania."

"Will you two," Ed said, "stop your squabbling." He leaned forward and touched a control. On the viewscreen, the void was replaced by what looked like a yin-yang symbol.

"Human-Vetch space," Ed explained. "We're that flashing dot, see."

She made out a blinking red light, crossing through the tail of the comma that was Vetch space. According to the diagram, they were about a third of the way through the alien territory.

Carew touched the controls again and the yin-yang symbol shifted to an edge-on perspective, so that the depth of the respective Human-Vetch space could be seen. Vetch space bulged, marked out in red light. By comparison, Human space was empty, just a thin blue wedge of stars settled on the edge of the space abutting Vetch territory.

"Makes one feel a little lonely," Ed said to himself.

"I wonder how the human colonists in the Devil's Nebula feel?" Lania said. "Really all alone out there."

"If they survived," Ed reminded her. "They sent out a mayday, after all."

Jed shrugged. "If they did survive, then that's what they wanted, wasn't it? A place far away from the rest of humanity?"

Ed smiled grimly. "Well, they've certainly got that," he said. "Anyone for breakfast?"

*   *   *

THEY ATE IN a lounge at the top of the ship, a long room with viewscreens set in each flank, affording a view of the void. Gorley and Choudri were already there when the three arrived, seated at the far end of a central table with mugs of coffee. The Expansion men had been chatting quietly, but now they fell silent.

Lania saw no reason not to be friendly. Ed seemed to have a grudge against everyone in any position of authority, but she would treat the pair as she would anyone else aboard the *Hawk*. To date she had found Gorley rather cold and remote, but the small Indian gentleman, Choudri, she rather liked.

She responded to the latter's smile and told him about her first real shift at the controls of the *Hawk*.

"I'm pleased the ship satisfies your expectations, Ms Takiomar," Choudri said.

"Call me Lania. I don't like formality, especially aboard ship."

Ed handed self-heating trays of food to Lania and Jed, and they sat around the table and ripped open their meals. "You'll find Lania, although a fine pilot, is not exactly conventional," Carew said.

"That," Commander Gorley said, "is a charge that could be levelled at all three of you."

Lania glanced at Ed. He sat back and gazed at the Commander, a slight smile playing over his thin lips. "Charged with being unconventional," he said. "Now, that is a compliment."

"It was, I assure you, not meant as one."

"So you like convention?" Ed said.

Lania chewed on a mouthful of reconstituted egg, watching both men. This should be interesting. Ed was never happier than when arguing with someone whose viewpoint he despised.

"For the smooth running of a stable and equitable society, Captain Carew, then yes, the conventional, the norm, is what helps maintain a status quo. A well-balanced society cannot sustain mavericks and anarchists."

"You think not?" Ed asked. "I would have thought that one of the necessary components of such a society, in order to counter-balance the force of repression represented by the likes of yourself, would be just such people, mavericks and anarchists. The Expansion is a big place, big enough for all forms of society – even radical societies, like those I would rather be a part of."

Lania turned to look at the severe Expansion man.

"Thankfully for all of us," he said, "You and your like do not hold the reins of power. It is a goal of our regime to spread homogeneity across the human diaspora."

"Homogeneity? A bland, sanitised society peopled by drones, easily manipulated and controlled?"

"A society bedevilled no more by those of a criminal tendency, like you and your crew."

Lania raised her coffee cup and smiled sweetly at Gorley. "And respects of the day to you, too."

Ed smiled. He looked across at Gorley. "Is that why you mounted this mission, Commander, to bring the cultists under your control? Or to ensure that they do not return with their ideals, one day, to infect the Expansion?"

Gorley pursed his thin lips, staring at Ed. "I've explained the reason for this mission, Captain. I assure you the Expansion has nothing to fear from the cultists, especially that they might one day return to Human space with their crazy ideas in tow."

Ed shrugged. "I hope they've managed to find a habitable world and start a free society." He paused and then went on, "What I fear is what you and your henchmen are planning once we locate them."

"I can assure you on that score, Captain Carew," the Commander said. "You have nothing to fear." He stood. "Now, if you will excuse me." He nodded to all present and strode from the lounge.

Ed watched him go, a smile animating his usually placid features. Lania laughed. "I think you got to him, Captain."

Choudri glanced up from his empty cup. He had been silent during the exchange, but now he said, "It would be a mistake, Captain, if you thought that Gorley and his like are representative of the political make-up of the Expansion."

Lania looked up, surprised. Ed was evidently taken aback, too. He stared at Choudri. "Are you saying that he isn't?"

Choudri shrugged. "Oh, he represents a certain reactionary viewpoint, but he is opposed by many in the ruling councils across the face of the Expansion. Myself included."

"Really?" Ed said. "Can you tell me where you stand on, first of all, hauling us before a kangaroo court, finding us guilty of transgressing Vetch space, ordering our deaths and then letting us off if we agree to fly you through Vetch space? Do you comprehend the hypocrisy of the Expansion's stance?"

Choudri smiled disarmingly. "I can only concur one hundred per cent with your analysis, Captain. Your error is in thinking that the decision to do this was a unanimous one. The Commander and his allies faced opposition on the matter, but they out-voted us. One of the reasons I volunteered to come along on the mission was to ensure that the old fashioned term... fair play... was adhered to."

Lania looked at Ed, who nodded, taking his time to reply, then said, "Perhaps you can tell me the real reason for the mission? Because," he said, leaning forward, "I don't believe for one minute what Gorley told us about ensuring the survival of the colonists and mounting a scientific mission of exploration."

Choudri was silent for a while, staring down as he turned his cup in his worn, brown fingers. He looked up at last and said, "The overt goal of the mission is just what the Commander told you, Captain."

"And the covert?" Ed asked.

Choudri smiled. "Would you believe me if I told you that even I, as Deputy Director of External Operations, do not know the covert – the *real*, if you will – aim of the mission?"

Across the table, Jed gaped, like an astounded goldfish. Lania smiled and looked at Ed.

"So you are not taken in by Gorley's claims?" Ed said.

The Indian shook his head. "Of course not, Captain." He looked from Ed to Jed, and then to Lania. "But this must not go any further than this room, do you understand?"

Ed said, "I assumed that Gorley had the entire ship bugged?"

"He did, but I took the precaution of having this area debugged."

Ed smiled. "I appreciate your candour, Director."

"Merely because we find ourselves on opposite sides of the law," the Indian murmured, "does not mean that we cannot see eye to eye on certain matters." He pushed his cup to the centre of the table, preparing to taking his leave.

Ed said, "One more thing. You've been surprisingly frank so far, but I wonder if you can give me one further answer?"

Choudri hesitated. "That depends on the question."

"It's simple," Ed said. "Why us? Why, among the hundreds, if not thousands, of other eligible crews, did you choose us?"

Choudri rose, his fingertips splayed across the table-top as he considered the question. "I told you back at the station that the reason was that you were the best. You were good, I admit that. But not the best. I was surprised, to say the least, when we did not employ one of our own navy teams."

"So why?"

Choudri shook his head, looking genuinely mystified. "I don't honestly know, Captain. The fact is that Commander Gorley and his cabal insisted that you crew the *Hawk*."

He excused himself and hurried from the lounge.

Lania was the first to break the silence that settled after Choudri's departure. "Well," she said, "do you believe him?"

Ed was leaning back in his chair, stroking the line of his long jaw. He appeared not to have heard her question.

Jed said, "He's an Expansion man. He's spinning us a line. Playing us for fools."

Ed said, "I'm not so sure about that, Jed. Why would he lie? What does he stand to gain by telling us what he's told us? Gaining our trust, for reasons of his own, entrenching our opposition to Gorley –

as if he really needs to work to do that! I honestly don't know."

"For what it's worth," Lania said, "I believe him. I've liked Choudri from the off. I think he's genuine."

Jed stared at her, incredulous. "You believe him? Are you insane? Can't you see? He's one of them. Against us."

"Hey," Ed said. "Calm down, Jed, okay?"

"Calm down? I don't believe what you're saying. The bastard's a reactionary. You're wrong to trust him a centimetre."

Ed looked at both of them. "Perhaps we should give the Director the benefit of the doubt for the time being, hm? We probably won't know where we properly stand until we see what gives at journey's end."

"Christ!" Jed spat.

Lania pushed aside her tray. She had finished the meal without realising she had done so. "Like I said, I trust the guy." She stared across at Jed. "It's good to know we have an ally aboard the *Hawk*, is how I look at it."

The engineer made a disgusted sound, stood quickly and left the lounge.

Ed watched him go. "What's eating him, suddenly?"

Lania shrugged. "Let him be, Ed. He'll calm down."

SHE LEFT THE lounge and took the dropchute down to her berth. She lay on her bunk for a while, feeling the vibration of the ship in her bones, but she was still energised from her time melded with the *Hawk* and couldn't properly rest.

She remembered then that the ship had a small gym on a lower deck and decided that a quick work-out was what she needed. One of the disadvantages with the *Poet*, she thought, was the space restrictions: she'd been forced to exercise in her own cramped quarters, which hadn't really been sufficient.

She stripped off her smartsuit, feeling it peel away from her nakedness like a shed skin. She was aware of being suddenly alone, denied instant access to limitless information. She flung the suit across the bed, pulled on a red jumpsuit, and stepped from her berth.

She took the dropchute to the lower deck and padded along the corridor to the gym. She was pleased to find that she had it to herself. She stood beneath the scanner and allowed the ship to program her a work-out regime to cover the next three days.

For the next hour she moved from machine to machine, starting with a slow jog and building up to a sprint, then moving on to weights and presses. It felt good to be exercising again, to have the endorphins racing through her system as she gradually increased her exertion and began to sweat.

Her thoughts strayed to past events, incidents with Carew and Jed – some funny, some dangerous – and then earlier, to her teens and childhood. She liked to think of Xaria, the beauty of her home planet, its glorious coastlines and mountains, but she could never dwell long on the geography of the world without coming up against the painful memories of her childhood. She had returned to Xaria in recent years in a bid to reclaim her past, and to a certain extent it had worked. But at times like these, when her body was active and her mind empty, painful thoughts flooded in to fill the vacuum.

She finished the last of the bench-presses and decided she'd done enough. She crossed to the shower, undressed and turned under the drumming heat of the jet, pushing old memories aside and thinking of Ed and his handling of the Expansion officials.

There had been a time, perhaps eight or nine years ago, when she'd thought that Ed might have been attracted to her. Events had proved her wrong, however; she had mistaken his concern for something more. She had been young – very young – and she wondered if his lack of interest was because of that and their age difference; he was, she admitted, old enough to be her father. She wondered if that was why she was attracted to him?

As far as she could tell, for as long as she'd been working for Ed aboard the *Poet*, he had never had a relationship – in the physical sense – with anyone on any of the many worlds they'd visited. It was as if he didn't need intimacy. He had told her, once, that he preferred ideas to people... and that felt true, to her. He would talk all night about abstruse ideas and philosophies, but clam up the moment she tried to get him to talk about himself and his emotions.

She was distracted by a movement across the room.

One of the guards had entered the gym and was stripping off his armour. He was a tall guy with a crew-cut, and stood with his back to Lania. He pressed the command console on his chest; sections of the golden armour lifted away with a hum of servo-mechanisms. Lania watched, the lengthy process bringing back a slew of painful memories.

Only when the guard lifted off the chest armour and laid it aside did Lania see that she was mistaken. The guard was not a man, but a woman in her mid-thirties: tall, tanned, athletically built and well-muscled.

Lania stopped the shower and activated the drier, and the woman turned and gave her a big smile. Underneath the armour, she wore a sweat-soaked one-piece, which she proceeded to peel off.

Lania stepped from the cubicle and pulled on her jumpsuit. She peered at the woman's armour, noting the insignia on the breast-plate. She smiled at her. "Based at Gerontious? You must have done your basic training on Macarthur's Landfall?"

"Don't remind me, girl. Three months of sweat, blood, more blood and a shitload of tears."

Lania smiled, remembering her own sweat, blood and tears. "How long have you been with the militia?"

"Just a couple of years. I worked for ten years as a cop on Mallarme, Arcturus." The woman wiped sweat from her face with her wadded one-piece and stepped into the shower. She turned under the jet to face Lania. "This is my second stint of active duty for the Expansion."

Lania laughed. "Escorting a bunch of criminals on a suicide mission through Vetch space. Someone didn't like you."

The woman smiled. "I'm Alleghri, Gina Alleghri."

"Lania Takiomar."

Gina frowned. "From Xaria, right?"

Lania sat down on a bench and leaned back against the bulkhead, watching the woman soap her lithe, muscled body. She had lovely breasts, full and dark-nippled. "How do you know?"

"I'm interested in the diaspora. Xaria was settled by colonists from Oceania a few hundred years ago. I reckoned Takiomar was an Asian name. Hey-presto."

"Quite the detective," Lania said. "I thought you might have been given our files."

Gina shook her head. "We were told very little. All hush-hush. Just that we were escorting a bunch of very dangerous crims through Vetch space." The woman activated the drier and turned. "If you don't mind me saying, you're the strangest looking set of criminals I've ever seen."

"Seen many?"

"My first posting was to Boronia, a prison planet. You don't exactly conform to stereotype. A dour, ageing captain, a fat slob of an engineer, and a beautiful pilot. Not exactly the Dorrigo Gang."

Lania smiled. "That's probably because we don't see ourselves as criminals." She shrugged. "We just sail close to the wind."

Gina stepped from the cubicle and pulled a fresh one-piece from a hold-all. She dressed, then assembled the armour around herself again. Lania found herself regretting that the show was over.

"That's not what I heard, girl. Word is you're dangerous killers who wouldn't think twice about..." She drew her finger across her throat.

"That's rubbish. We've never killed a soul. We wouldn't."

Fully-armoured now, Gina dropped into a squat before Lania and smiled. "No? But you supplied arms to the rebels on Ballantyne's World?"

"Before my time," Lania said. "I'm sure the captain had his reasons. All we've done is salvage a few wrecks – and I admit one or two of those might have been classed as theft." She shrugged. "Run some samizdat literature between colonies. Transported a rogue telepath. And then we went to Hesperides on a damned-fool errand for an art dealer. When we lifted off, the authorities pounced."

"Tough."

"Even tougher – we were sentenced to death, with a get-out clause: take the *Hawk* into Vetch territory, or die." She gestured. "Didn't take a lot of thinking about."

"You shouldn't complain, girl. I'm here on routine duty – I didn't do anything wrong, just ordered to get my shit together and here I am."

"You a conscript, or did you volunteer?"

"Volunteer. Dreamed about being in the militia since I was this high. Thought about nothing else. Got my grades, was accepted at the military academy on Borussia, then trained on Macarthur's Landfall."

Lania considered the woman's dancing blue eyes. She said, "That bastard Colonel Lansdowne still terrorising the recruits?"

Gina's eyes widened. "You know Lansdowne?"

"I was on Macarthur's, too. Only I wasn't a volunteer."

She liked the woman, even though she was a grunt, and she would have happily confided in her had the ship's alarm not blared through the gym just then.

"Shit, what the hell?" Gina said, moving like lightning for the exit.

Lania followed, making a detour to her berth to

collect her smartsuit. She was still pulling it on when she entered the flight-deck.

Jed was in his sling, hands dancing over the controls. Choudri and Gorley were peering at a screen, Ed beside them.

"What's going on, Ed?"

"We've been detected. A Vetch ship's on our tail."

The image of a squat, black and yellow Vetch interceptor appeared on the viewscreen, tiny against the grey void. Choudri said, "It's about a minute behind us. Not yet within firing range, but those things carry sufficient..."

Lania was already in her sling and integrating her suit with the ship's smartcore. Within seconds, her awareness of the activity on the flight-deck fell away as she felt the ship slip into place around her. The engines became her heart, the logic-matrix her brain. She lost her sense of self; she was now, to all intents, the *Hawk*.

She heard a voice: her own. "Power, Jed?"

"Achieving maximum," she heard, as if from far away.

She gave a subliminal command and the *Hawk* accelerated. She felt it surge; they had been cruising at something like a third of their maximum speed; now they were at eighty per cent of their potential and accelerating. She knew it was only an analogue, her smartsuit channelling the sensation of tremendous speed to her sensorium, but she felt as if she were flat on her back and sliding at speed down a luge track. She was ten again, with her father in the mountains of Xaria, and she was laughing breathlessly at the top of her lungs, screaming with the heady delight of her speed.

Behind the *Hawk*, the Vetch interceptor accelerated in a bid to keep pace, but little by little it was falling behind – and Lania felt a surge of triumph. The Vetch had sent their best to nail the *Hawk*, and they were leaving the interceptor in their wake. A minute later, the vessel failed to register on the *Hawk's* sensors.

Lania remained melded with the smartcore, reluctant to relinquish the link. She maintained the *Hawk* at eighty per cent of its maximum speed and monitored the running of the engines, feeling their power as if they were a part of herself. She summoned a schematic of the space through which they were travelling, and in her mind's eye the yin-yang shape appeared: the flashing red light that was the *Hawk* was now almost three quarters of the way through Vetch territory.

She eased the engines back to something like fifty per cent of their capacity and withdrew from the meld. Her senses returned, the awareness of her surroundings. She closed her eyes and heard sounds, the steady thrum of the drives, soft voices in the background.

Choudri was speaking. "...philosophers say that the void is the reality towards which we are all destined, Captain Carew. Nirvana. Some pilots claim they attain oneness with the void, an abolition of the self."

"With respect, Director," Ed replied, "as a materialist, I cannot accept the idea."

Choudri laughed. "I give thanks that I am not a materialist. My religion gives me another dimension to existence. I would be loath to think that this is all there is to being alive. How can you live with it, Captain?"

Ed was silent for a time, before replying cryptically, "We are all prisoners of our experiences, Anish."

Lania opened her eyes. Choudri stood at the apex of the triangular flight-deck, staring out into the immensity of the void, hands clasped behind his back. Ed sat with Jed at a small table, playing some kind of board game.

She eased herself from her sling and stretched. Choudri turned. "Welcome back, Lania."

Ed smiled at her. "Good work. We're impressed."

She smiled. "Thank the *Hawk*, Ed. All I did was give a few commands. The auto-pilot would have done just as good a job."

"You know that is not true," Choudri said. "It would not have responded as quickly, as adeptly. It's a machine. The human element, I think, is necessary."

"How long have I been in there?"

Jed looked up from the board game. "Just under twenty-four hours, Lania. We've had a couple of meals and slept."

"A day? You're joking, right? I thought more like a couple of hours."

"How do you feel?" Ed asked.

"An odd combination of wired and tired. I'm going to lie down. Let's just hope no more Vetch ships try to apprehend us."

She made her way to her berth and stretched out on the bunk, hands laced under her head. She recalled a stray memory from the meld. She was ten and on a summer vacation with her father, this time swimming in the sea beside their holiday villa.

She realised she was crying. She sat up, wiped away the tears and hurried to the lounge for a tray of food. She took it back to her room and ate alone, relishing the curry – her first meal for over a day.

A chime sounded at the door. She hoped it was Ed, come to talk to her. For some reason, right now she wanted his soft voice, his wise words, to console her.

She commanded the door to open. Gina Alleghri stood in the corridor, wearing a form-hugging blue jump-suit and carrying a flask of wine.

"Heard about your stint in the sling, girl. Thought you might like a drink."

Lania smiled. "You're joking. I could kill for one. Come in."

Gina sat beside her on the bunk and poured two tumblers of red wine. They toasted the *Hawk* and laughed.

Gina lay a hand on Lania's knee, smiling at her. "Where were we, Lania? I think you were telling me that you were on Macarthur's Landfall too, only you weren't a volunteer."

Lania lay a hand on top of Gina's. "Mind if we don't talk about the past? Only, it's kind of painful."

"Hokay. So, what shall we talk about?"

Lania felt something catch in her throat as she said, "Let's not talk."

She reached out and touched the woman's cheek, a mere brush of her fingertips, but it was enough to bring Gina's lips close to hers.

They kissed, and Lania felt a sudden need deep within her.

CHAPTER NINE

ALL THAT DAY, ever since sunrise, a dozen Flyers had circled in the air high above the clearing.

Now the great sun was half-set, a vast bloody dome straddling the horizon, and the Flyers moved away, sailing high above the jungle – all, that is, but for one of their number.

Maatja sat with her people in the clearing, as the heat of the day diminished. Leah and Rahn were positioned at the front of the gathering, cross-legged. She ignored her friends' idle speculation as the Flyer disengaged itself from the procession heading north; it circled the clearing once, then came in slowly to land before the gathering.

High in the sky, the Flyer had appeared small, certainly no larger than a family hut. But as it descended, it seemed to expand and expand. Now it settled before them on the clearing, almost twice the length of a long-house, a bloated grey monstrosity like a Harvester, but without the tentacles at the head-end, or the sphincter at the other. Along its flank was a string of what looked like suckers, and at its front end what might have been tiny eyes sunk into the grey flesh of its domed face. Maatja could make out no evidence of a mouth or nose.

She wondered what important information the creature wanted to impart and how it would speak to them without a mouth.

The Flyer settled, its flanks rolling outwards as it sank onto the ground. A gasp went up from the crowd. An air of excitement filled the clearing like the charge in the air before a thunderstorm.

As she watched, Leah and Rahn stood and moved towards the domed front end of the Flyer. They paused before the creature and each held out a hand and touched its wrinkled grey hide.

They held this pose for perhaps a minute. Beside her, Jaar whispered, "They're communicating telepathically with the Flyer."

Another boy said, "Telepathy's impossible!"

"No it isn't," Maatja corrected. "My father told me that there were telepaths aboard the starship that brought our people here."

Leah and Rahn dropped their arms and backed away from the Flyer. They sat down before it, staring at the creature's blank grey face.

Seconds later, something happened which brought a gasp from everyone in the clearing.

Beneath the two deep-set eyes in the head of the Flyer, a horizontal split appeared. At first it resembled a mouth, a pair of lips opening in a long grin. Then it widened to resemble a wound, scarlet with blood.

Then something slipped from the bloody gap and everyone jumped in startlement and revulsion.

Maatja felt her heart beating quickly as she stared. A small, upright creature stood before the gathering, a spindly thing on two legs, with long arms and a big, domed head. It was blue-purple, like a Sleer but much smaller. Its body was naked and glistened with what might have been streaks of blood and a white, fatty substance.

It stood on bent legs, staring around the clearing with big black eyes; it had a tiny nose and slit lips and looked, Maatja thought, evil.

Her father had once told her that the Weird came in many forms. They were able to mould flesh just as humans had once used metals to make machines. Her father said that the Weird made their people to suit the various environments they inhabited, which was why the Flyers were able to travel through space. Maatja thought that the Flyer looked like a living creature – but was it nothing more than a fleshy spaceship that contained ugly little manikins like this one?

The creature took a step forward, then another, bobbing horribly at the knees as it moved towards where Leah and Rahn were seated.

When it reached them, it dropped into a crouch before the Elders.

It stared into their eyes and spoke.

Maatja was too far away to hear its harsh, rasping words. She stared intently at its face, but the creature seemed to articulate whatever it had to say without the slightest trace of expression. Its big eyes stared and its lips moved minimally as its rasping whisper imparted information to the Elders.

Maatja willed it to finish, so that Leah and Rahn might communicate to their people what the creature had said.

She looked around her and smiled at the open-mouthed, staring faces of the children in her group.

The creature stopped speaking and climbed slowly to its feet – like an old man with joint problems – and moved back to the Flyer. Maatja stared in wonder as it reached out, arms above its head like a diver about to leap into a pool. It leaned forward, inserted its hands into the bloody slit in the Flyer's head and appeared to be sucked off its feet. In a moment, it had vanished.

Slowly, with no apparent means of power, the Flyer rose into the air. Silently it turned and climbed and Maatja watched as it sailed off over the treetops, its bloated outline silhouetted against the light of the dying sun.

Leah stood and turned to face her people, Rahn beside her.

"The Weird," Leah said, "came with important news."

She paused, and a flurry of excited speculation passed around the gathering. She silenced it with a gesture and continued.

"Humans from the Expansion are on their way to World," she said, and hurried on. "They are coming to aid the Weird, to help expand the beneficence of the Weird throughout the Expansion."

Someone close to Maatja whispered, "What does ben... beneficence mean?"

Jaar replied, "It means food. The Weird want to give phar to all the humans across the Expansion."

Maatja looked at the boy. He sounded authoritative, but she didn't believe his explanation.

Leah was saying, "The humans will come here in a great golden ship. Though the people in the ship are one people, they are divided – some are good, and others bad. Some will help us, and others will not. The Weird want us to accommodate them as our guests, until the humans move to the lair, downriver."

One of the adults called out, "Will the Weird be moving across space to the Human Expansion?"

Leah inclined her head. "Though my contact did not say as much, I suspect this is so. We have enjoyed the benefits of the Weird for many years, and now the time has come for us to share with our fellow humans the full wonder of our benefactors."

An appreciative murmur passed through the gathering. Someone asked, "When will the humans arrive?"

"Within days," Leah said, "though my contact was not specific. We will hear their ship's approach, and the Sleer will notify us when the crew disembark so that we might prepare a suitable welcome."

The gathering broke up a short while later, but not before Leah announced that, to celebrate the good tidings, naar would be circulated and they would drink as the sun went down.

As the adults drank and the children played, Maatja slipped away and slithered down the bank of the fissure. She came to her tree and shinned her way up, until she came to the wide, accommodating fork and sat with her back against the trunk.

She reached out, plucked a freer fruit and sucked the sweet juice from its flesh.

She stared at the spread of stars that was Vetch space and the fainter sweep of far suns that was the Expansion. Hard to believe that, right now, a human ship was on its way to World.

She wondered at what Leah had said, about the Weird spreading into human space, and what the Outcasts might think about that.

She was startled, a short while later, by a commotion from the clearing. She heard a cry, followed by a ragged cheering and then a chant.

She slid down from her perch and climbed the steep incline until she came to the edge of the fissure and peered over.

Everyone, adult and child, was gathered outside the long-house where her people conducted all their important meetings. The adults were chanting, their blood warmed with naar. Maatja wondered if Leah was giving a speech: the crowd seemed to be gathered about some focal point, staring and cheering at something Maatja could not see.

She scrambled from the fissure and hurried across the clearing. She wormed her way through the crowd, using her elbows to part reluctant adults. She eventually emerged through the press, then stopped dead in her tracks.

A giant Sleer, shadowy in the twilight, stood under the thatch of the long-house. It was holding something aloft, something reduced in its mammoth grip to the dimensions of a carved doll.

As Maatja's eyes adjusted to the gloom, she saw that the Sleer was holding a body – the body of a human being.

"An Outcast!" someone cried and another cheer went up from the crowd.

Then the body, which Maatja had assumed was dead, set up a feeble groaning, and she felt suddenly sick. She stared at the Outcast's face, hoping that it was not Kavan, or one of the other Outcasts she had met the other day.

She did not recognise the limp figure – but that did not make her feel any better.

Leah stepped forward and spoke to the Sleer, and the creature slung its burden over its shoulder and stepped from the long-house. It passed within a metre of Maatja, and she caught the reek of its body, and of something else, the stench of the Outcast, who had soiled himself in terror. The crowd parted and the Sleer loped down the length of the clearing.

"To the Harvester," Leah called out, and the cheering crowd followed the Sleer and its feebly struggling victim.

Maatja remained where she was, not wishing to witness the grisly disposal of the Outcast. Tomorrow, she would go to the ghala clearing and tell Kavan what had happened, and apologise on behalf of her people.

Now she rushed behind the nearest hut and vomited onto the floor.

She heard the desperate screams of the Outcast as he approached the Harvester.

CHAPTER TEN

CAREW STOOD BEFORE the viewscreen and stared out at the swirling grey of void-space. The scene was hypnotic, strands of sourceless light twisting like smoke in an ever-shifting monochrome kaleidoscope. He thought he could make out images, definite outlines. It was said that if you stared long enough into the void, you would see whatever you wished to see. But that way lay madness.

Director Anish Choudri stood beside him. The Director had summoned the chart of this sector of space, showing them as having passed from Vetch space and on the cusp of the Devil's Nebula, fast approaching the system from which the distress signal was issuing. Behind the two men, Jed and Lania were phasing the *Hawk* from the void.

"How did you come by your crew, Captain Carew?" Choudri asked now, apropos of nothing.

He glanced at the diminutive Indian. "Why do you ask? And call me Ed, by the way."

"Very well, Ed. I asked because I'm curious. You are three very different characters, in age, background, temperament, and yet you seem to get on very well."

Carew smiled. He had never really given much thought to it. He'd had quite a few combinations over the years, but he had to admit that Lania and Jed were the best – the best at their jobs and the people he liked the most.

"I guess I... found them."

Choudri repeated the word, smiling.

"I found Lania on Rocannon's End. She was... drifting. She was around eighteen at the time, living by her wits in the pit city and looking for a better life. She'd had training – she could fly a starship and she could fight like a cat. But she was on the run from something. She told me that she couldn't sign aboard a legitimate ship. So I took her on for a trial period, and that was ten years ago."

"Did you ask her what she was running from?"

Carew shook his head. "She never volunteered the information, so I never asked. Privacy is important when you're living on top of someone in a cramped salvage vessel."

"Are you curious?"

"To tell the truth, I'm not."

Choudri laughed.

"What?" Ed asked.

"You're a very personable individual, Captain Carew. You're intelligent, superficially amiable, and yet there's something about you, a distance, an aloofness. Often with aloof people there's also a certain arrogance, but I do not detect that in you. A cynicism, yes, a weariness with the ways of the world, but no conceit."

He wondered if the Indian was right in his assessment. "I'll take that as a compliment, Anish."

Choudri looked at him. "You do realise that Lania is in love with you?"

Carew stared at the Director. "What?" The idea was ludicrous.

Choudri laughed. "No, of course you don't. Your aloofness precludes you from truly apprehending the needs of others. I hope you don't mind my speaking frankly. But" – the Indian gestured with a fine, thin-boned hand – "the fact remains that Lania Takiomar loves you."

"What makes you think...?"

Choudri held up his right hand and counted off points on his fingers. "The way she speaks to you. The way she watches you when you're talking to other people. The way her admiration almost radiates from her. She's devoted to you, Ed."

He shrugged. "She's grateful to me for saving her from a life of hardship, that's all."

"That isn't all. Open your eyes, man."

"I'm old enough to be her father, for heaven's sake."

The Indian shrugged. "She's lonely, Ed. Show her a little compassion, hm?"

The silence stretched and Carew was happy for it to do so. He hoped Choudri would drop the subject.

The Indian said, "And Jed? You found him too?"

Carew nodded. "That's right, only Lania found him. She was in a bar on Replenish, and he tried to pick her up. They got chatting and she pretty quickly worked out he was on the run. As it happened, he'd sprung himself from a prison ship and didn't have the funds to buy a new identity. He said he was a ship's engineer, so Lania brought him back to the *Poet*. We needed an engineer – I was doubling in the post, after sacking the last one. So I hired him, and the rest is history."

"I suppose you haven't enquired too much about his past, either?"

Carew smiled. "I didn't have to enquire. Jed was only too willing to tell us. Ran away from home at the age of fifteen. Taken on as an engineer's apprentice a year later, worked for the Addenbrooke Line for five years before killing a man in a bar brawl. After that, it was all downhill. Five years in jail, out for a few months before falling in with the wrong crowd and getting himself caught raiding a munitions plant. Jailed for three years, escaped. Captured again." He shook his head. "He was heading nowhere, in a manner of speaking. And then Lania found him."

"Your ship is a veritable refuge for waifs and strays."

Carew stared into the void and said bitterly, "Well, it was."

Choudri laughed. "Knowing your propensity for extricating yourself from tight situations, I'm sure everything will work out for the best."

"I hope you're right, Anish. I sincerely hope you're right."

The Indian hesitated, then said, "When all this is over and we're back in Expansion space, I'll do my best to ensure you get on your feet again, as it were."

Carew looked at the Indian. "Isn't that a strange thing for an Expansion Director to say to an unreconstructed outlaw?"

"It might be, put like that. But it isn't an odd thing for one human being to say to another, Ed."

From behind them, Jed called out, "Phasing in three, two, one..."

The scene through the viewscreen flickered. The grey of void-space stuttered, then faded. A cluttered spacescape filled the screen.

Jed whistled. "Would you look at that!"

Carew stared out, wondering if this was one of the reasons why he could not lead the life of a planet-bound citizen. He needed vistas like this one to renew his sense of wonder in the universe.

A quarter of the screen was filled by a fulminating supergiant. It blazed like a coal, giving off frequent geysers and plumes of superheated plasma. Before it, strung out in perspective along the plane of the ecliptic, were perhaps thirty planets ranging in size from gas giants to tiny, ice-bound planetoids.

The solar system was majestic in its absolute silence.

Behind it, the orange drift of the nebula provided a dramatic backdrop.

"Welcome to the threshold of the Devil's Nebula," Lania said, extricating herself from the pilot's sling and stretching. She joined them before the viewscreen and smiled at Carew. He nodded in reply, recalling what Choudri had told him earlier, and returned his gaze to the view.

The hatch at the far end of the flight-deck sighed open and Commander Gorley strode into the chamber.

He came and stood beside Lania. "I must congratulate you on getting us safely through Vetch space, Ms Takiomar."

Lania's response was formal. "It's what you hired me to do, Marshall."

"Have we located the source of the signal yet, Director?" Gorley asked.

Choudri said, "Apparently it hails from a planet closer to the sun and at the moment on its far side."

Lania pointed. "What's that?"

Choudri touched a slide on the frame of the screen, homing in on the object Lania had indicated.

At first, Carew thought it was an irregular-shaped satellite in orbit around an icy outer planet, but as the screen magnified the image it became obvious that the object was not natural. As vast as a moonlet, Carew realised, and *manufactured*.

Choudri looked at Gorley. "Should we take a closer look?"

Gorley nodded minimally.

Lania returned to her sling and guided the *Hawk* through space towards the object. Choudri returned the screen to its default setting. The object shrank suddenly and then proceeded to grow as they approached.

Ten minutes later they hung in front it, dwarfed by the immensity of the thing.

It was approximately cuboid, but the irregularity Carew had noted earlier was the result of a great section of its top right-hand corner having been sheared off.

It was dark grey and pitted as if with missile impacts, its face scorched and blackened. Where the corner had been blasted away, Carew made out interior cells, like those of a vandalised beehive.

Jed said, "Looks like some kind of orbital emplacement to me, boss. And it looks like it came off second best in the battle, too."

Only then did Carew see the debris that floated in the vacuum all around the fortification. He asked the Indian to increase the magnification again. Choudri homed in on the drifting wrecks of shattered starships, the lifeless casualties of some long ago war.

"There must be hundreds of them," Lania said.

Perhaps even thousands, Carew mused; everything from eviscerated liners to tiny, mangled shuttles. The wrecks were blasted, burned out.

Jed said, "You think the Vetch did this? Attacked the race who inhabited this system?"

"Who knows," Carew said.

Choudri looked to Commander Gorley. "Perhaps we should take a closer look at the planet down there," he said.

Gorley nodded. "We did come here in the spirit of scientific investigation, after all. Ms Takiomar, takes us down to the surface, please."

"Aye, aye, sir," Lania said, winking at Jed as she instructed the *Hawk* to begin its spiraldown.

The beleaguered fortification drifted off-screen as the *Hawk* banked and approached the planet far below, a small world scarved with dun and ochre coloration, which resolved to reveal vast deserts dotted with cities.

They dropped quickly and Lania flew them low over the arid surface. Carew stared out at approaching cities, one after the other, strung out across the desert wilderness. Surprisingly, the cities and towns appeared undamaged; Carew had been expecting to find them as devastated as the orbital emplacement. But they appeared pristine, if deserted, like the forgotten sets of some high-budget holo-vision extravaganza. The only signs of the battle that had raged above were the remains of crashed starships of alien design, half-buried in the shifting desert sands.

Ahead, the largest city of all appeared on the horizon, as eerily quiet and deserted as all the others.

Lania called out. "Should I bring the ship down there?"

Gorley nodded. "Look for a suitable landing place within the city itself."

The *Hawk* approached slowly, sand-coloured domes and towers passing beneath them. Carew searched for the slightest sign of movement, but all that stirred between the buildings was the wind-driven sand.

Choudri said, "There's no sign of vegetation anywhere. It's totally lifeless."

They moved gradually over the wreck of a downed starship, conjoined with the wreckage of the building it had destroyed.

Lania brought the ship down beyond it, in a plaza surrounded by low, round buildings, ochre brick domes, and the occasional towering minaret. Carew imagined a time when the city square had heaved with alien life, when citizens had gone about their lives, oblivious of the apocalypse to come.

The *Hawk* landed in a sandstorm of its own making, impacted gently and bobbed on its stanchions.

"Atmosphere content?" Carew asked.

"Oxygen-nitrogen-argon mix," Lania said, reading from her screen, "but rarefied. We'll have to go out there with breathing apparatus. And it's damned hot out there – over forty Celsius."

Gorley said, "I'll send out a team of militia first and then whoever would care to disembark may do so. I'd advise we venture out in teams of three, until we've ascertained that it's safe out there."

Much as Ed wanted to find something to object to in Gorley's orders, the Commander was following sensible landfall protocol.

He returned to the screen and stared out at the dead city. Ten minutes later, three militia moved out from under the nose of the *Hawk*, suited up and masked, looking like insects. As he watched, one of their number looked up at the viewscreen and waved. Beside him, Lania smiled and returned the salute. Carew looked at her, but Lania's expression told him nothing.

"A friend of yours?"

She nipped her top lip between her teeth, as if to stop herself from smiling. "Something like that," she said.

THIRTY MINUTES LATER they received word that all was AOK on the surface of the alien world and Carew prepared to disembark with Lania and Choudri. Jed said he might take a look later, and satisfied himself in the interim with a cold beer.

With Lania at his side, Carew took the dropchute to the exit hatch and stepped out onto the hot sand. They moved from the shadow of the *Hawk* into the glare of the alien sun: it was a vast orange hemisphere low on the horizon, setting over the desiccated city and casting long shadows across the square.

"Where to begin?" Choudri said.

A trail of scuff-marks in the sand, left by the militia, crossed the square and approached a stone-built dome topped by a tower. Carew indicated the building. "Why not over here?" Beyond it was the wreck of the starship they'd seen earlier.

They crossed the square to the domed building.

Carew had visited perhaps a hundred different worlds in his lifetime, and while many of them had sported alien landscape, flora and fauna, they had all been settled by humans and therefore shared a basic similarity, or familiarity, of architecture. He had never really felt totally alienated on an alien world.

But here it was different. The strange architecture told him he was on a world where humans had never trod before.

The stone domes that surrounded the square were windowless, their entrances thin slits, and Carew could only assume that they had been places of cool refuge from the daytime heat of the supergiant. It was twilight now, but even so, he judged the temperature to be in the high thirties.

They came to the curving wall of the dome and examined the entrance, tall and narrow, as if made for creatures half again as tall as humans and extremely thin. Carew turned sideways and edged through the gap; he had expected it to be dark within, but light flooded the great circular chamber.

Lania and Choudri followed him in.

He looked around and saw how the dome was illuminated. Light was channelled down the spire that sat at the apex of the dome, where angled mirrors reflected the dying light of the sun.

Lania moved around the perimeter of the dome, staring at something on the wall. He joined her.

"Carvings," she said, her voice muffled by her breathing apparatus. "They look ancient." She reached out, gently touched a bas relief design depicting a tall, insect-like creature holding what might have been an agricultural tool. Or, then again, it might have been a weapon.

They moved around the dome, staring at the frescoes showing aliens in all manner of activities, none of which were readily comprehensible.

Choudri said quietly, "I wonder what happened to them?"

They left the dome and walked around its perimeter, following a cobbled channel that led to a long, straight road, arrowing off into the city between domes. Carew made out what might have been vehicles; small, rusted wrecks mired in drifts of sand.

They moved to the first of the wrecks and peered within. At first glance, the vehicle appeared empty, but Lania placed a hand on his arm and pointed to what seemed to be a driver's seat mounted before a control column.

Piled on the seat was a jackstraw collection of bones, bleached white by the sun. Carew made out the skull, long and thin, which corresponded to the carved heads of the aliens portrayed in the dome.

Choudri touched his earpiece, listened attentively, then said, "Understood. We'll be right with you."

He turned to Carew. "That was Alleghri, leading the militia. They've found something. This way."

His curiosity piqued, Carew followed the Indian along the main road, threading their way between even more wrecked vehicles, until they came to a turning beside a dome whose walls were cracked and stove-in like an eggshell.

They passed between buildings and came to another wide open area. Carew made out three armoured figures – the sight of them human and comforting in the alien landscape – standing on the edge of a great pit. They were staring down, their bowed heads granting them an air of reverence.

One of the figures turned and lifted its arm in a wave. Carew recognised the crew-cut woman who'd signalled up to the ship earlier: Lania's new friend.

They joined the trio at the edge of the pit and stared down.

At first, Carew failed to take in the enormity of what lay before him. His mind registered the hundreds of stick-like objects at his feet, and then he realised suddenly that they were bones and that they went on and on and on, a macabre landscape of tangled skeletons of thousands, perhaps even hundreds of thousands, of aliens extending for at least a kilometre.

Two of the guards were running tests on the nearby bones, scanning the remains with sensors connected to smartcores within their armour.

The woman, Alleghri, said, "We've found skeletal remains all over the city, practically everywhere we've looked. There must be millions of them."

"Any idea what might have happened to them?" Lania asked.

The woman shook her head. "Judging by the wrecked fortifications and the ships we saw in orbit, there seems to have been some kind of war. But here" – she swept out an armoured arm to indicate the city – "there's no sign of war damage. It's as if the populace suffered a plague."

One of the militia stood and read something scrolling across a screen embedded in the forearm of his armour. "The remains are approximately a hundred and twenty years old, give or take a few years."

"Any idea of cause of death?" Choudri asked.

"Impossible to say, at the moment. I'll run tests back at the ship, but I'm not hopeful we'll find out soon."

"But no signs of violence?"

"None that we can discern."

Lania looked out across the sea of bones. "A mass burial site? Is this where the survivors came to lay their dead?"

Alleghri looked at her. "What survivors?"

Lania shrugged. "Survivors who themselves succumbed to whatever killed their fellows?" She shook her head. "It's unimaginable."

Alleghri said, "And this is representative of what we saw on the way in. City after city, dead and deserted. The entire planet, dead for over a hundred years."

Choudri said, "On the scale of things, that's not long at all."

A thought occurred to Carew. "When did the colony ship from Vercors set off?"

Choudri thought about it. "About a hundred years ago, Ed. It was a slow-ship, the colonists in suspended animation. They wouldn't have arrived at this system for twenty, thirty years."

"So it can't have been humans bringing some form of disease."

Lania shook her head. "No. And it wouldn't account for the orbital destruction," she pointed out.

"I wonder if this was the result of bacteriological warfare?" Carew said. "They fought an orbital battle with invaders, but lost when their enemy resorted to germ warfare?"

"We might know more in a few hours," Choudri said.

Carew looked around at the skyline of the dead city and found what he'd been looking for. The broken back of the downed starship emerged from the rubble of buildings, perhaps half a kilometre away.

He pointed. "I'm going to take a look at that."

Lania came with him, along with Choudri. Alleghri gave orders to the two militia-men to conduct further tests, then fell into step with Lania. The pair exchanged smalltalk as Carew led the way through the city, their words too quiet and muffled for him to pick up.

He had been obsessed with starships of all kinds since his youth on Temeredes. He'd lived near the starport there and spent all his free time in the observation lounge, watching the ships come and go. His imagination had been fired by the bigger ships, the colossal cargo liners and supply ships, and the farther they had travelled through space to get to Temeredes, the greater his interest. He wondered what the boy he had been would have thought of his future self, thousands of light years from home, and approaching the wreck of a vast alien starship.

They climbed over sand-blasted rubble and came at last to the great curving flank of the vessel.

Lania turned and stared at him, her brown eyes intense above her breathing mask. "Remind you of anything, Ed?" she murmured.

He reached out, his finger-tips tracing the familiar scrolls and whorls etched onto the metal. He stepped back and looked up, following the swirling design across the arching superstructure.

He said to Lania, "It's almost identical, wouldn't you say?"

She nodded. "Right."

Choudri was watching them. "To what?"

Lania said, "On Hesperides, we found the crash-landed wreck of a starship. It was obviously alien." She reached out and touched the swirls engraved on the metal. "The design was identical to this."

Carew took in the lines of the ship, the sweep of its scimitar fins. "The ship, too, resembled this one."

"The same provenance, then?"

"It would seem so."

He left the group and moved to where a panel in the side of the ship had parted company with its neighbour and hung open like an inviting doorway. He pulled it further back and eased his way through, the soles of his boots grating across a fine drift of sand.

The others joined them and he led the way along corridors – broken and angled, which made navigation difficult – towards the front end of the ship. Along the way they came across alien skeletons clothed in the shredded remains of uniforms, attenuated creatures with long, narrow skulls.

They arrived at the flight-deck, a circular amphitheatre surrounded by banked consoles and screens. Carew counted twenty dead aliens littered around the chamber.

"I wondered if the ship belonged to an invading race," he said. "But I think not."

Choudri agreed. "The frescoes showed creatures that appeared very much like these. They were an advanced, star-faring race."

"Which sent a vessel all the way across Vetch space, only for it to crash-land on Hesperides."

Lania said, "They sent more than one vessel, Ed. Remember what Jed said about seeing that crashed ship on Tamalkin, way back?"

Carew looked at her. "I wonder if it had anything to do with this, the death of their civilisation? Perhaps they were fleeing something?"

"Fleeing the war, whoever was attacking them?" Lania suggested.

Carew thought about it. "That's all very well. But if you recall, there was no sign on the ship on Hesperides of any survivors, or the bodies of those killed on impact. If there had been survivors, then we'd surely have heard about it. And on Tamalkin, too."

Choudri was watching him. Carew frowned at the Expansion man. "What is it?"

"There were other crash-landed wrecks like this one, all across the Expansion. They arrived in our space more than a hundred years ago, over a five year period."

"I never heard about it," Carew said.

"The Expansion authorities kept it under wraps, didn't let word get out."

Lania asked, "And why was that?"

The Director paused, then went on. "We investigated the wrecks, but the odd thing was that they appeared to be empty, unmanned. And... and they hadn't been running on auto-pilot, either. To be honest, we didn't know what the hell was happening, so we threw up security cordons around the ships and maintained a complete news black-out."

"Any theories?" Carew asked.

Choudri shook his head. "We were completely mystified and still are."

Lania said, "Perhaps we'll find out more clues here?"

Something occurred to Carew. "The cultists from Vercors, Procyon... Jed said something about a cult on Tamalkin, worshipping some kind of crashed starship."

Choudri nodded. "As did the cultists on Vercors," he said.

"So they set off aboard the colony vessel, heading for this very star system. It can't be just coincidence."

"It would appear not," Choudri said and in an aside to Carew, "I wonder how much Gorley knows, and isn't telling me?"

"Perhaps," Carew said, "we should return to the *Hawk* and go through what we've found. Then the Commander might be more forthcoming."

Choudri laughed at that. "You are an optimist, Captain Carew."

They left the ship and made their slow way back through the desiccated city.

* * *

ONE HOUR LATER they ate a meal in the lounge of the *Hawk*. The atmosphere was subdued. Commander Gorley, they discovered on their return, had left the ship along with the remaining three militia.

When they finished the meal, Carew turned in his seat and stared out through the long viewscreen. The sun had gone down a little further; now only a quarter of the bloated red disc showed over the horizon, and a bloody light suffused the eerie landscape.

Alleghri was speaking. "...And that's another strange thing. We've detected not a trace of anything living on the planet, right down to the microbial. Nothing. It's as if whatever accounted for the aliens wiped out every other form of life, too."

Carew watched Lania as she smiled across at the strikingly handsome woman. "What could have done that?"

Alleghri shrugged. "Search me. I've seen nothing like it before."

"And you're an expert in such matters?" he asked.

Alleghri stared at him, her expression neutral. "Degree in microbiology, Borussia University. I was seconded for two years to the Expansion's Scientific Unit."

"Not just," Lania said, looking across at Carew, "a pretty face."

Carew turned and stared through the viewscreen, wondering at Lania's sudden friendship with the woman. He considered what Choudri had told him earlier, about Lania's feelings for him, and wondered if she'd taken up with the guard in some kind of convoluted mind-game.

His only worry was that the woman might be manipulating Lania for her own ends; he wouldn't put it past Gorley to have ordered Alleghri to work her way into his pilot's affections. He'd have a word with Lania later.

Outside, the three militia men and the comparatively slight Gorley were crossing the square. A minute later Carew heard the sigh of the chute as it deposited the men in the ship, then the thud of heavy footsteps as the militia moved to their quarters.

In due course, Gorley joined them in the lounge.

Carew told him about the crashed starship, but Gorley interrupted him and said, "I know. I investigated the wreck myself. It appears it belonged to the natives of this planet."

"The same race," Carew said, "that sent identical ships across Vetch space to the Expansion."

Gorley lowered his water flask and stared at Carew. "You appear extremely well informed, Captain."

Across the table, Director Choudri leaned back in his seat and stroked his chin.

Carew said, "However hard the authorities try to suppress information, Marshall, it inevitably leaks. As it happens, we also came across a downed ship on Hesperides."

"I know very little about the other alien ships," Gorley said. "Not my department."

"No? Not even when the cultists we're going after turn out to hail from one of the planets where an alien ship came down? Not even when they formed some kind of cult around the same starship?"

Gorley's severe hatchet face gave nothing away. "What are you trying to say, Captain?"

"Merely that I think you know what's going on here. Probably not everything, but more than you're letting on."

Gorley took another long swallow of iced water. He looked around the group, every one of whom was watching him. "You seem to know as much as I do, Captain. Over one hundred years ago, seven alien starships entered Expansion territory. Only two were detected at the time and tracked by our interceptors. Like the other five, which we discovered later, they came down on sparsely populated colony worlds." He hesitated, then went on. "I will tell you this: when we made investigations on the crashed ships, we discovered no signs of life aboard them. The mystery has remained until this day."

Choudri said, "And what we've discovered here only deepens the enigma."

Gorley went on, "A cult grew up around the starships, perhaps an inevitability given the mystery of their provenance and mission, and the susceptibility of the human mind to superstition."

Carew said, "How did the cultists from Vercors know where the starship came from? Did they discover something aboard the ship?"

Gorley smiled, an unfamiliar expression on his face. "That, we do not know. Another mystery to add to all the others."

Carew considered the Expansion man. "And the Expansion knew nothing about the colonists' mission to cross Vetch space before they embarked on it?"

"Captain Carew," Gorley said evenly, "I suspect you are paranoid in assuming that the Expansion has spies on every planet, but may I remind you that this is not so. And anyway, this was over a hundred years ago, and Vercors was then not part of the Expansion hegemony. We had no idea, and little interest, in cultish groups setting off on fool missions across enemy territory."

Carew smiled at the Marshall. "Then isn't it all the more strange that now, a century later, you're suddenly interested?"

Gorley returned his smile. "By no means. It would be perverse of us if we were to ignore the distress call of fellow human colonists, would it not?"

Alleghri murmured something to Lania, then rose from the table and strode from the room. A minute later Lania excused herself and left the lounge. Carew watched her hurry off. He chastised himself for feeling responsible for her welfare. He was not her father, after all. But he'd known Lania over ten years now, and old habits died hard.

One of the guards, out of armour, came into the lounge and murmured something to Gorley, who listened attentively. The guard withdrew.

Choudri looked at Gorley and said, "Well?"

"They ran a series of analyses on the alien remains," he said, "and not unsurprisingly, they found no trace of any bacteria or virus that might have been responsible for the deaths."

He finished his meal and stood. "I'll give the order for our departure from the planet in one hour," he said. "Gentlemen."

When he'd left the lounge, Carew turned to Choudri. "I'm tempted to say that he was playing his cards close to his chest."

The Indian nodded. "I'll talk to him later, alone. I might be able to elicit a little more."

Choudri rose and made to leave the lounge. As he was passing, Carew restrained him with a hand on his sleeve. "Anish, might I ask why you're siding with me in this matter?"

He watched the Indian closely as he replied.

"Are you familiar with the old saying that it is often wise to make one's enemy's enemy one's friend?"

Choudri nodded to Carew and left the lounge.

Carew remained where he was seated on the banquette, drinking his water and watching the sun slide imperceptibly over the horizon.

As much as he liked Anish Choudri, he was aware that there was always the possibility that the Director was a hard-line Expansion man through and through, and was playing some sort of double bluff.

He would have to tread warily in the days ahead.

As for Lania...

He left the lounge and moved to the flight-deck. Jed was in his sling, examining readouts on the screen. "Where's Lania?"

"Still in her berth. She'll be down shortly."

Perhaps thirty minutes later, Lania strode onto the flight-deck, a spring in her step.

"A word, if I may, Lania."

He moved to the nose of the ship and stood before the viewscreen, staring out at the sun. Lania joined him. "I always think sunsets are so romantic, don't you, Ed?"

He looked at her. "I just want you to be careful, okay?"

She looked taken-aback. "Careful?"

"With the militia-woman... What's her name? Alleghri. I want you to remember that she's Expansion, understand?"

She stared at him, and he thought he detected a sudden flare of anger in her chestnut eyes. She said, "You're not my keeper, Ed."

"Listen, Lania – you can do whatever you want, with whomever you want. That's none of my business. But... I don't want to see you get hurt by someone who might – I say *might* – be using you, okay?"

She said, emphatically, "Gina isn't using me," and strode over to her sling.

Carew sighed and turned back to the view as Director Choudri and Commander Gorley entered the flight-deck and took their seats.

Five minutes later, the *Hawk* rose slowly from the square and Carew watched the dead city fall away beneath them.

CHAPTER ELEVEN

As much as Lania may have hoped Ed's words of caution about her affair with Gina were the result of jealousy, he was probably incapable of that emotion. He was just being solicitous of her welfare – which was probably as good as it was going to get.

She slipped from her sling and stared through the viewscreen.

They had moved a lot further in-system since leaving the outer planet, and now the fiery sun took up fully half the viewscreen. Straight ahead was a vast blue planet, striated with chiffon strips of cloud, a small grey moon in transit across its azure face. Lania thought that she had probably never seen a system so beautiful.

She stretched in her sling and smiled across at Jed. "How long was I out?"

"Less than an hour."

She shook her head. "Felt like minutes."

She thought of Gina, in her arms a little over an hour ago. The big, tough militia-woman had told Lania that she felt safe in her embrace. And Ed had said that Gina might be using her!

"So the colony ship is somewhere down there?" she said.

The world was colossal. She took in the calibrations that stretched across the foot of the viewscreen and checked its magnification. According to these readings, the planet was four times the size of Earth and five astronomical units from its supergiant primary.

She wondered if the colonists had found a suitable, Earth-like world on which to settle.

But why the distress signal?

Ed was beside her. "The signal didn't come from down there, Lania." He pointed to the small, grey moon. "It came from there."

She flashed him a look, but found it hard to feel resentment. She smiled. "The moon? It doesn't look that hospitable to me."

He nodded. "I agree."

Choudri and Gorley were standing before the viewscreen, talking. Choudri nodded, then turned and said to Lania. "Could you take us down to the moon? We'll make a few orbits and home in on the signal."

She nodded and integrated with the smartcore. The ship flowed around her, moving to her commands.

When she emerged and placed the *Hawk* on auto-pilot, the view through the screen was of a rocky grey world with a close, curved horizon.

Ed pointed. "There!"

She saw the streak of silver on the horizon, took control of the *Hawk* and slowed its approach. She brought them down gently beside the long, boxy colony vessel, the *Hawk* dwarfed by its mammoth dimensions.

Choudri said, "Well, at least it seems to be in one piece. I was fearing that it might have been destroyed on landing."

Jed was reading from his screen. "That's the good news. The bad news is that there's no atmosphere out there."

Lania looked at Director Choudri. "When did the ship arrive here?"

"I can't say exactly, but perhaps sixty, seventy years ago."

Ed nodded. "With luck, if all the systems are running at optimum, then the colonists will still be in suspension. What were the operating parameters on those old suspension units?"

Gorley said, "Perhaps two hundred years, if conditions were optimum."

Lania thought of being a colonist, woken from cold sleep over a hundred years after setting off, to find an Expansion vastly different from the one they had left.

If they agreed to being returned to the Expansion, that was.

She looked at Director Choudri. "Just what are your plans for the colonists, Director?"

"Our plans?"

"If they're still in there, sleeping, are you going to haul them back home?"

He looked at Commander Gorley, who said, "Our remit is to locate the colonists and assess the sustainability of any colony they might have founded. It would appear that the latter is a futile hope, now. Our first task is to assess the condition of any survivors. Only then, and in consultation with the colonist's elected representatives, will we make any decision as to their future welfare."

Ed said, "You must have had contingency plans for this situation, Marshall?"

If Gorley did, then he was reluctant to divulge them. Instead he said, "I'll take three militia over and report back."

Lania said, "I'd like to come, too. I've brought you all this far – I want to see inside the ship."

Gorley was looking at her, his thin smile making him look like an amused goat. He nodded. "Gina will no doubt help you suit up."

Colouring, she hurried from the flight-deck and found Gina Alleghri.

THE SURFACE OF the moon was as grey as gunpowder and as fine as talcum. The regolith kicked up with their every step and hung eerily in the low gravity.

She looked up, and the view took her breath away. Above the becalmed colony vessel, the vast bright blue planet hung silhouetted against the even vaster supergiant. This close, she could see great spurts of fiery ejecta and loops of molten matter spewing millions of kilometres from the sun's surface.

A tinny voice sounded in her earpiece. "Beautiful, isn't it?"

She looked at Gina, beside her. The woman was gazing through her faceplate at the view, her expression transfixed.

"I've seen plenty of suns in my time," Lania said, "but never one like that."

"I was born and brought up on Dancer's Drift, Antares, so I saw this kind of thing every day. But I haven't been home in years. This brings it all back."

Gina's commanding officer up ahead snapped, "When you two've finished admiring the view?"

Lania grinned at her and moved across the surface to the main group: two bulky militia, their armour reflecting the red light of the sun, accompanied by the suited figures of Gorley and Choudri.

They were staring up at the entrance hatch of the downed colony vessel. It was sealed. So far as Lania could make out, the ship had suffered no structural damage on landing.

"Three of us go that way," the militia captain ordered, indicating the rear of the ship. "You three that way. We'll meet on the other side and consider how we'll board the ship, okay?"

Lania, Gina and Choudri moved along the flank of the ship towards the bulbous command section. Its superstructure was as unremittingly grey as the regolith, its original livery excoriated by passage through the void. Here and there Lania made out the ghost of old insignia and numbering, and towards the front end of the ship the outline of the word *Procyon*.

The Pride of Procyon, she thought. There was nothing proud about the sad old ship now.

They came to the bull-nosed front end. Slit viewscreens, on three levels, banded the great hull. Lania jumped up in the light gravity and landed on a projecting fin. She moved along it towards the body of the ship and peered in through the screen.

"Make anything out in there?" Gina asked.

"Not a thing."

Had she been expecting to see the skeletons of the flight crew, she wondered? Or signs of fire, or some other catastrophe? The flight-deck looked like the darkened set of a holo-movie, emptied of actors and technicians.

"Lania! Everyone! Here!" Gina called.

Heart thumping, Lania jumped from the fin and looked around for Gina. A trail of footprints led around the nose. Lania followed, bouncing in the low gravity, once or twice almost losing her footing.

Gina was standing before the flank of the ship, hands on hips, staring up at something. Choudri was beside her, mimicking her stance as he too stared up at what they had found.

Beyond them, the two other militia and Commander Gorley were bounding towards them.

Lania reached Gina and stared up.

A metre above her head, a hole punctured the metal of the flank. It was perhaps two metres across and perfectly circular.

Gorley's voice sounded in her earpiece, "That certainly wasn't made by a meteor."

"Look at the edge of the incision," Gina said. "The metal looks burnt."

The surface had bubbled around the hole and dribbles of metal had run like candle wax. "What the hell could have done that?" she found herself saying.

"Dunno," the militia captain said. "But we've found ourselves an entrance. Wait here while I recce."

He bent his legs, sprang up and took hold of the lower lip of the circular hole. He hauled himself up, climbed aboard and disappeared from view.

He was gone for perhaps two minutes, and then reappeared at the opening. "Looks deserted to me."

He knelt, then reached out a hand for Gina.

One by one they scrambled aboard the colony ship.

They stood in a long, lateral corridor, brightly illuminated by their collective headlamps. Choudri was kneeling beside the hole, examining the perfection of its incision through the ship's outer skin, its insulation and wiring, and two inner membranes.

"Whatever did it, it cut through with great heat, or maybe acid."

"If there were any colonists out of suspension and awake," Gina said, "they would have died quickly with the decompression."

Choudri said, "The ship landed, which suggests the maintenance crew were conscious."

"So where are the bodies?"

Lania gestured towards the hole. "This wasn't an accident. Something did this intentionally."

Gina grinned at her. "Give the girl a coconut," she jibed.

"We split up," said the captain, "go through the ship in pairs. Draw your arms. Maintain radio contact. Meet back here in thirty minutes. Understood?"

Gina took Lania's arm and steered her towards a side corridor, opposite the circular hole punched through the skin of the ship. Gina led the way, Lania following her dark, bulky shape.

It was oddly eerie, walking through the semi-darkness of a ship that had left the Expansion over a hundred years ago. There was something of the museum experience about it, familiar and yet strange. She had watched holo-vision programs about aged ships and seen old scrap in junkyards, but to see superseded fittings like strip-lighting instead of glo-tubes, staple-ladders instead of chutes, gave her a shivery sense of temporal displacement. She hurried to catch up with Gina.

"Back there in your cabin, girl..." Gina was saying now.

"Gina! Shh!"

"S'okay. This links just the two of us. You don't think I'd let my bastard captain know, do you?"

"Well, Gorley knows something. And Ed."

Gina turned and smiled at her through her faceplate. She reached out. "I just wanted you to know, you're special."

Piqued by something she could not easily identify, Lania said, "Yeah, that's what Ed says."

Gina stopped and stared at her. "You and him?"

Lania found herself saying, "Sometimes. It's on and off, Gina. I don't let myself get too close."

Gina made a sound like a disapproving sniff and continued to lead the way along the corridor.

Now why the hell did I say that, Lania wondered? She followed the armoured woman.

They came to a wide central aisle that ran the length of the ship, and Gina turned right. A minute later they arrived at a pair of double doors. Blocky lettering above the entrance read, "Cry-sus units 1-500."

Gina turned to her. "This is where they'll be, girl."

Gina reached out and palmed a sensor panel beside the entrance. The doors refused to move. She slapped the sensor again, swearing. "Stand back."

Lania did as instructed and covered her eyes as Gina lifted her laser and turned the sensor panel to dripping slag. She applied the muzzle of her weapon to the seam between the doors and prised. She was able to part the doors a centimetre, then worked her fingers into the gap. With brute force, assisted by her suit's servo-motors, she dragged open the door. The mechanism broke and the door sprang back into its housing, almost skittling the militia-woman in the process.

She laughed at herself and led the way into the suspension chamber.

Lania stepped over the threshold.

The chamber was v-shaped, the banked walls on either side housing the cryogenic suspension units – two hundred and fifty, she estimated – along each side.

"Come and look at this, Lania."

She moved to Gina's side. The curved lid of the first pod was retracted and the coffin-like container was empty. Gina gestured along the row, diminishing in perspective. "And they're all the same. Every one of them. Empty."

Lania moved to the other side of the chamber. Likewise, every pod had its cover retracted and every pod was empty.

"Where the hell could they have gone?" she murmured.

Gina had opened radio contact with her captain. "Sir, we're in the cryo-suspension chamber 1-500. Only the colonists aren't here, sir."

"Copy, Sergeant," the captain said. "Move to the rear of the chamber and you'll find an exit hatch. Pass through it. You'll find us on the other side."

They walked the length of the chamber, Lania checking that every unit was indeed empty, and arrived at the hatch at the far end. It was open; Gorley and the militia captain stood outside. Choudri and a militia-man emerged from a sliding door adjacent to the first chamber.

Gorley said, "We've checked every suspension chamber, now, and they're all the same. There's no trace of a single colonist."

Lania looked along the corridor, where ten identical hatches gave access to the chambers.

"This doesn't make any kind of sense to me," Gina said. "The moon's airless. No one can survive for a second out there. They can't be somewhere else in the ship?"

Her captain grunted with derision. "Sure. They're in the lounge, drinking coffee. All five thousand of them."

Gina glared at the man. "I was thinking more of the holds."

The other militia-man shook his helmeted head. "They're not. We checked."

A sudden heat swept through Lania's head and she said, "They've been taken."

They stared at her. Gina said, "What?"

"The colonists. They've been taken... somewhere. Whatever came in through the hatch, it took them."

The captain snapped, "We've no proof of that."

"Then where the hell are they?" Lania said. "There's a big hole drilled neatly in the side of the fucking ship and the colonists are gone."

Gina said, "I don't know. Perhaps they suited up, left the ship."

Choudri said quietly, "There would have been evidence of their departure, Gina. The regolith out there was undisturbed until we came along."

They stood in silence, each with their own thoughts.

"So," Lania said at last, "I'm right, aren't I? Whatever made the hole, it got in here and took them. Didn't it?"

Gorley said, "If it did, then why isn't the regolith disturbed directly outside where the hole was made? You'd think the egress of five thousand colonists would leave some trace."

The captain said, "Some kind of ship, an alien vessel. It approached the ship, drilled the hole, and they entered. They got the colonists and departed with them through an umbilical."

Gorley said, tentatively, "If that happened, then it would have taken time. Perhaps the maintenance crew had time to leave some form of record."

The captain said, "If they did, then the best place to look would be the flight-deck."

He set off along the corridor, followed by Gina. Lania hurried after her, taken by a sudden dread she knew to be groundless; even so, she didn't want to be last in line.

She thought of the colonists, woken to be confronted by aliens and ordered off the ship. The terror they must have experienced, the sheer horror of the unknown.

What else, she wondered, as she hurried after Gina, might account for what had happened here?

They walked along the lateral corridor and came to the hole in the flank. They slowed as they passed it, each one of them pausing to examine the incision again. As if this time it might offer up more clues, she thought.

A minute later the captain rounded a bend in the corridor and stopped. "Well," he said, "here's one colonist who didn't get off the ship."

He moved aside to let the others see.

"Christ," Gorley said. "What happened to him?"

If Lania had felt the first stirrings of terror earlier, at the absence of the colonists, she was clutched by panic now as she looked down at the corpse of this lone, hapless human.

He had been mummified over the decades, his skin flash-freezing and then drying, contracting over his skull and bones, so that the remains seemed shrunken, his fraying uniform half a size too big. But it was not the process of mummification that frightened Lania, horrendous though that was.

The corpse was plastered to the lower bulkhead of the corridor, its upper half intact, but the bones of its pelvis and legs – without material or skin – fused and welded to the wall.

His mouth was open in a silent scream of pain.

Lania closed her eyes and moved away.

The captain said, "He has a weapon. Look."

Lania opened her eyes long enough to take in the small blaster clutched in the corpse's left hand.

"I wonder if this was why he was killed?" Gina said. "He showed resistance, fought?"

They filed past the corpse in reverent silence.

The captain led the way to the flight-deck, encountering no more bodies on the way.

They entered the flight-deck and moved around the oval chamber, taking in its old-fashioned design, its bulky flight couches in lieu of slings. Even the consoles and screens were bigger, bulkier, than those of today.

"What are we looking for?" Gina asked.

"Well, probably not a hand-written note saying 'We're being invaded,' Sergeant," her captain said.

Lania slipped into a couch and tapped the console. As she had expected, there was no response.

"They stored data on needles, back then, right?" The captain was on his knees, examining the interface of a com-stack.

"A hundred years ago? Yes," Gina said. "Coiled fibre storage was still twenty years off."

"So you'd think the needle storage units would be full of back-ups and blanks, right?"

Choudri crossed to him. "And they're not?"

"All empty."

"Here, too," Gina called. "It looks like an entire com-stack was unbolted and taken."

Lania said, "But why would they do that? Take a whole com-stack? It doesn't make any kind of sense."

Gina stood, hands on hips and looked around the old flight-deck. "What does, girl?"

Commander Gorley said to the militia captain, "Get the others over here. Go through the ship from top to bottom. And have Novak rig up a power system, okay? I want all the data possible copied from this ship's core matrix – have Thomas go through it for any clues as to what might have gone down here." He sighed. "And here I was, thinking we might find the colonists happy and settled on some idyllic colony world."

The captain grunted. "You really expected that?"

"I hoped."

Lania looked across at Gorley. For the first time ever, the man sounded almost human.

Commander Gorley led the way from the flight-deck and along the corridor. Lania averted her gaze as they approached the dead colonist, and wondered at her sudden squeamishness. She had seen far worse sights in her early years – and once or twice since joining Ed Carew, as well – but for some reason the sight of this corpse gave her the terrors. Perhaps it was the unknown circumstances of his death, at the hands of who knew what alien horror? Or perhaps the utter loneliness of his death, so far away from home.

Or perhaps I'm just getting too sensitive, she thought.

The captain jumped down through the hole and assisted the others out one by one. Slowly, weary now after being out for over two hours, they made their way around the starship and across the churned regolith to the *Hawk*.

Ed was standing in the reception foyer, his long face wearing a worried frown, when Lania cycled herself through the air-lock.

He came across to her and touched her shoulder in an uncharacteristically familiar gesture. "What happened? You look shattered."

"I'll just get this off and I'll be straight up. Fix me a hot coffee and I'll see you in the lounge, okay?"

He nodded and stepped onto the chute.

She shucked off her suit, then took a quick shower and rode the chute to the lounge, feeling a little better. Well, cleaner, at any rate.

Ed sat on the banquette beneath the strip screen, which showed a breathtaking view of the supergiant and the swelling blue world. He had a drink clasped in both hands, and his eyes were on her as she sat down opposite and sipped her own coffee.

"Mmm... that's good." She smiled up at him. "Amazing how good coffee tastes. I suppose it's familiar."

"What happened?"

She considered the events of the past couple of hours, then told Carew what they'd found. "The colonists are gone, Ed."

They discussed the situation, Carew adding nothing constructive to what had passed back and forth aboard the colony ship.

"In the circumstances," he said, "speculation is pretty futile."

She was silent for a time, then said, "Ed."

He smiled at her. "What is it?"

She shook her head. "I don't know. I don't get frightened easily. You know me. What did you say, once? That I didn't have the imagination to be frightened?"

"I said that? I don't remember."

"Well, you did. Anyway, maybe I have the imagination now. I'm frightened. Whatever happened to the colonists... They were taken, Ed. Taken, and by something that might still be..."

He reached across the table and squeezed her hand. When was the last time he'd done that? She smiled. He said, "You've got to remember that this was a long time ago, Lania. What, seventy or eighty years? The chances are that whatever took them is long gone now. And the *Hawk* and the militia pack a hell of a lot of fire power. The *Procyon* was virtually unarmed." He smiled. "Don't let it get to you. We'll be fine, okay?"

She finished her coffee, asked if he'd like another, and fetched two more.

They sat and chatted.

At one point he said, "I'm sorry if what I said earlier hurt you, about Gina."

She shrugged. "I know you meant well, Ed. I was being over-sensitive." She smiled at him. "I just can't see that Gina is using me. We're just having a fling. It's fun, nothing more."

"It's just that I don't want to see you getting hurt, like that time on... I'm getting old. I can't remember where it was. You fell head over heels for that police cadet."

She looked away. "Chalcedony, Delta Pavonis," she said. "I don't know what happened. It was the first time it affected me like that."

"You wanted me to find him a job on the *Poet*."

"Don't! You were right – he was a bastard. One of the few times when your dislike of authority figures paid off."

"It was seeing him with at least three other women while stringing you along that I didn't like."

She looked at him and laughed. "Ed, it wasn't that that bothered me. He wanted to borrow my smartsuit to help out on a case – that's the only reason he was interested in me."

"You never told me that."

She shrugged. "I don't tell you everything, Ed."

"I'm sorry. I must sound like your father sometimes." He hesitated, and she feared he was going to say that she'd never spoken about her father

– then Commander Gorley and Director Choudri entered the lounge and sat down at the table.

Choudri fetched two coffees.

Ed said, "An eventful foray, by the sounds of it?"

Lania watched Choudri sip his coffee. "Has Lania filled you in?"

Ed nodded.

"There's not a lot to add," Choudri said, "other than the fact that Novak has been through the *Procyon*'s core."

"And?"

"Nothing. It's wiped. Which is unusual in itself, but added to the fact that all the back-up pins are missing, along with a com-stack."

"Aliens interested in our technology?" Carew said. "Or the cultists being ultra-cautious and not wanting anything to fall into the wrong hands?"

Lania said, "Either of which sound highly unlikely."

"Have they analysed the remains of the colonist you found?" Carew asked.

Gorley nodded. "He was killed by a weapon we've never come across. Lasers don't do that kind of damage, or pulse-guns. His bones were fused to the wall."

"Acid?"

Gorley lifted his thin shoulders. "We don't know, and to be honest I don't want to come across the creatures responsible."

Lania could see Carew stopping himself from saying what he was thinking, and she could well imagine those thoughts. She was thinking them herself: that the Marshall's sudden squeamishness was odd in someone responsible for the punishment of those he considered enemies of the Expansion.

She stood up and said, "I'll leave you to your speculations, gentlemen. See you later, Ed."

She left the lounge and took the upchute. She had intended to lie down and rest for a while, but as she was passing Gina's berth she heard the sound of the shower's water jet. She paused and knocked on the door.

"Come in, Lania."

Smiling, she slipped inside. "How did you know it was me?"

Gina turned in the shower stall, laughing. "Who else was it likely to be? Care to join me?"

"I've just showered," Lania said. "But I could be persuaded to have another one."

She shucked off her smartsuit, left it in a puddle on the floor and stepped into the shower. They kissed, and Gina slipped a soapy hand between Lania's legs.

Later they lay on the bed, Lania's head on the older woman's shoulder.

"What's it like, working for the militia these days?" She thought back twelve years, to the months and months of discipline, the penalties for breaking the rules. She'd had to get away.

Gina pulled a face with the effort of peering down at her. "Probably much like it was in your day."

She'd often wondered what life might have been like if she'd toed the line and worked at it: she would have a cushy job somewhere, maybe even settled down with someone, kids...

The thought repelled her and at the same time made her laugh.

"What?" Gina asked.

"Just thinking about what might have been, if I'd not got away and hooked up with Ed."

Gina said, "For an ex-militia-woman and a feared criminal, Lania, you're nothing but a little pussycat."

"Grrr," she said. "A pussycat with claws."

"And one that likes lapping."

She thought about events aboard the *Procyon*. "Your Captain seems like a real bastard, if you don't mind me saying."

"Evans? Oh, he's okay. He's just another prick in love with his rank, is all. He's good at his job."

Lania smiled. "A good Expansion man," she said.

"Is there anything wrong with that?"

She thought about her father. "No," she said at last. "No, nothing at all."

"Hey, are you going to tell me how you managed to skip Macarthur's Landfall and get off-planet without tripping the slightest security rig?"

She smiled and stroked Gina's cheek. She wondered why she hadn't told her yet. Was it something to do with what Ed had said, about being careful? Didn't she trust the big, sexy militia-woman?

"Maybe one day," she said.

Lania's earpiece bleeped. It was across the room, discarded with her smartsuit. She jumped off the bed and slipped it into her ear.

"Yes?"

"Lania," Ed said, "get yourself down to the flight-deck. I thought you'd like to see this."

"What is it?" She struggled into her smartsuit.

"You'll find out soon enough. And a message from Commander Gorley: we're taking off in thirty minutes."

"On my way." She dressed, kissed Gina on the lips and slipped from the room, wondering what

Ed wanted her to see. She took the downchute and stepped onto the flight-deck.

She stopped as she saw what was on the viewscreen. "What the hell are those?" she asked.

Ed was standing before the screen, with Choudri and Gorley to his right and left. Jed was in his sling, staring at the viewscreen. Lania slipped into her own sling.

Choudri half turned towards her, as if not wanting to tear himself away from the screen. "Thomas detected them an hour ago, while doing telemetry analysis on the blue planet. He saw them drifting through the upper atmosphere. This shot is magnified ten thousand times."

There were a dozen of the things, great bloated ovals, dark grey in colouration, floating in procession through the upper clouds of the blue world. Their hides were puckered and striated with wrinkles, and here and there on their adipose, limbless bodies she made out what looked like suckers.

"They're alive, aren't they?"

"Without doubt," Carew said.

"How big are they?" It was impossible to tell the size of the creatures, with nothing else in the shot.

Choudri said, "Approximately fifty metres long, twenty broad and high."

"They're huge."

"Even more amazing," the Indian went on, "is that they're space-going. Thomas saw them when they were in orbit, high above the blue planet."

"You don't think they're..." – she thought of a phrase to describe them – "biological spacecraft, with the real aliens inside them?"

"Who knows? I suppose anything's possible."

They watched the floaters drift leisurely across the screen, one behind the other – not dissimilar to a procession of terrestrial elephants, albeit that these creatures were without tails or trunks, or legs for that matter.

They dropped behind the cloud cover and vanished from sight.

Lania said, "Surely they can't be the creatures that abducted the colonists?"

"Unless they posses telekinetic abilities," Commander Gorley said dryly. "But they might not be the only alien creatures dwelling on the blue world."

She looked at him. "You want us to go down there?"

"That was the general idea, yes."

She looked at Carew, who was holding his chin, looking thoughtful. "If we go in carefully, cautiously, Lania. And get out at the first sign of trouble."

Gorley nodded. "That goes without saying."

Lania integrated with the smartcore. "To the blue planet it is, then."

She gave the command for the *Hawk* to lift-off.

CHAPTER TWELVE

THERE WAS AN air of excitement and anticipation among the fissure people, such as Maatja had never experienced before. Everyone was talking about the starship coming from the Expansion and what this might mean for World. Jaar, the eldest of her group of friends, held forth as if he were an Elder-in-waiting and declared that as the first humans to experience the Weird, it would be the duty of their people to go forth into the human Expansion and spread the good word.

Privately, Maatja thought this unlikely. The Weird were powerful enough to spread the 'good word,' or to enslave humans across the galaxy, without the help of her people.

But she said nothing, merely smiled to herself as Jaar went on self-importantly.

At midday, with the giant sun directly overhead and everyone seeking the shade, Maatja saw her parents leave their hut and hurry to that of the Elders, Leah and Rahn. They were greeted with solemn hugs at the door and stepped inside.

Maatja left her patch of shade beside the family hut and slipped behind the huts, running parallel with the jungle until she came to the Elders' hut.

She crouched beside the wall, found a split in the weave and peeped through.

Her parents were sitting cross-legged before Leah and Rahn, and they were all eating dried phar.

Rahn was speaking; Maatja strained to hear his words. "...what the Weird want from us, but I do know in my heart of hearts that we are here to do their bidding. They saved us when we came to World, fed us and showed us the ways of this strange place."

Her parents raised gourds of liquid, murmured ritual thanks, and drank.

Leah said, "It is my time of Passing very soon. I will go to serve the Weird."

Maatja stared through the weave and saw her father smile. "I will be there already, Leah."

Maatja's heart jumped into her throat and she felt a pounding pulse at her temple.

Her mother gripped her father's hand. "We are so proud," she murmured.

"To be one of the Chosen," Leah said, "is an honour not accorded to everyone."

Her father said, "But why me?"

Rahn smiled. "I can only assume that you have exhibited qualities the Weird deem worthy," he said. "Loyalty and bravery, diligence and insight. You are a worthy Chosen One."

Maatja felt tears spring to her eyes. Her throat felt sore with the effort of suppressing her sobs.

"Have you prepared?" Rahn asked.

Her father said, "All that remains is to tell Maatja and Hahta."

There was a pause, then Leah said, "Maatja is a singular girl."

"We love her, but..." Her mother hesitated. "But she is not like the others. She spends time alone, in the jungle."

Rahn said, "We know. We have observed her. We know that she has contact with the Outcasts. Yesterday we sent a tracker to follow her, hoping that she might lead us to their dwelling place. But the boy she was with was too fleet."

From the expression on her mother's face, she clearly had no knowledge of this. Her father reached out and took her hand, consolingly.

Leah said, "There will be time in future to trace the Outcasts and eradicate them, and Maatja will play her part in this."

Maatja crouched, frozen. She was gripped by fear. She felt as if the slightest move, the merest breath, might be detected by the adults.

They knew of her meetings with Kavan. They were using her, biding their time before they took the opportunity to follow her to the Outcasts' tree-top retreat.

She heard stirrings within the hut: her parents were rising to leave.

She stood shakily and ran back to her own hut and dropped to her place in the shade outside. She curled up and closed her eyes and tried to come to terms with what she had learned that morning.

Her father was leaving them for the lair of the Weird, one of the Chosen. And her people knew that she was in contact with the Outcasts.

She knew, then, that she had to be very careful in her meetings with Kavan, or not meet him at all in future, for fear of bringing death to his people.

Her thoughts were interrupted by her mother's voice. "There you are, Maatja. Would you please come into the hut?"

Obediently, Maatja stood and followed her mother inside. Hahta was already there, sitting in front of her father. He smiled at Maatja as she sat down next to her sister.

Her mother joined them and they sat in a circle and after a long pause, her father spoke.

"A wonderful event occurred three days ago," he said. "Leah and Rahn were informed that the Weird had selected someone from our people to join them in their lair."

Hahta interrupted excitedly, "You, Daddy! You were Chosen!"

Maatja saw her sister's unbridled enthusiasm and felt sick.

He smiled. "I was chosen, and today I will leave for the lair of the Weird. It is an honour I can still hardly bring myself to believe, and I hope you will share with my and your mother's joy."

"Daddy is a Chosen One!" Hahta chanted.

Her parents looked at Maatja. "Maatja?" her mother said.

She forced a smile. "I don't know what to say..."

"Say nothing," her father said, "but rejoice."

"Let us eat a celebratory meal of phar," her mother said, moving off to prepare their very last meal together.

Maatja ate without tasting a thing, her senses numbed. Hahta chattered excitedly and her parents answered their younger daughter's questions as best they could. A small part of her wished, then, that she had eaten phar for years so that she too could feel happiness now, not this intense, gut-aching sadness.

After the meal, her mother took Hahta from the hut, leaving Maatja alone with her father.

He smiled at her and took her hand. "I know this is especially painful for you, Maatja."

She gripped his hand. "I don't want you to go!" The idea was so vast and painful she could hardly comprehend what life might be like without her father's presence.

"You must understand that this is what I want."

"What? To leave us?" she cried.

He said, "Both Hahta and yourself have reached the age of independence. I could never have been a Chosen one before now. You are both almost women, able to look after yourselves. Maatja..." He paused. "When I am gone, I want you to be careful. Do you understand? Do not venture into the jungle alone, and especially do not meet with the Outcasts. Nothing but tragedy for all concerned will come of these meetings."

She found herself staring at her father and nodding.

He reached, cupped her cheek and thumbed a tear from her eye.

That afternoon, Maatja, Hahta, her mother and all the fissure people attended the Ceremony of Leaving, and gathered in the clearing as Leah and Rahn announced that her father had been chosen.

Maatja felt the phar sitting heavily in her stomach and she wondered if it was this that was numbing her to the awful idea of her father's going. She felt as if her emotions had been ripped from her, as if her ability to cry was gone for ever.

At sunset, as the last of the bloody light bled from the sun and filled the clearing, her father, accompanied by Leah and Rahn on either side and followed by Maatja and Hahta and their mother, strode to the edge of the fissure, then paused.

Her father stepped forward and embraced first her mother, then Hahta and then Maatja. She held on tight, feeling his solidity, breathing in his odour. She did not want to let go, but he eased himself from her gently and kissed her forehead.

She watched him walk down the steps cut into the bank of the fissure and pass from sight, wanting to scream at him to come back. She looked at the people around her, her mother and sister, and felt disbelief at the sight of their joyous smiles.

As the sun sank fully and darkness enveloped the clearing, she returned to the family hut with her mother and Hahta. She curled in her bed in the darkness, her father's absence almost palpable, and considered what to do.

She spent a disturbed night, woken by nightmares of pursuing Sleer and dead Outcasts and her father smiling at her.

In the morning, as the first light of the sun speared through the weave of the wall, she knew what she was going to do.

Before her mother and sister stirred, she gathered her fruit basket, slipped from the hut and crossed the clearing. She slipped over the edge, found a freer fruit bush and gorged herself, then began collecting fruit and berries for the journey. She would be gone for days, she thought, and did not know if there would be food bushes downriver.

"Maatja!"

The sound of her name startled her. She looked up. Hahta was peering over the edge of the fissure. "Maatja, what are you doing?"

Maatja scrambled up the incline to her sister and pulled her into the cover of a bush. Hahta stared at the laden basket, her eyes wide.

Maatja thought about what to tell Hahta, then said, "I am going away for a short while, but I'll be back."

"But where are you going?"

She hesitated, then said, "To the lair of the Weird."

Hahta stared at her with massive eyes. "Why?"

Why indeed? To try and find her father, to find out exactly what to be a Chosen One meant. And then to return here and join the Outcasts with her knowledge...

That was her plan, at any rate.

She said, "I want to see where father has gone, Hahta."

"But he's gone to serve the Weird, Maatja! He is Chosen."

Maatja embraced her sister. "I'll be back in a few days, okay? Don't worry about me."

Hahta began to cry. "Don't go, Maatja. Don't leave me!"

She wiped away her sister's tears. "Don't cry. I will be back and everything will be... alright again. Please, trust me."

Hahta nodded bravely and Maatja said, "Now go back to the hut and tell mother. Just tell her that

I have gone away, but not into the jungle with the Outcasts, okay?"

Hahta nodded and they embraced again and Maatja watched her little sister stand and cross the clearing to the family hut. When she was safely inside, Maatja turned and hurried down the precipitous incline.

As she went, she told herself that her lies to Hahta had been necessary. Perhaps it would be better, for all concerned, if she did not return to the clearing, but joined the Outcasts immediately upon her return. She thought of Hahta, waiting for her, and tears prickled her eyes.

She reached the river an hour later. The sun was fully up by now, but this far down the fissure was still in dark shadow. The river was a placid black ribbon, murmuring at her feet.

She found a fehl tree, reached up and embraced one of its massive seed pods. With all her strength she wrested it from the branch, almost tipping backwards into the water as it came away with a snap. The pod was open at the top, ready to shed its load. She reached in with both hands and scooped out the dry, thumb-sized seeds.

She had heard the adults talking, and knew that the lair was situated in the mountains a little more than a day downriver. She would keep an eye out for the jetty built below the entrance to the lair, where the returning Harvesters were unloaded from the ferry.

She wondered what she might find at the lair of the Weird, and tried to suppress her fear.

She was about to lower the seed-boat into the water when she was startled by a great explosion overhead.

She looked up as the thunder rolled, but knew that it was not yet the rainy season.

The sleek shape of a starship, golden in the light of the sun, swept along the narrow gap of the chasm high above. Maatja gasped in wonder as it banked and disappeared from sight.

The humans, she thought, come to do the bidding of the Weird.

She lowered the seed-boat into the water, stepped wobblingly into it and pushed herself from the bank.

CHAPTER THIRTEEN

THEY MADE A dozen orbits of the blue planet, each pass varying by a few degrees, so that by the end of the twenty-four hour period they had scanned the entire world from pole to pole.

Carew returned to the flight-deck after a short sleep to find Jed in his sling. The militia-man, Thomas, was poring over a console, flanked by Choudri and Gorley.

"Lania?" he asked Jed as he took his seat.

"She's sleeping, boss. We're on automatic."

The scene on the viewscreen was one of limitless jungle, split by black fissures, like negative images of forked lightning.

Carew said, "We should call this the green world, Jed."

He thought of Lania and the conversation they'd had in the lounge back on the moon. It was strange, but in the ten years he'd known the woman, he'd never felt closer to her than he did now. He wondered if that was because they were far from home, in an unfamiliar situation: he was seeking comfort from what was familiar, in this instance the friendship of the person he'd known the longest. Which was strange, because he didn't usually allow himself to get close to others. He must be weakening.

He looked through the viewscreen. There was no sign of the vast floating creatures they'd seen earlier from the moon.

"Have you located the colonists?" he asked Choudri, who had risen from his swivel chair to massage the small of his back.

"We're pretty sure we have. There's a concentration of life-forms situated in a big settlement just north of the equator, with others scattered in much smaller groups further north. Unless they're native to the planet, then we think they might be the colonists."

"Have you calculated how many there are down there?"

"Approximately a thousand in the main group, and hundreds scattered."

"From an original crew of five thousand?"

Choudri frowned. "Life down there might have proved inimical," he said. "Anyway, we're going in for a closer look. We should be overhead in ten minutes."

"So the atmosphere's breathable."

Choudri nodded. "Very much Terran-norm, with a trace more nitrogen. The gravity is slightly higher, but not much more given that it's such a big world. We suspect it's light in metals."

"What about those floating things we saw earlier?"

"They came down in one of the fissures about fifty kilometres from the settlement – actually descended into the fissure and vanished."

Carew peered at the screen. "How deep are the fissures?"

"According to telemetry, they range from a kilometre to three kilometres deep."

Carew whistled. "Amazing features."

"We surmise that they're relics of seismic activity, long in the planet's past. The world is riddled with them, and the rest is jungle in a band covering everything but the polar regions, with a few vast lakes."

Carew thought through what Choudri had told him. "If they are indeed the colonists," he said, "then I'd like to know how they got down there, who brought them here and why."

Choudri nodded. "That's what disturbs me. The motives of whoever brought them here."

Jed said, "Maybe they were just being helpful? The ship came down on the moon and the natives of the blue world saw it and gave a helping hand?"

Carew smiled. "I wonder why I think that wasn't the case, Jed?"

The door slid open and Lania stepped onto the flight-deck. She gave Carew a smile and sat next to him on his couch. "What's happening, Ed?"

He gave her a condensed version of what Choudri had told him, then gestured towards the viewscreen. "The settlement should be coming into view any second now."

"How high are we?" she asked.

Jed glanced at his console. "A kilometre. The viewscreen's on plus three magnification."

As they watched, the dense jungle down below was interrupted by a sandy clearing perhaps a kilometre long by half a kay wide, lying to the north of an ink-black fissure. Carew made out a row of perhaps a hundred small timber huts on stilts, and two longer constructions, one situated halfway along the row and the other at its western end. In the clearing between the huts and the fissure, he saw what looked like regular, upright, bi-pedal life-forms: human beings, going about their everyday business.

"Up the magnification," Gorley ordered.

Seconds later the scene jumped and Carew saw that the figures in the clearing were indeed human.

"They look primitive," Lania said. "I was expecting... I don't know, a technological civilisation, perhaps. At least something a little more developed that this."

The humans appeared Caucasian, though deeply tanned by the supergiant sun, and simply dressed in loin cloths. One group appeared to be working with rudimentary tools, knives and axes, with which they were shaping timber.

"And to think that a couple of generations ago," Gorley said, "their ancestors were navigating starships through the void."

"I wonder how much knowledge they retain of their history?" Carew said.

He peered at the long-house at the western end of the clearing. It had a thatched straw roof and what appeared to be open sides. There was something within it, but the angle prevented him from seeing what it was with any certainty.

He indicated the long-house. "Any chance of homing in on that?" he asked.

Lania peered. "What is it?"

"A hut, obviously. It's larger than the others, presumably important. What I'm interested in," he said, "is what it contains."

The scene jumped, and when it resolved the long-house practically filled the screen. Thomas adjusted the image, pulling it out a little, and Carew saw that his earlier assumption had been correct.

"Good God," Gorley said. "What is it?"

"One of the floating creatures," Carew said, "or something closely related to it."

The long-house enclosed a vast, grey, bloated creature, its sides bulging obscenely, spilling out between the upright supports.

Carew looked across at Choudri. "Should we land?"

"I see no reason why not," the Indian said. "But perhaps if we came down some distance from the clearing and made our way there on foot, our arrival might not prove so traumatic for them."

Gorley said to Thomas, "Prepare the militia. Four of you will accompany the landing party, while two will remain with the *Hawk*."

Carew said to Gorley, "I'd like to take my team along."

Gorley conferred with Choudri, and the Indian said, "Very well, but ensure that all three of you are armoured."

Carew said, "And armed?"

Gorley smiled. "The only members of our party who will be armed are the militia, Captain. Ms Takiomar, kindly bring us down three kays from the clearing."

Lania eased herself into her sling. The *Hawk* banked and, in a few minutes, came in to land, incinerating a great swathe of the jungle canopy and the undergrowth as it did so.

TWO BULKILY ARMOURED militia led the way, and two more brought up the rear. Between them, Carew and the others marched in single file through the ash path created by the leading militia-men.

The vegetation here was alien and grotesquely swollen. What appeared at first glance to be tree-trunks turned out, on closer inspection, to be the probosci of things that lived in the high canopy and hoovered sustenance from the jungle floor. There were bona fide tree trunks here and there, but they were bulbous and etiolated and covered with spines that writhed and surged as if questing for victims. Leaves and flowers were overblown and much bigger than anything Carew had seen before; he felt like a dwarf passing through some kind of crazy, genetically-engineered wonderland.

After an hour of solid marching, Gorley called a halt.

They sat around in a circle, watching the swinging probosci of a canopy creature come snuffling across to them: thicker than a man's torso, fortunately it was a herbivore and harmless. It merely sniffed its way around the group, probing and patting like an affectionate elephant's trunk, and then went on its way.

Strange flying creatures, part insect, part bird, moved around them so swiftly that the eye could not properly focus on their iridescent darting forms.

Carew drank ice-cold water and watched Jed's wide-eyed fascination at the world around him.

Lania said, "How could any human being adapt to this?"

Gorley smiled. "You'd be amazed at how adaptable we are, Ms Takiomar. Even across the Expansion, humanity has adapted itself to survive on what we might think of as inimical worlds."

Jed said, "The ice planet of Kergulen, for instance."

"Or even more hostile," Choudri put in, "Hellebore, Sirius II. Its atmosphere has a higher than normal carbon dioxide content; colonists must be genetically adapted to breathe there."

Jed laughed. "Why do they bother?"

"They mine diamonds," Choudri said. "A one-year stint can make a man a millionaire, or kill him."

Lania grunted, "Give me Xaria any day."

Carew said, "Anyway, the fact is that the colonists here didn't choose the blue world, or whatever they call it. They were *brought* here, after all."

It was a fact he could not dismiss: the colonists had travelled light years through the void and across hostile Vetch space, to end up on a terrifying world at the behest of the floating aliens.

He thought of the bloated creature in the long-house and, not for the first time, wondered what the hell was going on.

They stood, shouldered their packs and set off again through the jungle, the leading militia-man clearing a path with timed blasts of his pulse-beam.

One hour later they came to the edge of the clearing. Gorley sent a militia-man to scout ahead. Carew felt his pulse quicken as he anticipated the reception they might receive. The colonists had been here for perhaps seventy years. Probably none of the original crew were still alive; these people would be the second and third generation, quite unused to meeting human strangers bearing all manner of technological apparatus they had never seen before.

The leading militia-man returned. "So much for sneaking up on them unannounced. They must have heard us coming. They've mustered a welcoming committee."

Gorley said, "Hostile?"

The militia-man shook his head. "I don't think so. Come and look."

Cautiously, the group followed him through the undergrowth, then came to a halt on the margin of the jungle. Carew, with Lania at his side, knelt and peered through a stand of thorny ferns.

Perhaps a thousand people – the entire population – filled the near end of the clearing. They sat crossed-legged, patiently staring into the jungle. Carew felt that every pair of eyes was boring directly into him. A man and a woman sat at the front of the group, their heads together as they conferred.

Gorley said, "We go together, hands raised, is how I think it's done. Alleghri, Thomas, stay here and cover us. If there's any trouble, fire only to stun, okay? On no account shoot to kill."

Self-consciously, Carew rose from his crouched position and raised his hands, aware of Lania doing the same beside him. Gorley and Choudri led the way.

Carew stepped from the shade and into the clearing and the first thing he noticed was the bloated sun on the horizon and the furnace-like blast of its heat.

The crowd stood as one, a wave of humanity coming to their feet with a murmur like surf. Their leaders remained seated, then turned and gestured. The crowd reseated itself in silence.

They were blonde-haired to a person, their bodies tanned deep brown. Carew had them down as Nordic, or perhaps Germanic, though short and slight.

He, Lania and the others remained on the edge of the jungle, arms raised, smiling rather tensely at the seated man and woman.

Slowly, their expressions serious, the pair rose to their feet and held out their hands.

"Greetings, strangers," the woman said, in a dialect hard at first to understand, the vowels drawn out and deep. "We have been awaiting your arrival."

Gorley was the first to voice their collective surprise. "You have?"

"We knew you were on your way, strangers."

Which was not, Carew thought, that surprising when he came to think about it; they were creatures of the jungle, alert to sounds that would give away the approach of all-comers.

Choudri smiled. "You saw us, or heard us?"

"Neither, stranger," the woman replied. "We were told of your arrival here."

"Told?" Gorley said. "By whom?"

The woman averted her gaze, looking at the sandy ground. The man spoke for the first time, "The sun is hot and you must be thirsty. You are our guests. Please, come into the shade and we will talk."

The man and woman stood and walked around the seated crowd, towards a long-house similar to the one, a kilometre down the clearing, in which the bloated creature dwelled. Gorley led the way around the crowd and Carew followed, aware of the curious scrutiny of the gathered colonists.

They came to the long-house and stepped into its welcome shade. They sat down, facing out across the clearing, where the crowd had moved swiftly and reseated itself. The man and woman fell into lithe cross-legged postures and gestured. A boy and a girl came forward bearing a tray – crudely fashioned from a platter of wood – bearing nine stone mugs of liquid.

Nine, Carew thought.

The woman smiled and said softly, "Your companions, in the jungle, must be hot and thirsty too. Do you have the means to communicate with them? I assure you, we mean you no harm."

Gorley smiled and spoke into his wrist-com, and a short while later Alleghri and Thomas emerged, rather sheepishly, from the jungle and joined the others in the long-house. Carew watched them sit down, their bulk contrasting with the slim-boned colonists.

He saw Lania pull the cuff of her smartsuit over her thumb and surreptitiously dip it into her mug. She nodded to Gorley and mouthed, "Safe."

The woman said, "Drar. A juice derived from a fruit of the jungle. Very high in vitamins. It is our staple drink."

Carew lifted the mug and tasted the sweet, viscous liquid. It was not unlike a mixture of banana and orange juice, with a sharp, peppery aftertaste.

"Although this meeting might be unprecedented," the woman said, "I think the protocol might be to introduce ourselves."

She was not at all what Carew had expected from colonists who had dwelled in this harsh environment for up to seventy years. Now that his ear had attuned itself to her dialect, he realised that she was eloquent and articulate, her manner at once assured yet placatory. He thought the pair perhaps in their fifties, their tanned faces surprisingly unlined.

"We are an exploratory team from the human Expansion," Gorley said. "I am Commander Edmund Gorley and my second in command is Director Anish Choudri." He introduced the rest of the team, and the man and woman smiled to each one in turn.

"You are welcome to World," said the woman, and the simplicity of the name seemed in keeping with what Carew had seen of these people so far. "I am Leah."

"And I," said the man, "am Rahn."

"We are the Council Elders. We do not rule our people, as such, merely guide. We lead, as you will come to see, a simple life here in the jungle of World. Our every need is assured. We are a happy people."

Carew wanted to ask her about the beast in the long-house, but thought that perhaps now was not the right time.

Gorley said, "You are descended from the colonists who set out from the Expansion world of Vercors, approximately one hundred standard years ago." He paused. "I was wondering if you still hold the same beliefs as your ancestors?"

The man replied to this. "Our fathers and mothers came from Vercors, where they followed the way of the Kurishen. We no longer believe what we once believed. Belief, in our experience, is an outgrowth of one's environment, and as such we have adapted our beliefs to suit the ways of World."

Gorley said, "Your ancestors came to this system in a ship, following the course of an alien vessel from the sixth planet of this system. We landed there and found it arid, lifeless. I take it that your people, too, found it thus and so moved on."

The man and the woman merely smiled.

Gorley pressed on, "We found your colony vessel on the moon of this world. We wonder how you came to be here?"

"That, Edmund Gorley," the woman said, "is a story longer to tell than there are hours remaining in the day. Observe, the sun is dying. Night will soon be upon us. We follow the sun, rising when it rises, sleeping when it sleeps. We have set aside accommodation so that you can spend the night here rather than return to your ship." She gestured through the open-ended long-house to three neighbouring huts. "In the morning, we will show you around our settlement and attempt to answer your questions."

Outside, as if at some unspoken command, the crowd rose as one and drifted across the clearing to their huts. Within seconds, the clearing was almost empty; only a few settlers moving towards their dwellings at the far end of the settlement remained in sight.

The man and woman rose, inclined their heads minimally in farewell, and left the long-house.

"Well," Carew said when they were alone. "What did you make of that?"

"One," Gorley said, "they said that they were *told* we were coming, which is rather odd. Two, they seem – and this may seem patronising – civilised."

Carew nodded, loath though he was to agree with the Expansion man. "The same thought occurred to me. I was expecting ignorant jungle dwellers."

Choudri said, "I'm curious to learn what belief system they adopted which is 'an outgrowth' of this environment."

Outside, the sun was sinking, bringing a rufous twilight to the clearing. In the jungle behind the long-house, the medley of strange birdsong and animal noises that had accompanied the daylight now quietened with the onset of evening.

Gorley said, "We all have blister-tents in our packs, equipped with security alarms. I suggest we sleep in them within the huts they've assigned us." He looked at his watch. "Assemble outside in ten hours?"

They left the long-house and found the guest huts. Carew, Lania and Jed took the first and Carew set up his one-person blister-tent beneath the low, dusty thatch.

He crawled into the tent, undressed and stretched out in the silence of the alien evening. He was thinking about what the woman, Leah, had said about their every need being assured, when Lania called from her tent, "Ed?"

"Mmm?"

"Can't sleep," she said. "Tell me a story."

He smiled. "There was once a starship called *The Paradoxical Poet*, and its crew of three travelled far and wide..."

* * *

CAREW AWOKE SUDDENLY and wondered where the hell he was.

He rolled onto his back and stared up into the darkness. His eyesight gradually adjusted, and he made out the shadowy curve of his blister-tent above his head, its frame illuminated by the red glow of the security unit.

"I am on a world called World," he told himself, "the guest of human settlers who seem too good to be true."

He looked at his wrist-com. It was over an hour before the time Gorley had assigned for their morning assembly, but he had slept solidly and felt wide awake. He dressed quietly and ducked from the blister-tent.

He stood and took a deep breath. He could smell the thatch, a dry pollen-like scent which irritated the back of his throat. He stepped outside, pushing open the loose door, again fashioned from thatch, and found to his surprise that the long clearing was bathed in light.

It was not sunlight, however: the supergiant was still well below the horizon. In its stead, two moons rode low on the western horizon. One, he thought, was the rocky, lifeless moonlet where the *Procyon* had come down, a misshapen gourd beside its companion. The second moon was huge and reflected the red light of the sun, filling the clearing with second-hand illumination like rosé wine.

High overhead, a scatter of strange constellations hung like errant chandeliers, and to the east was the orange-pink mass that was the body of the Devil's Nebula. He found the stretch of stars that was Vetch space – and beyond it the faint stars of the Expansion. Somewhere out there was the small, G-type star under which he had been born, now Vetch property.

He crossed the clearing towards the escarpment that marked its southward edge. The ground was sandy beneath his feet and his passage kicked up a cloud of fragrant dust. In the starlight, he saw that it settled faster than his senses were accustomed to. It would take some adjusting to the greater gravity here, and not only the odd effect of feeling heavier than usual: objects fell faster than normal, as he had found last night when discarding his clothes – they had seemed to drop as if whisked away by an unseen hand – and now the ground pulled at his boots as if they were magnetised.

He was exhausted by the time he came to the edge of the escarpment and looked down. He'd thought the drop would be sheer, a vertical fall to whatever lay a kilometre or two below, but the fissure fell away at an angle of perhaps seventy degrees, cloaked in shadowy jungle.

Even in the roseate moonlight he could see no more than a few metres into the chasm. He wondered what the settlers did for water in the jungle, and if a river lay at the bottom of the fissure.

He stared along the length of the clearing, wondering if he might be breaking some form of etiquette if he were to make his way to the second long-house and investigate the penned creature.

He was about to set off when he noticed, with a start, a shadowy figure to his right. He thought at first that it was Lania, sans smartsuit, for the figure was small, feminine and semi-naked.

Then he saw that it was a settler, a young girl of perhaps ten. She stepped towards him and in the moonlight he saw her face for the first time and gasped.

"Maria?" he said.

He was mistaken, of course, but she bore an uncanny resemblance to Maria, and the sudden sight of her had fazed him. He peered at the girl, who stood before him unsurely, a frightened expression on her tanned, triangular face.

He smiled. The resemblance to his dead sister was remarkable. Or was his mind playing tricks? Was it just that she was tiny, bird-boned and very blonde – and his guilt was doing its best to make him see Maria in the settler?

She said in a tiny voice, "I am Hahta. You are a stranger from the stars."

His racing pulse slowed gradually. "I am Ed Carew. And yes, I am indeed from the stars."

"In a golden ship, yes? It said you would be coming."

He looked at her. "It?"

She looked bemused. "The Weird in the Flyer."

He repeated her words to himself. He looked around. They were quite alone in the clearing, next to the fissure.

He eased himself to the ground and sat cross-legged, gesturing for Hahta to do the same.

"The creature that lives in the..." – he pointed down the clearing, to the long-house – "is the creature in there a Flyer?"

She trilled a laugh and said, "No, that creature is a Harvester!"

Carew thought about it and said, "So it was a Weird *inside* a Flyer which knew we were coming?"

"It told us that you would soon be here, in your golden ship."

"How did it know, Hahta?"

She shook her head. "The Weird just know. They know everything. They give us all we need to live, and sometimes we are Chosen." She looked at him and beamed. "My father was a Chosen One."

Carew repeated the word. "What does it mean?"

"It means that the Weird said my father was special and he has gone to their lair."

She fell silent, then whispered, "Only, yesterday Maatja left the clearing and went down the river to find him, and I'm frightened for her safety and want her to come back."

"Hahta, slow down." He reached out, took her small hand in his. The feel of it was painful, as was the sudden look of trust in her blue eyes.

"Now, first of all, who is Maatja?"

"Maatja is my older sister. She is seven."

He was thrown, momentarily, until it dawned on him that their years were based, of course, on the passage of their own planet around its primary.

"And you say that she has gone downriver?"

She held out a thin, tanned arm and pointed into the fissure. "Down there. She wanted to follow our father to the lair of the Weird. He was a Chosen One, and those that make the journey to the home of the Weird, they never return."

Carew nodded, trying to make sense of her words. What he did know, now, was that the simple world of the settlers, portrayed by Leah and Rahn earlier, was nothing of the kind.

"And what will your father do when he reaches the lair of the Weird?"

"He will help them," Hahta said.

"Help them in what way?"

She shook her head, frowning. "He will do what they want him to do, but I don't really know what that is. But, I want my sister back, Edcarew. I begged her and begged her not to go, but she would not listen. And now I beg you, will you try to find my sister and bring her back to me?"

He took a deep breath, then said, "I don't know whether I'll be able to do that, Hahta. Your people might not want me to do that. Do you understand? They might try to stop me."

She nodded and said in a small voice, "I know. They did not want Maatja to go. When they found out she had left, they sent a Sleer after her."

"A Sleer?"

"Oh, a kind of Weird. They are used to track down and capture the Outcasts."

"And who are the Outcasts?" he asked.

"The Outcasts are bad people who once lived with us but then left and now they live to the north and try to kill the Weird."

He nodded. "I see."

She looked up, shyly, through her long lashes and said, "Do you think you might be able to find my sister, Edcarew?"

It had occurred to him that this might be a trap, a ruse set up by the Elders to test him and his team. And yet, he thought not. She seemed genuine in her distress.

He said, "And you say that down there is the home of the Weird?"

"Straight down is the River of Life," she said. "A long, long way down. The Chosen Ones are led down the five thousand steps by the Elders, and then they are taken in boats along the River of Life, and then they go deep underground to the lair of the Weird. My father will be there by now, but perhaps Maatja has not reached the lair, yet. Perhaps there is time to save her still."

"Hahta," he said with a sigh, "believe me, more than anything I would like to help you, and I promise you that I will try. But you must realise that I am only one person and against me is the will of your people and the will of the Weird. Do you understand?"

"I understand that you are strangers from the stars, who the Weird said will come to World and bring a time of change."

He stared at her. "It said that? A time of change?"

"It said that you will help the Weird, that you will help the Weird spread all across the stars. They will not just be here, on World, but on every planet of every star."

He was aware of the thudding of his heart as he stared at the young girl, who had told him so much. "What else did the Weird tell you about us, Hahta?"

"They said that though you come as one people, in one golden ship, really you are two people, some good and some bad. Some will help my people and some will not." She smiled up at him with childish simplicity. "So you are good and will help me, Edcarew?"

He smiled and squeezed her hand. "I will do my very best, Hahta," he said, with a heavy feeling in his heart.

She looked away from him, to the east. "The sun is coming up. A new day. Soon you and the Elders will talk and they will tell you all about the Weird and how they help us. Please do not tell anyone that I asked you to find Maatja. My mother says she is lost to us now, for disobeying the Elders." He saw sudden tears glisten like crystals on her cheeks. "But I don't believe that!"

She jumped to her feet suddenly, slim and lithe, and dashed back across the clearing to one of the huts.

Carew watched her go, and wearily climbed to his feet as the first filament of the new sun rose above the jungle canopy. He stopped and stared at its fiery magnificence, at the dance of crimson magma cast lazily from its circumference as if in slow motion.

He made his way back to his hut.

Lania was up and stretching outside the hut. She watched his approach, smiling. "I saw you chatting to the..." She stopped, staring at him and said, "What's wrong?"

"Where to start?" he said wearily.

"Ed, what is it?"

"There's more to the settlers than seems apparent, Lania. Fetch me a flask of water and I'll tell you what the kid said."

She brought two flasks from his tent and they sat in the entrance of the hut as the sun rose, and he recounted everything Hahta had told him about the settlers, the Weird and the Outcasts.

"And they knew we were coming, Lania. They said that though we came in one ship, we were two people, one set good and the other bad."

She stared at him. "Well, that pretty much describes us and the Expansion people, Ed, depending on which side you're on. But how the hell did the Weird know that?"

"I don't know. But don't let on to the Elders that we know, okay?"

She nodded. "Are you going to tell Gorley and Choudri?"

"I don't see why not. We seem to be all in this together."

"And the kid? Her sister? You can't do anything about that."

He looked at her. "Can't I?"

"Ed, it'd be madness."

He almost told her, then, about how his inaction, forty years ago, had cost the life of his sister, but then Choudri and Gorley emerged from the neighbouring hut and joined them. Carew decided to tell them what he had learned from Hahta, now before the Elders arrived.

A silence greeted his words when he finished speaking some ten minutes later, and before the debate could begin, he made out Leah and Rahn walking towards them down the length of the clearing.

A posse of settlers followed in their wake.

As they had the day before, the nine guests from across space sat in the open long-house and Leah and Rahn sat cross-legged before them, the other settlers massed behind them in the clearing. The sun rose above the jungle canopy and a bloody flush fell across the sand.

Carew searched the faces of the massed settlers, but could not see Hahta.

"You said you came from the Expansion on a mission of exploration," Leah said in her soft, deep voice. "Did you come specifically in search of my people?"

Gorley replied. "We received the distress signal from the *Procyon* and mounted a mission both to investigate what became of the ship and the colonists and to explore this as-yet uncharted region." He hesitated. "We found the *Procyon* on the moon, its suspension pods mysteriously empty, a hole in the flank of the ship."

"I can see that it must have puzzled you."

Choudri said, "We couldn't work out what had happened."

"The explanation is simple," Leah said. "We came down on the moon when our ship suffered a mechanical dysfunction. I do not know the details, as this of course happened before any of us were born. My father told of great desperation among the maintenance crew of the *Procyon*, as repairs were considered impossible."

"What happened?"

Leah smiled. "My people were rescued. A Flyer arrived on the moon, and then more and more. They communicated with the maintenance crew and said that they could save the five thousand colonists and take them to a place of safety."

Carew said, "The creatures, the Flyers, spoke your language?"

Leah smiled. "They did not need to. They read our minds and placed their thoughts in our heads." She gestured. "Of course, we could only accede to their offer, the alternative being death on the arid moon. In relays, the Flyers brought us to World."

"We saw a dead colonist aboard the *Procyon*," Carew said. "What happened to him?"

"He was the first human to apprehend the Flyer when it sent a... a Sleer into the ship."

"A Sleer?"

"Another of the Weird, the aliens of World," she said. "According to the story, before the Sleer could establish mind contact, the colonist fired upon it, and the Sleer responded in self-defence."

"The colonist's bones were fused to the metal of the ship," Carew said.

Leah gestured sadly. "The Sleer are hunters," she said, "and they sometimes use acid weapons. The Weird much regretted the death, but the fact was that they saved my people from extinction."

"So they call themselves the Weird," Carew asked, "or is that your name for them?"

Leah smiled. "A little of both. Their name for themselves sounds a little like 'weird,' and our ancestors adapted the sound."

Gorley said, "And they brought you here, but for what purpose?"

At this, Rahn smiled ingenuously and said, "For what purpose? You judge others by your own values, sir. The Weird had no ulterior motive in saving our souls than simply that – an act of altruism that needed no explanation, as far as they were concerned."

Carew looked beyond the pair to the crowd. The colonists watched the proceedings in attentive silence, their faces expressionless.

Lania said, "So they brought you here approximately seventy standard years ago."

"Or almost forty years ago, as we calculate the passage of time."

Lania nodded. "There were around five thousand of you then, but..." – she hesitated, glancing at

Carew – "from orbit we calculated there were approximately a thousand settlers here, around the clearing, and a few hundred more scattered in the jungle north of here."

The Outcasts, Carew thought.

Lania went on, "Over a period of seventy years, we would expect your numbers to have grown, not fallen."

Rahn nodded. "The early years here were not easy," he said, "despite the ministrations of the Weird. We took time to adapt to this world, and we suffered many casualties to disease. Also, there was conflict between our people. There were those who adhered to the old ways, the belief in the way of the Kurishen, and others who disavowed the old beliefs and instituted new ones more in keeping with World, and our life here with the Weird."

Lania said bluntly, "You fought?"

"Sadly, yes. This was before my time," Leah said. "Before any of us here were born. Over a period of years, the adherents of the new way prevailed and pushed their opponents out into the jungle. Their descendents still dwell out there, but we have little communication with them."

Carew heard a racket of animal calls from the jungle at his back, a low, regular whooping bellow and a painfully high sound chipping away like the blade of a chisel striking an anvil.

Gorley said, "And those beliefs, the new beliefs and your relationship with the Weird?"

Leah smiled, as did Rahn beside her. It was as if the mere name of the aliens brought cheer to their hearts.

"They saved us, many years ago," Leah said. "They showed us how to live here, to adapt to the jungle. They gave us everything we needed to survive. Before, my people worshipped a race of aliens known as the Kurishen, from the sixth planet of this system, a peace-loving people who fled their planet when it became uninhabitable."

Carew recalled the wrecked space stations circling the planet, the destroyed fortifications. "They fought a war with another race?" he said.

"Perhaps, a long time ago, this was so, but it was long before our time. My people found the crashed starships of the Kurishen and decoded their books and took on their beliefs. But they were the beliefs of a dead race, which had no relevance or value to the settlers of World. Over the years, we came to revere the Weird."

Carew asked, "But the ships of the Kurishen, when they came to the Expansion, were found to be empty, with no trace of the Kurishen."

Leah smiled. "Perhaps that mystery only added to the appeal in the eyes of my ancestors. It is an enigma I cannot hope to answer."

A silence lengthened, before Gorley asked, "And your relationship with the Weird, your beliefs...?"

"It is not a complex system of belief, my friend – there are no great lengthy screeds or tenets that must be obeyed, rather a series of simple facts that cannot be denied. There are no rules that followers must obey for fear of punishment."

Carew considered what Hahta had said, that her people had sent a Sleer to track down and bring back her sister, Maatja, and that Sleer were used to capture those known as the Outcasts. Was this the action of a belief system which claimed to use no punitive measures?

"The simple facts are that the Weird, in the many forms they take, whether Harvester, Flyer, Shuffler, or any other, give us life, and we for our part give the Weird life in return."

Gorley inclined his head as if in understanding, then asked, "In what way does this transaction work?"

Leah and Rahn leaned towards each other and spoke in lowered tones; Rahn nodded and Leah looked up and smiled. "If you would care to follow us to the domicile of the Harvester."

The Elders stood and moved from the long-house. Outside, Leah spoke to her gathered people. They remained seated as Gorley led the way from the shade and into the blasting heat of the sun.

Lania fell into step beside Carew as they made their way down the length of the clearing. "This should be interesting."

"I've never been introduced to an alien god before."

She smiled. "That's how she made it sound, isn't it? I can't imagine what her people can give the Harvester that it can't get itself."

"Or what it gives in return," he said.

Ten minutes later they approached the long-house within which the alien creature dwelled.

He had only seen it at a distance before, but even then it had appeared gross. At close quarters, its corpulence was hideous and obscene. It filled the length of the long-house, great bulges of grey fat swelling out between the timber supports. Each bulge was slit laterally with what might have been a mucous membrane, suppurating with a rank green ichor.

A team of attendants made its way around the long-house, placing crude ladders on the flank of the beast and mopping away the ichor with what looked like sponges.

The stench was eye-watering, though clearly Leah and Rahn and the other settlers were unaffected.

The pair led the way around the long-house to the creature's rear, where a thick tentacle hung. Leah spoke to a pair of cleaners, who approached the tentacle. The first woman grasped its thick base, while the second directed the trunk-like appendage towards a wooden bucket.

The first woman then squeezed the tentacle, easing her hands expertly along its length until, from a raw pink sphincter, a thick milky fluid oozed into the waiting bucket.

Within seconds the receptacle was full and the woman replaced it with a second.

"We dry the phar," said Leah in lowered tones, "and it provides our staple form of nourishment."

Lania exchanged a glance with Carew and pulled a face. Carew smiled and murmured, "Don't criticise until you've sampled it, Lania. It might taste exquisite."

Gorley said, "And in return, you give the Harvester...?"

Leah smiled and led the way to the front of the long-house.

Carew had expected to find a face, or at least a semblance or eyes and maybe a mouth. Instead, the head of the Harvester sported multiple tentacles which snuffled around the sandy ground, sucking up husks of some dried fruit placed there by the cleaners.

"The Harvesters find the rind of the ghar fruit a delicacy, and as it is inedible to humans..." Leah gestured at the probing trunks.

"A wonderfully efficient system," Choudri commented.

"And this forms the basis of your belief system?" Lania asked, and Carew detected a note of sarcasm-cum-incredulity in her question.

Leah smiled. "A small part of it; merely one of the bases on which we found the belief we call Sacred Circularity."

Rahn stepped forward and addressed the group, "Later today, one lhan before sunset, approximately two of your hours, we will perform the ceremony of Return. We will remove the Harvester from its resting place here and transport it" – he gestured across the clearing to the fissure – "to the bank of the river. From there it will be taken downriver to the lair of the Weird and a new Harvester will take its place. Thus the Great Circularity is continued. This ritual is the highpoint of our calendar, and we would be honoured if you would attend."

Gorley replied, "And we feel honoured to be allowed to attend."

Leah led the way back across the clearing. "If you would care to retire to your huts until the commencement of the ceremony, my friends, I will have food brought to you."

"The phar?" Lania asked.

Leah inclined her head. "A little phar, but also the less nutritious fruits of the jungle."

They parted company outside their huts and sat in the shade, watching Leah and Rahn as they rejoined their people and dismissed the crowd.

"Well," Gorley, "what did you make of that?"

Lania said, "What she told us about the diminished numbers of settlers..."

Carew looked at her. "What about it?"

"I don't buy her explanation. They started with five thousand and now there are only around a thousand settlers here and a few hundred in the jungle? Given the fact that their numbers should have at least quadrupled in almost seventy years, the figures don't add up, even if there had been conflicts and hardship."

Carew considered what Hahta had said. "Also, this give and take thing, the Great Circularity. Hahta said that her father had gone to 'help' the Weird. Another aspect of the circularity? Leah mentioned nothing of this."

Two serving boys ferried trays laden with phar and spiky green fruit across the clearing and set them on the sand beside their guests. Then they brought gourds full of drar juice, then bowed and departed.

Carew regarded the trays. The dried phar resembled a slab of cheese, pale and sweating in the midday heat.

Lania tested it with her smartsuit, then smiled at him. "Full of good, healthy bacteria," she said, "but nothing harmful."

He broke off a chunk as the others watched him. "There's an old saying, 'When in Nova Roma.'"

"Don't do it, boss!" Jed said.

He slipped the phar into his mouth and chewed. It was dry and sour, not at all the delicacy he had been expecting.

CHAPTER FOURTEEN

TWO HOURS LATER Carew stood beside the long-house where the Harvester reposed. Leah and Rahn were nearby, murmuring a commentary to Gorley and Choudri. The settlers were massed in the clearing. They had set up a low monotone hum which according to Leah was the song which signalled the commencement of the transportation ceremony.

"I've watched the Pan PharmOlympic games on New Athens," Lania murmured to him, "and I've seen the grand final of the Expansion skyball contest on the Persephone trading station – but I think this might beat them all."

The same team of a dozen cleaners which had ministered to the Harvester's needs now began to dismantle the long-house. They did it with the practised expertise of a circus team bringing down a big top at the end of a show. They swarmed up the timber supports – using the blubber of the alien as foot-rests – and withdrew pinions from the roof joists. Within moments they were lifting the thatched roof and sliding it down the far side of the creature, then pushing it back to rest upside-down against the margin of the jungle.

Next, the team lifted the timber support columns from pits in the ground, abrading the flesh of the Harvester as they did so. When the posts were removed, the creature, its tonnage released, sagged outwards – its colossal flank barred with pale indentations.

Rahn stepped forward, anointed the Harvester's proboscis with fluid and intoned something under his breath.

A great chant rose up from the gathered settlers, followed by a rhythmic stamping of feet. This ceased suddenly and an eerie silence filled the clearing.

Reverently, heads bowed, a hundred men and woman emerged from the crowd and moved around the splayed, stranded alien. Leah stepped forward and raised a hand.

"And so the eightieth Harl ceremony of the year 42 commences."

The crowd cheered, and the bearers moved into position. They knelt and, on a shouted command from Rahn, gripped a series of timber handles projecting from beneath the monster's bulk. Then they lifted the vast catafalque in one fluid motion.

Carew had expected the bearers to struggle, the catafalque to teeter under the great weight, but the bearers were well practised and strong, and the great beast never so much as wobbled as it rose into the air. The bearers lodged the timber handles across their necks and shoulders like yokes, and on another shouted command, this time from a woman at the front of the team, they walked in step across the clearing towards an archway constructed from curved tree-trunks on the edge of the fissure.

Leah and Rahn escorted their guests behind the catafalque, followed by the mass of the settlers.

"Impressed so far?" Carew murmured to Lania as the procession neared the lip of the escarpment.

"Beats the hell out of skyball," she said. "But how the hell will they carry it down five thousand steps without the thing sliding off?"

Carew tried to banish the vision of the Harvester slipping from the catafalque and tumbling all the way down to the bottom of the fissure.

"They've had plenty of practice, Lania."

She grunted. "Hell of a lot of work to appease the appetite of a minor god," she said. "And all the settlers get from it is a daily slab of tasteless goo?"

The bearers had reached the archway of trunks. They passed beneath it, slowed and turned laboriously, negotiating the esplanade of packed earth at the top of the flight of steps. When they were parallel with the fissure, they stepped forward and negotiated the first of the steps.

Now Carew saw how they accomplished the operation without any embarrassing mishaps. The steps were shallow and wide, so that they proceeded down the incline at an obtuse gradient; the bearers at the front kept the handles on their shoulders, while those in the mid-section and to the rear lowered the handles and gripped them at waist-height – effectively keeping the Harvester level.

Lania moved alongside Leah and said, "Isn't it odd to have a race divided into so many different... types?"

"Strictly speaking," Leah said, "they're not divided, as such. Many years ago, the Harvester here was a Flyer, and before that a Shuffler, and before that a Sleer. Before that, they were a series of other... manifestations... many of which do not show themselves for human inspection."

"And the Harvester?" Lania asked. "What will that change into?"

Leah smiled, like a holy disciple asked the true nature of her god. "Ah," she said at last, "that we do not know."

The packed-earth stairway zigzagged down the side of the fissure. Some stretches were long, others short, taking in the nature of the gradient. Carew imagined the back-breaking work it must have taken to hack the path through the jungle which clung to the side of the ravine. He peered over the edge of the path, but the bottom of the fissure was lost in shadow.

They passed from direct sunlight into shade and the temperature fell by at least twenty degrees. He pulled his water flask from his backpack and took a long drink, offering it to Lania and Jed. The engineer accepted, but Lania shook her head. It was at times like these that Carew envied his pilot her smartsuit, with its thermostatic facility which kept her body cool in the punishing heat of the day.

An hour passed and Carew found himself thinking of the girl, Hahta, and what she had told him early that morning. She had said that her father had been 'chosen' by the Weird, selected to go to their lair in order to 'help' the aliens.

Presumably he had come this way, followed by his other daughter. He wondered what fate had met her father. Hahta had said that the Chosen never returned – but what about Maatja?

He looked over his shoulder at the mass of descending settlers straggling down the zigzag path: there were humans of all sizes, youngsters and their parents – but, he realised for the first time, no old people amongst their number. He wondered about that.

"What?" Lania said, watching him as he scanned the settlers on the flight of stairs directly above them.

"I've only just realised, Lania – I haven't seen a single settler over the age of, say, fifty."

Lania looked up reflexively, frowning. "Come to think of it..."

"What the hell do they do with the oldsters?"

She shrugged. "Okay, how about this. They live such healthy lives, eating all that fruit and Harvester shit and stuff, they don't age as obviously as we do? Perhaps Leah and Rahn here are eighty, but only look fifty?"

He pursed his lips. "Or perhaps they lead such relatively primitive lives, with no drugs and healthcare as such, that they die off in their fifties and don't reach old age."

Ahead, the bearers came to a gradual halt. "The halfway point of the descent," Leah said.

As Carew watched, they eased their burden onto a framework of timber struts erected in a widened area of the pathway. The bearers, relieved, exercised their tired arms, stretched and talked animatedly amongst themselves.

Serving boys and girl circulated with great jugs of liquid, from which first the bearers drank and then the followers. The guests were offered a jug and Leah murmured, "It is customary at this juncture for all gathered to drink to the success of the ceremony."

Carew took the heavy jug, lifted it to his lips and drank. The fluid was thick, white, and he recognised not so much the sour taste as the slightly chalky texture. He passed the jug to Jed who drank, then lowered the jug and wiped his mouth with the back of his hand, frowning at the less than refreshing draft.

"What is it, boss?"

Carew turned to the elder. "Leah?" he asked.

"Fresh phar," she said, "before it has had time to dry out and solidify. At this stage it's at its most nutritious."

"Hear that?" Carew said to an appalled Jed. "The best meal you've had in days."

The others took the jug and drank sparingly, while Lania put a solicitous arm around Jed's shoulders and lectured him quietly about cultural relativism.

Before the bearers resumed their descent, Carew said to Leah, "You maintain a healthy diet, and no meat?"

"We are vegetarian, Ed Carew. As were our ancestors. We take all the nutrition we need from jungle fruits and phar."

"It keeps you looking young, or..." He paused. "If you don't mind my asking, what is the life-expectancy of the settlers on World?"

She regarded him, her gaze level, as if considering what to tell him. At last she said, "We live into our third decade, Ed Carew; fifty years, by your reckoning. Short lives, perhaps, by your standards, but long enough for us to fulfil our purpose."

With that she walked off and addressed the bearers before Carew could continue his questioning.

He exchanged a look with Gorley and Choudri. Lania said, "'Fulfil our purpose,' Now what the hell did she mean by that?"

The descent recommenced. The bearers took their burden and Carew and his colleagues followed at a respectful pace. As he walked, he wondered how old Leah and Rahn themselves might be, and if they were approaching the age where they judged they had fulfilled their purpose?

They worked their way deeper and deeper into the fissure and the temperature dropped appreciably. Soon, a dim twilight maintained. The vegetation, so abundant high above, thinned out so that for the last hour of their journey the steps were hewn from bare earth. There was no birdsong this far down, nor the calls of other life-forms, and an eerie quietude accompanied the last leg of the descent. Even the following crowd was strangely silent.

Carew looked up and saw high above his head a thin strip of roseate sky, darkening towards sunset.

A little later Lania lay a hand on his arm and whispered, "Look."

She pointed over the edge of the path; perhaps two hundred metres below them, Carew made out a slick of oil-black water. It flowed between the rocky banks without the slightest ripple, silent and eerie. On the riverbank, half a kilometre distant, a wide timber jetty projected into the river.

Journey's end, he thought. At least for ourselves and the celebrants.

"Strange," Lania said, at his side.

He smiled at her.

"It makes me wonder at the many other rites and rituals, bizarre and unbelievable, going on across the galaxy," she said.

"My bet is that there are far stranger things happening out there."

"But involving human beings? The Expansion is perhaps too sanitised, but this..."

He glanced at her. "It makes you uneasy?"

She nodded. "Yes, it does. These people, for all their outwardly idyllic lifestyle... they seem in thrall to these things. I mean, their lifespans, for one thing. And do they have things like literature, art? The things that make humans... human?" She smiled suddenly.

"What?"

"And there I was, preaching to Jed, and who's to say that these people are any less human for the life they lead?"

Carew shook his head. "No, I agree with you. The set-up here makes me uneasy, too."

They had reached the foot of the stairs, and before them, the bearers slowed as the path levelled out. They made a slow, careful turn and carried the Harvester to the end of the jetty. There, they lowered it to the timber boards, stood and retreated to the path.

The mass of settlers remained on the bank of the river, where a flat area had been cleared, as if for the express purpose of providing a vantage point.

Leah and Rahn stepped forward and invited their guests to join them at the very end of the jetty. Carew and the others walked along its length and stood beside the Harvester, staring downriver.

"And now?" Lania asked.

"Now," Leah replied, "we wait."

Carew was perhaps an arm's length from the Harvester. The slits along its length had parted as its mass spread, and now they resembled nothing so much as open, suppurating wounds. The smell at such close quarters was appalling, as if the flesh of the beast was rotting from within.

Rahn smiled and pointed downriver. "Look."

Only then, in the dimness and distance, did Carew make out the small shape of a raft making its way up-river towards them, paddled by perhaps twenty settlers. As everyone watched, the raft gained solidity in the twilight, and Carew saw that borne on the surface of the raft was a smaller, slimmer version of the Harvester.

The raft manoeuvred itself alongside the landward end of the jetty, its deck flush with the wooden walkway. The bearers lashed the vessel fast to the timbers, and the rowers laid aside their oars and fell to the task of easing the new Harvester from the raft and onto the jetty. Like the larger creature, this one reposed upon a great timber catafalque, and the rowers lifted it by means of timber handles and moved it little by little onto the jetty.

The watchers on the shore started up a low, monotone chant.

Carew examined the new Harvester. Except in its dimensions, the creature was identical in shape and colouration to the outward-bound Harvester. This one's flesh was without the indentations made by the timber posts, however, and the lateral slits in its sides were sealed tight and did not ooze fluid.

When the new Harvester was safely placed upon. the jetty, the bearers began the delicate task of easing the bloated Harvester onto the raft. It proved to be a laborious process, involving much shouting and yelled commands. The raft wobbled as it took the first of the load and when the entirety of the creature was lowered onto its deck, the vessel sank a metre into the water.

A great sigh went up from the watchers on the riverbank.

The rowers took up their positions on either side of the creature, their elbow room much restricted now, and on the jetty Leah and Rahn stepped forward and took it in turn to recite what sounded like lines of verse, though in a dialect so broad Carew was unable to make out a single word.

The raft cast off and floated serenely down the sable river.

Carew said, "And what happens to the Harvester when it reaches its destination?"

"In two sunsets," Leah replied, "it will make the transition."

Carew repeated the last word. "And that is?"

"That, my friend, is the most glorious stage in the life-cycle of the Weird. It is the time of moving from this realm, to the exalted other realm."

"The Weird equivalent of Heaven?"

Leah smiled. "Not as such. The Harvester will move from this universe to the next one, and it is the duty of one Council Elder, in this case myself, to witness the ultimate transition." She paused and turned to take in her guests. "I leave at full sun up in the morning, and I would be honoured if you, as our guests, would accompany me on the journey to the home of the Weird."

Choudri and Gorley conferred, then looked around the group; no one demurred. Choudri said,

"We would be privileged to witness the transition."

Leah beamed at them. "The journey downriver is in itself an experience I am anticipating, a time of meditation for an Elder coming to the end of her tenure."

Gorley looked at her. "You are stepping down?"

She laughed. "You could put it like that, my friend. Rahn and I have served our people, and the Weird, for ten of our years now, and it is time for younger souls to take on the responsibility."

She turned and addressed the bearers, who fell to their knees on either side of the catafalque. They rose and bore the new Harvester high, their faces showing none of the strain or contortion they had exhibited on the descent.

They moved from the jetty and began the long ascent up the five thousand stairs.

Carew and his group, led by Leah and Rahn, walked slowly after them.

Lania fell into step beside him and murmured, "There's something I don't understand about all this, Ed."

He smiled. "You're not alone, Lania, I assure you of that."

She looked at him. "So you've noticed the anomaly?"

"Anomaly?" he said. She looked exasperated, and slowed her pace so that they fell further behind Leah and Rahn.

"So the fat, bloated Harvester gets shipped off home and is replaced by a smaller, slimmer version."

"I'm following you so far."

"And the new Harvester is fed the husks of that jungle fruit and shits out phar which the settlers consider a delicacy. You don't see the anomaly there?"

He thought about it, admitted defeat and said, "Enlighten me."

"It's just this, Ed – *how does the Harvester grow so damned fat?*".

He nodded. "You're right. There can't be much nourishment in the husks, and Leah did say earlier today that that's its only foodstuff." There must, he thought, be a simple explanation, but for the life of him he couldn't think of one.

"Well done, Lania."

"I thought there was something odd going on, and I didn't need my smartsuit to tell me."

"Any ideas?"

She screwed her lips into a frown and shook her head. "Beats me. I'll work on it, though."

They came to the halfway point, where the bearers eased the Harvester onto the timber supports and took a break. This time, to Jed's evident relief, there was no refreshment in the form of liquid phar.

High overhead, the strip of sky was darkening rapidly. Stars were beginning to appear, bright in the indigo heavens.

Lania was chatting with Jed – joshing him about the phar – when a small figure wormed its way through the crowd of settlers and sidled towards Carew.

"Hahta," he said, glancing around. The others were facing up the incline, and Leah and Rahn were talking to the bearers.

"Edcarew," the little girl piped. "Have you decided yet? Can you help me?"

"Hahta, I can't talk here, okay? Not when so many people..."

She interrupted, "But you are going downriver with Leah, no? To the lair of the Weird? So you can find Maatja, yes?"

"Hahta, we need to talk. But not here. I'll meet you later. Is that possible?"

She nodded, her blue eyes bright in the light of the stars. "Tonight, at moonup. Where we met before, Edcarew."

"Very well. I'll be there."

She flashed him a grin and ran back into the crowd.

He looked around, nervous that their conversation had been observed. Lania looked at him. "What did she want?"

"She knew we're accompanying Leah downriver."

"News travels fast. She asked you to look for her sister?"

"I said I'd talk to her later. I think she knows a lot more than she's told me so far. It's just a matter of knowing the right questions to ask. I'm meeting her later tonight."

She looked at him. "Mind if I come along?"

He thought about it. Why not? Lania might have more insight into the mind of the girl, know which questions to ask. He nodded.

The bearers resumed their burden and the climb recommenced.

THAT EVENING, TO celebrate the success of the Ceremony of Transportation, Leah and Rahn invited their guests to a feast at the long-house where their initial meeting had taken place.

A mat on the ground was stacked with a dozen different fruits and the obligatory dried and sliced phar. Fruit juice was on offer, as well as a special drink called naar which, Rahn announced, was alcoholic. Guttering candles fashioned from vines and tree sap illuminated the gathering, and Leah and Rahn toasted the installation of the new Harvester.

Jed sipped the naar and pronounced it an improvement on the liquid phar, and Carew joined him in a cup. It wasn't exactly the finest malt whisky – it was fruit-based and more like a liquor – but he found it more than palatable.

They ate and drank and exchanged small-talk. Carew wanted to ask about the anomaly of the Harvester's diet, but the occasion never arose. Gorley and Choudri were telling the settlers about the Expansion, and Leah and Rahn listened wide-eyed to the stories of the technological wonders described.

Carew had a second cup of naar, feeling his senses become pleasantly muzzy. He placed a hand over the cup when a settler tried to refill it, and Lania smiled at his wisdom. "Well done, Ed. You know you can't take your drink." She was drinking fruit juice herself.

A sudden silence descended on the gathering and one of the settlers rose to his feet. He raised his gourd mug.

He spoke, and though his accent was heavy, Carew made out the words, "We drink to the passing of Leah and Rahn."

At this Leah stood and lifted her mug. "And we, in turn, drink to celebrate the coming of Jarl and Keer."

"Thus the Great Circularity continues," Rahn said.

Jed looked up drunkenly and focused on Leah and Rahn. "And you two?"

"We have fulfilled our service and now we make way for younger, fresher minds. Such is the way."

Carew exchanged a glance with Lania.

Gorley said, "And you, Rahn, won't be accompanying us to the lair of the Weird?"

Rahn smiled. "The male of the Elders does not witness the transition," he said. "On the very first occasion an Elder followed a Harvester to its home, over forty of our years ago, the *Procyon's* captain happened to be a woman. And so it goes. Traditions are what bind society together, they are the warp and weave, if you like, of the fabric of a people. We will not forgo that tradition, not break the thread."

Leah passed the jug of naar. "More drink!" she said, insisting on refilling Carew's empty mug.

He drank, but sparingly, while the evening continued around him and the guests became slowly more inebriated. At one point he looked from the long-house, into the dark sky above the clearing, but the moons had not yet risen.

The party broke up an hour later and Carew and Lania grabbed the arms of an insensate Jed and half-carried him to their hut. The others retired to their dwellings, and within minutes a silence had settled over the clearing.

They eased Jed into his blister-tent and in seconds he was snoring.

Lania sealed the front of the tent, then turned to Carew. "All that talk about the passing of Leah and Rahn, Ed? Are you thinking what I'm thinking?"

"That they've come to the end of their usefulness, for whatever reason." He paused, looking at her in the half-light. "Euthanasia?"

"That's what I thought. But why? I mean, they're still young."

The average life-span in the Expansion, given the latest healthcare and bionics, was in the region of two hundred standard years. The thought that Leah and Rahn would live for only a quarter of this, for reasons connected to the Weird, sickened him.

"Perhaps Hahta will be able to tell us more," he said.

Lania moved to the door of the hut and peered out. She waved Carew over.

"Look," she said.

Over the jungle on the far side of the fissure, the huge moon was rising, its pocked face flushed with the light of the supergiant. Riding high above it was the smaller moon, and their combined light filled the silent clearing.

He stepped out into the pleasantly warm night; a cooling breeze blew across the fissure. He looked towards the place where he had spoken with Hahta that morning, but there was no sign yet of the girl.

He heard movement from a hut further down the clearing to their right. Hahta, he thought, leaving to keep her rendezvous.

The figure that emerged from the hut, however, was not Hahta. He watched as Leah stepped out into the moonlight. She turned, beckoned and a second figure joined her: Rahn.

And with him was a third settler.

Lania whispered, "It's the girl..."

His first thought was that the Elders had found out about the rendezvous, and were preventing it.

But there was no signs of struggle or protest from Hahta; she walked off down the clearing, between Leah and Rahn, as if this late night promenade was a regular occurrence.

Lania said, "She looks... drunk, or drugged."

Carew stared at the girl and saw that indeed there was something mechanical about her movements, unresisting and compliant.

The trio moved off down the clearing, passing the serried huts, until they were almost lost from sight.

"I wonder where they're going?" he murmured.

Her tongue nipped between her teeth, Lania looked at him. "There's only one way to find out." She grabbed his arm. "Come on."

They crept from the doorway of the hut, the double moonlight sending their shadows sprawling to their right as they followed the three figures. Lania lay a hand on his arm, counselling wariness, and they slowed their pace.

Carew expected the trio to turn into one of the huts at any moment, but they kept on walking and, perhaps five minutes later, passed by the last of the huts. Lania's grip tightened on his arm. "They're heading for the long-house."

She dragged him into a gap between two huts. They came to the margin of the jungle behind the huts and ran west, parallel to the clearing. In a few minutes they came to the last hut and paused, ducking down and watching the trio approach the long-house.

The Harvester beneath the thatch was a dark shape, and at this distance it was impossible to discern the slightest detail. The trio came to the long-house and stepped into its shadow, and Carew saw that there were other settlers there who greeted them.

Lania leaned towards him and whispered in his ear, "Into the jungle, Ed. We'll be able to get closer to the long-house, see what's going on in there. And they won't be able to see us. Okay, keep close."

Then she was gone, a fleet figure at his side one second, and the next vanished into the jungle: in her jet black smartsuit, it was as if his shadow had detached itself from him and fled.

He followed. She was waiting for him, took his arm and pulled him along after her.

They passed through the undergrowth without a sound, moonlight flashing through the fronds like blades of silver. He felt his heartbeat loud in his ears.

Lania slowed, turned and placed a long finger before her full lips. She trod with exaggerated steps through the shrubbery, as stealthy as a stalking cat.

Something eclipsed the moons to his left: the dark, square bulk of the long-house. Lania continued for another ten metres, then settled into a crouch. He knelt beside her and she reached out and eased back a broad leaf.

A group of settlers stood in silence before the head-end of the new Harvester. Carew watched as Leah knelt before the creature's probing trunk and offered it something – a husk of fruit? – then stood and made way for Rahn to do the same. Then it was Hahta's turn and Carew knew then that she was definitely drunk or drugged: she stared ahead with wide, unseeing eyes, and her movements were stiff, automatic.

Behind her stood the two younger settlers, Jarl and Keer, and when their turn came, they too offered the swinging proboscis a chunk of gourd.

It appeared, from the reverence of their movements, that they were making an offering to the new Harvester – supplying the creature with the first of many meals to come.

Carew wondered if that was the extent of this ceremony; they had fed the beast and now they would return to their huts. But another voice told him that there was more to come.

He glanced at Lania and was struck by how beautiful she appeared in the moonlight, with her rounded brow and flat nose, her jet hair swept back and gathered behind her head.

She saw him looking and pulled a grim face.

He returned his attention to what was happening within the long-house.

The five settlers had moved from the head-end of the creature and now stood with their backs to the jungle, facing the flank of the Harvester. Carew judged they were perhaps three metres from Lania and himself. His breathing sounded loud in the silence and his knee joints creaked as he shifted position minimally. He winced, fearing discovery, and tried to control his breathing.

One of the settlers was intoning something, some religious incantation, some paean to the mighty Weird, the giver of all that was good in the universe.

Then Leah and Rahn turned to face each other. They remained like this, face to face, for perhaps a minute, their expressions in shadow. They reached out and embraced, and Carew thought that the embrace had about it the finality of a farewell gesture, while the rational part of his mind told him that this could not be so.

Then they disengaged and Rahn turned and faced the flank of the Harvester.

Jarl and Keer stepped forward and approached the creature. They were carrying something between them, a container into which they dipped their hands. What they did next disturbed and surprised Carew – and evidently Lania, too, as she jerked back involuntarily and glanced at him, her expression screwed up in distaste.

Jarl and Keer reached out and anointed a slit in the flank of the Harvester. Jarl began at the top, Keer at the bottom and massaged their hands – smeared with a thick, oily fluid – up and down the length of the pink, shining labia, something almost sexual in the passion with which they worked.

Slowly, the vertical slit responded to their ministrations and began to part.

Jarl and Keer, their duty done, stepped back.

Carew's heart pounded. He felt dizzy. He didn't want to watch what was about to happen.

A second later Rahn stepped forward. At that moment a frond fell before Carew's face, and when he waved it away Rahn had disappeared.

He blinked. He looked at Lania, saw his shocked expression mirrored in her face.

He looked back, but there was no Rahn. He had vanished, as if he had never been.

Then Hahta stepped forward, walking like a zombie, and Carew wanted more than anything to shout out loud, to leap forward and stop whatever was about to happen.

Hahta moved towards the glistening slit in the flank of the Harvester, and as he watched the aperture opened wider to receive her, and she was drawn inexorably within.

He felt a hand on his arm as Lania grabbed him and hauled him away, through the jungle. He stumbled after her, his only thought to get away from there, to get back to the others and warn them.

Only then was he hit by the thought that the girl, Hahta, had been punished for speaking to him.

Lania gave an abbreviated scream to his left and he heard a brief, frantic struggle. He turned in panic. Something whipped around his waist and lifted him off the ground. He tried to scream but a warm wet mass fastened around his mouth – something soft and rubbery and terrible.

He was pulled off his feet, dragged through the undergrowth, carried by a creature which possessed immense strength and speed. Then whatever had taken him climbed and swung through the air, and he had the dizzying sensation of travelling high, far higher than he should have been if his abductor had been a mere human being.

"Lania!" he called out.

Then his head connected with something solid.

CHAPTER FIFTEEN

LANIA SCREAMED AND knew terror as she had never known it before.

What was happening to her was unbelievable, could not be happening. She screamed again, not wanting to believe that she was thirty metres above the jungle floor and travelling at speed in the arms of... of what?

She was like the rag-doll plaything of an ape, except that whatever had abducted her was supporting her back and head solicitously. She was aware of its great strength as it swung through the jungle canopy, leaping and diving, and she knew that, had it intended to kill her, it could easily have done so. Therefore, it wanted her alive. And Ed?

She rose and fell with the creature, the motion making her feel sick. She saw flashes of green vegetation, a starlit sky, then the ground far below. She tried to twist her head to see what was carrying her, but the thing held her fast in arms. It felt slick and wet and rubbery. No, not arms – she was gripped merely by one arm, while the other was employed to swing through the treetops. This she could see, a thick, muscular appendage that grabbed and released branches and vines in quick succession, launching itself from tree to tree with great powerful swings. She thought back to what she had seen just minutes ago: Rahn and then the girl Hahta, absorbed into the Harvester, and her mind revolted.

She cried out Ed's name, then made a concerted effort to twist her head and look to her right where she heard a clattering through the foliage.

She saw Ed, floppy in the arms of...

She closed her eyes and screamed, but when she opened them again the monster and Ed were no longer in sight.

Had she really seen the thing that held Ed as it swung through the jungle canopy, or had she hallucinated?

It had been man-shaped, but of an umbilical, new-born purple-blue, a hideous thing corded with veins, with great powerful arms and legs, a domed head featureless but for two great, black, circular eyes.

Why had the settlers not mentioned these monsters that haunted the jungle? Why had they kept quiet about these simian tree-dwellers when they had told of the Weird?

Unless, of course, they *were* the Weird.

For a second she found herself almost upside-down, gasping and staring down at the jungle floor. And there, far beneath her, she caught a fleeting glimpse of two tiny human figures, darting through the forest and looking up at her from time to time.

The sight filled her with hope. The settlers had sent people after her, to wrest her away from these monsters. She wondered if they were armed. She tried to recall if the settlers had carried weapons, or had spoken of them, but she had no recollection of either. How, then, would they effect her rescue?

She tried to fight, to kick her legs and move her arms so that she might swing at her captor. But the single arm pinned her tight to the hot, wet torso and she was powerless to resist her abduction. She closed her eyes and fought to keep the contents of her stomach in place as she pitched and rolled through the air. She had once piloted the *Poet* through a meteor hailstorm in the Barnard's Star system, but though fearful, she had been fuelled by adrenaline, in control of the situation, confident of surviving the ride. Now she had no such confidence, was not in control, and felt not an iota of the same adrenaline course through her, just fear.

They seemed to swing through the treetops for hours on end: she would not have been surprised to see the hemisphere of the supergiant heave itself into sight, heralding the end of night. Would their flight ever cease? Where were they taking her, and why? One scrap of comfort was the fact that she was not alone, that the monsters had taken Ed too.

Then it seemed that the creature slowed in its manic swinging from tree to tree; it felt as if it were walking upon something solid. She screwed her head away from its chest in order to see where they were going.

They were in the very upper canopy of the jungle, and a scintillating dazzle of starlight, like a chandelier, illuminated a magical scene. Pendant from high branches were dozens of orange globes; at first she was unable to work out how big they were – the size of flyers or as small as oranges? – until she saw that they were connected by a network of walkways, and upon these swaying bridges scurried the tiny figures of human beings. She saw a woman duck into one of the orange spheres and knew them to be dwelling places high in the jungle canopy.

They slowed still further and she saw that the creature was carrying her along one of the walkways. At length they entered a globe, and she found herself inside a circular space with curved, ribbed walls.

The creature placed her in a sitting position against the wall, and she leaned back against the pulpy interior, and before she knew it her captor had forced something into her mouth. It was bitter and jelly-like and before she could spit it out, it dissolved on her tongue. She heard a sound outside and the creature bearing Ed ducked in through the tiny opening and set him with surprising gentleness, given its size and strength, against the wall opposite her. Then the creatures made for the exit and paused to look back – a pair of bloody embryonic monstrosities with featureless faces and great domed insect eyes – before slipping from the globe and disappearing.

She felt a great drowsiness sweeping through her body and knew that the lozenge forced into her mouth had been a sedative.

She looked across at Ed, her heart leaping with joy at the sight of him. His head was bloody from a gash that split his brow, and he was unconscious. Her last thought was that perhaps he was not unconscious, but dead. She felt a moment of futile panic, and then slipped into oblivion.

*   *   *

"Lania?"

She opened her eyes.

Ed was kneeling beside her, stroking her cheek. She smiled up at him, lifted her hand and touched the dressing at his forehead. It was not the synthi-flesh patch she might have expected, but a wad of leaf held in place by a loop of twine. But the fact that it was there at all suggested the possibility of kindness on the part of their captors.

She saw a gourd of liquid in the centre of the floor and next to it a palm leaf bearing two yellow fruits split into segments. Breakfast.

"What happened?" Ed said. "Something grabbed me. The next thing I knew..." – he reached up and touched his head – "I head-butted a tree or something. The odd thing is, I don't feel a thing now."

She smiled. "These jungle remedies." She sat up and moved to the opening. A grey, fungal walkway connected the dwelling to the crown of a tree, perhaps thirty metres away. All around hung similar globes. There was no one in sight, neither humans nor monsters. She looked down, made out a sea of leaves broken here and there by a vertiginous view of the jungle floor.

She said, "Why did they give Rahn and Hahta to the Harvester, Ed?"

He looked at her. "I wondered if they gave Hahta... because she talked to me. I wondered if it were my fault –"

"But they gave Rahn, too." She recalled what Rahn had told them. "He said that it was time to make way for younger, fresher minds."

"Perhaps that answers the anomaly you noticed, Lania. Now we know how the Harvesters get so fat. They feed on people: those who have reached a certain age and... and undesirables."

"That's sick," she murmured. She sank back against the soft pith of the wall, reached for the jug and drank. Some kind of fruit juice, indeed the finest drink she'd ever tasted. She passed the jug to Ed and he drank.

She inspected the fruit, sniffed it, then ate; it tasted sour at first, then sweet, and filled her mouth with an effervescent juice.

"We're in some kind of giant fruit," she said. "The good news is that there are humans about. I saw them last night."

"What took us, Lania? Did you see them?"

She nodded. "Humanoids. Bipedal. Imagine skinned, bloody apes, but with big black eyes like locusts. The way they moved through the jungle, their speed and power..." She shook her head at the recollection of their headlong flight.

She wondered at the humans she had seen tracking their progress through the jungle canopy. Last night she had assumed they were settlers from the clearing, but now realised that she might have been wrong. Had they been the tree-dwellers, complicit in their abduction?

"These people must be the Outcasts, Ed."

He nodded. "The girl, Hahta, she told me the Outcasts were 'bad people' – that they tried to kill the Weird."

"Bad people who tended to your wound and left food and drink for us."

"Bad is relative. I wonder what the Outcasts think of the settlers?"

Lania reached up and touched her ear, and found that her earpiece was missing.

Ed raised his hand to where his own should have been. "Mine too."

"You think they were dislodged in transit?"

He shook his head. "More likely removed. The Outcasts don't want us communicating with the others, obviously."

They were silent for a time. Ed moved to the opening, sat and stared out. Lania asked, "What do you think they want with us?"

He shook his head. "They might just be curious. We're the first visitors to their planet for seventy years. These are people opposed to the ways of the settlers. They might see us as allies."

She smiled at him. "Are you just saying that to try to make me feel better?"

"No – I'm trying to make myself feel better." He picked up a segment of fruit and began eating.

She stared out at the dome of the rising supergiant. It must have been an optical illusion, but from this vantage point, a mere fifty metres closer to the sun than at ground level, she seemed to be able to make out more detail on its fiery orange surface: the great sunspots, the rising spirals of fire, the geysering molten outbursts. It was colossal and majestic and strangely moving.

She found herself reaching out for Ed's hand and holding on tight.

She said in little more than a murmur, "Have I ever told you about my father, Ed?"

He looked at her and shook his head. "No. No, you haven't."

"Haven't told anyone about him. Never wanted to; or rather, I've wanted to, but never felt close enough to anyone to tell them, to trust them enough." She thought she saw him wince at that, but she might have been mistaken. "I was close to him."

"What happened?"

She sat in the opening and stared out at the fulminating supergiant. "My mother died when I was two. My father told me it was a heart attack." She shrugged. "So he brought me up, spent all his free time with me when he wasn't at work."

"What did he do?"

"He was a cop." She laughed. "Really. He was an Expansion cop working on Xaria. Working for the enemy, Ed. Anyway... one day when I was fourteen, we went swimming in the sea, well away from anywhere. We went there every holiday, just the two of us, and swam and dived and played with the narns – these things like dolphins – and just had a great time."

She stopped. "I'd like to go back to Xaria, buy a villa on the coast where we spent the holidays, and lay the ghosts to rest." She realised she was crying. When she glanced at Ed, he was looking away, pretending he hadn't seen the tears streaming down her cheeks.

She said, "Then one morning we were out swimming, diving off a rocky ledge into the sea. Daddy wanted to impress me, so he climbed higher and moved a little further along the ledge, to where we hadn't jumped from before. And when he dived for the last time he hit something under water and I was watching, and when I got to him, swimming through the blood... I think he was already dead. I dragged him to the beach, managed to haul him ashore. Found his com and called emergency, but by the time they got to us it was too late."

Ed put an arm around her shoulders and pulled her close.

"And things just got worse from then on. I had no relatives, so I was taken to an orphanage in the capital, only the orphanage was militia run, right? So a year later they came recruiting, dangling all these pretty holos and virts in front of our young impressionable eyes. Join the militia and see the universe – that kind of thing."

"And you joined up?"

"And I joined up, and a few months later, realised I'd made a terrible mistake. And for the next couple of years I played the hard-working rookie in the boot-camp on Macarthur's Landfall, and all the time I was planning how to get the hell out of there." She paused, thinking back to the innocent kid she'd been, and the image of herself back then brought on another flood of tears.

"Then I had the opportunity. I'd saved a lot of money and I was trusted. I was on port patrol, and a tanker crewed by a bunch of freeloaders from Mars had landed a week before, and I'd made myself known to the captain. He was the sort who'd take on a stowaway for a couple of thousand, no questions asked. The night I skedaddled, I stole my commanding officer's smartsuit, told a couple of friends I was going to go back to the south where my father died... and took off aboard the tanker."

The silence stretched and she felt good in Ed's embrace.

He said, "And a few months later, I found you in that bar on Rocannon's End."

She smiled. "Best thing that ever happened to me," she murmured.

He squeezed her shoulders. "Hey, dry those tears, Lania. I think we have company."

She swatted her cheeks with the cuff of her smartsuit. Outside the opening, she saw the walkway swaying. Two men were moving nimbly towards the dwelling fruit, one young and the other old, followed by one of the skinned monsters from the night before.

She and Ed retreated to the far end of the globe and sat back against the pithy wall.

The men paused outside the entrance, and as she watched, a curious thing happened. She thought it must be some form of ritual, a rite they enacted before entering these strange fruit dwellings. The men stood before the threshold and looked at each other, and then the old man closed his eyes. He seemed to be concentrating. Perhaps fifteen seconds later he opened his eyes and they spoke together in low tones.

Lania exchanged a look with Ed, who just shook his head in mystification.

The two men ducked through the entrance, nodded to Lania and Ed, and sat between the curved ribs of the wall. The monster, she saw, took up a position outside, sitting cross-legged on the walkway; it was fully twice the size of a man and filled the entrance with its slick, blue-veined bulk.

The young man looked across at Ed. "How is your head this morning?"

Ed raised a hand to the makeshift dressing. "Fine. I can't feel a thing."

"It was an unfortunate accident. We're sorry it happened."

The young man appeared to be in his twenties and wore nothing but a loin-cloth, his torso a perfect example of muscular definition. The old man, she saw on closer inspection, looked ancient. His long grey hair was tied back, emphasising his lined face. Oddly, he was not dressed like the rest of the human settlers on World, but wore an ancient pair of spacer's radiation silvers, cut off at shoulder and thigh.

He was staring with disconcerting intensity at her.

Lania looked at the monster sitting outside the door, its head bowed. Its surface rippled with petroleum highlights; it looked, she thought, like the anatomical diagram of a flayed corpse.

"What," she asked, "is that?"

The young man replied, "A Sleer. They're incredibly strong and fast. They brought you here."

Ed said, mystified, "A Sleer? But they're Weird..."

The young man inclined his head. "Early stage Weird. They assist the Fissure People."

"Then how...?" Lania began.

"They send them after us, to capture us and kill us. But now and again we manage to capture them, tame them and train them to do our bidding."

"They're monstrous," she said.

"Not as monstrous as what they become, later."

Ed said, "The Harvesters?"

"But before that, the Shufflers, ambulatory Harvesters, if you like."

"And Harvesters are the ultimate form?" Ed asked. "We were told that each Harvester returns to the Weird home and makes the transition from this universe to the next one, whatever that means."

The young man nodded. "And in making that transition they become Servers, so that, as their title suggests, they can serve the Weird Mother."

Ed repeated the name.

"We have never witnessed the creature, just heard tell of it. A vast, static mind which controls every one of its many... parts."

Ed looked from the oldster – who had yet to open his mouth – to the young man and asked, "That's all very well, but what do you want with us?"

"I am Langley, and my friend here is Villic." At this the old man nodded minimally, his face expressionless, as if set in stone.

"Carew and Takiomar," Ed said. "But you haven't answered my question. What do you want with us? Why did you bring us here?"

Langley and Villic exchanged a glance, and the latter nodded minimally. "We want to know why you came to World," Langley said. "We want to know who you brought with you."

He was interrupted by a sudden movement outside the globe. The Sleer stirred, restless, and made a sound like the low bellow of a tethered bull.

Villic, closest to the door, turned and stared at the creature, and instantly it ceased its moaning and settled down.

"It's hungry," Villic spoke for the first time, his voice gravely.

"It can eat," Langley said. "I'm sure our guests will not attempt to escape."

Villic turned again and stared at the Sleer, and a second later it rose to its full height and sloped off along the walkway.

Lania stared at the old man, suddenly uneasy.

Ed said, "Why should we tell you that? You abduct us, have your monsters drag us through the jungle..."

Langley raised a hand. "By abducting you, as you say, we very likely saved your lives. Please listen to me: you can trust us. We know what the Fissure People said to you, the lies they told about the Great Circularity, about the idyllic lives they lead, their supposedly mutually-beneficial relationship with the Weird. But it's all lies."

Lania said, "We saw the... before the Sleer took us, we saw what the Harvester did."

Langley looked at her, sympathy in his eyes. "That's only one aspect of the evil of the Weird," he said. "Did you not wonder at the scant population of the Fissure People? Did you not question why there were not ten, twenty times their number?"

"They told us that disease took their people, before they discovered the Weird," Ed said, "and that they fought battles with you, the Outcasts, which further reduced their numbers."

The old man smiled and shook his head.

Langley said, "The truth is that they feed their old, their hopelessly injured, and their dissidents, to the Harvester. It is what the Weird demand."

"And they do this willingly?" Lania said.

The old man smiled. "You saw the ceremony. You saw Rahn give himself to the monster. You saw the girl, Hahta, step without protest into the Harvester."

"But I assumed she was drugged," Lania said.

Langley replied, "They are *all* drugged. All the fissure People."

Ed said, "The phar?"

Langley nodded. "It is a wonderfully efficient system that the Weird have devised. The Harvesters are fed the naar husks, which they metabolise and secrete, along with hormones which act as a mind-altering soporific on the Fissure People. This makes them mere drones to the Weirds' bidding, passive and compliant. Is it little wonder that they smile so much?"

Lania thought of Rahn and how he had gladly stepped to his death – and that, she thought, was the true horror of what happened, the willingness with which he had given himself to the Weird.

"And every month," Langley was saying, "they transport the Harvester downriver to their subterranean lair and a new one takes its place, and so the cycle starts over. The Harvester ingests the old and the truculent, for despite the phar, occasionally certain Fissure People do raise themselves from their lethargy and protest." He smiled. "We have managed to save a few, and they live here with us now."

Lania said, "So the Weird, the Harvesters, all those cycles... the end result is that they do it for food, for human corpses?"

Langley considered her question. "In the early days, when they brought us here, they wanted our knowledge, and physical ingestion was their way of ingesting our collective knowledge also."

Ed interrupted. "Hold on. When they *brought* you here?"

Langley smiled. "Of course." He looked at Villic, who nodded silently, and Langley went on, "It is a long story, my friends, and begins when the Weird found the means to pass from their realm into ours."

"Can you rephrase that in more scientific terms?" Ed asked.

Langley smiled. "Forgive me. I did make it sound mystical." He paused, then said, "The Weird dwell in a realm that underpins the void, just as the void underpins our reality, or universe. Just as we have learned to breach the void and use it to aid our passage between the stars, so the Weird in their own way found how to locate a weakness in the fabric of their reality and penetrate *through* the void, into this universe." He parted his hands. "I'm afraid that that's about as scientific as I can manage. The end result is the same, however it is described. The Weird, having spread throughout their realm, now wish to inhabit ours – and in human beings they have found the perfect species to assist them in this desire."

Lania said, "You said they brought you here?"

"Over two hundred Terran years ago," Langley continued, "the Weird broke out of their universe and discovered this one. This planet was uninhabited. But the sixth planet of this system was populated by a race of space-faring aliens called the Kurishen. The Weird observed them for a while – for decades – and then devised a way to use the Kurishen. They infected them with mind-parasites and controlled certain of their numbers, and used them to instigate a war between factions of the Kurishen."

Lania said, "We saw the results of that war when we entered the system."

Langley nodded. "The Weird then took the Kurishen's ships and crewed them with Sleer, then sent them out across Vetch space and into the Expansion."

"The ship we found on Hesperides," Ed said, looking at Lania, "the others on Vercors and Tamalkin."

"There were seven in all sent to human space, and others which landed in Vetch space. On arrival, the Sleer disassembled themselves, broke down into thousands of parasites – mind-parasites, like those they inflicted on the Kurishen. Many of these perished in the unfamiliar atmospheric conditions while waiting for suitable human and Vetch hosts, but many survived and infected the unwitting."

"On Hesperides," Lania said, "we found an old Vetch ship beside a crashed Kurishen vessel. The crew of the Vetch ship were dead, shot by one of their own, who had then turned his weapon on himself."

Langley said, "The Vetch were well ahead of humans in combating the threat of the Weird. They had developed surgically-enhanced telepathy long before us, and they used it to root out those infected by the Weird mind-parasites. The Vetch crew sounds as if it were infected, and the telepath did the only thing possible in the situation."

Lania shook her head, recalling the mummified Vetch corpses. She stared at the young man. "Vercors," she said. "A Kurishen vessel came down there. A cult grew up around it."

"My ancestors formed that cult, abetted by the Weird mind-parasites. They manipulated hundreds of my people, had their leaders form the cult and work towards the grand plan: to take a starship full of colonists through the void to the Devil's Nebula, where they would live in paradise with the Kurishen. It is testimony to the weakness of the human race that even many of the uninfected believed this."

"But what did the Weird want with you?" Lania asked.

"Lania," he said, "you must understand that the Weird do not manipulate matter as we do. They are not a technological race. They are a hive-mind, controlled by a great mother-mind, a vast central nervous system, back in their own realm. They manipulate genes and their own fleshly matter, but their evolution has never needed to manipulate their environment and manufacture machines. So in order to spread themselves across our universe, they must utilise the technology of first the Kurishen and then the Vetch, and now we humans.

"They brought the *Procyon* to this star system in order to study it and its people, to probe their minds so that they might come in time to understand the means by which we worked physical matter. However, there were competing factions aboard the *Procyon* who understood the threat and tried to sabotage the mission. They brought the ship down on Kurishen's moon, but the Weird boarded the ship and quelled the rebellion and brought the colonists here, to World."

Langley paused and looked at Villic.

The old man nodded, looking from Lania to Ed and said, "Back in the time before I joined the crew of the *Procyon*, I was an Expansion agent."

Lania stared, amazed, and tried to work out how old Villic might be.

Villic smiled. "I am over ninety years old – standard years, that is. I've actually lost count, as the years on World are much longer than Terran standard. But at any rate, between ninety and a hundred. And I was twenty when I was assigned to infiltrate the Vercors cult and report back to my Expansion paymasters. Which I did, though my story was so... so bizarre that I fear they didn't believe me." He paused, smiling as he thought back over the years. "I had the cut when I was eighteen and I was still attempting to hone my ability, to come to terms with what I was."

Lania stared at him. "The cut?"

She noticed that Ed was smiling, a step ahead of her.

Villic went on, "When I was eighteen, I tested psi-positive and I had the operation to make me telepathic. Then, my ability still weak and almost driven mad by the side-effects of my powers, I was assigned my first case. I infiltrated the cult and discovered that many of their leaders were infected with the Weird parasite. I reported back, but I think my handlers thought me mad. I was determined to prove myself right, and to this end I signed up on the mission aboard the *Procyon*." He paused, his gaze reflective, then said, "I have led a long and interesting life, here on World."

Lania thought: he's a mind-reader. Everything I think, my most private memory, is open to him. She gave a mental shudder, all too aware that he would be reading her involuntary loathing.

To his credit, he didn't react to her thoughts – if, that is, he was probing her then.

Ed said, "There were com-stacks missing from the *Procyon* and data-needles. Who took these?"

Villic replied, "The infected took them. The Weird have technical facilities deep under World, run by the Fissure People, humans trained by the original settlers in the use of com-technology. It's all part of the Weird drive to understand our ways."

Lania saw movement outside the entrance. The Sleer had returned, swinging a globular green fruit in its massive, skinless fist.

She looked across at Villic and asked, "What happened when you were brought to World?"

"The Weird had the area by the fissure cleared and we built the huts and long-houses. They told us what was safe to eat; most of the animals of the jungle contained toxins, which is how we became vegetarian. Then the Weird introduced us to phar, to supplement our diets, and that's when things began to go wrong. A few of us realised what was happening and we formed a breakaway faction."

Ed asked, "Did you read the Weird, what they intended?"

Villic shook his head. "I could pick up their mentation – but it was like a language I had no hope of understanding. Over the years I concentrated and learned to recognise the simple emotions of the most basic Weird we had contact with, the Sleer, which is how I can control them now."

"So that's why they're working for you," Ed said. "It's nothing to do with their volunteering?"

Villic laughed. "Of course not. They're Weird through and through, though at this stage of their development they're simpletons. They're muscle, no more, in the main controlled by the Weird mother-mind. From time to time I can wrest them away and control them, but only for short periods. Within weeks, they grow in mental strength and overcome my power, or the mother-mind regains control." He looked through the entrance at the Sleer, which was noisily eating the fruit.

Lania said, "And then?"

"We put them to death," Villic said, "quickly and painlessly." He returned his gaze to Ed and Lania. "So we broke away, started separate colonies in the jungle tops. We found that if we hollowed out these grambo fruit, they provided not only good sustenance but wonderful accommodation. At first the Fissure People came after us, and we did fight, but not so that our collective numbers were reduced as much as they would have you believe."

"And you?" Ed asked. "Did you try to alert them to what was happening?"

"Of course! In the early days we did nothing else. Then they protected the clearing with more and more Sleer and we became wary. We still have successes, however – individual Fissure People who, for whatever reasons, don't take to the phar and seek another way."

Ed said, "A girl called Maatja. Her sister told me about her. Her father went to serve the Weird and she followed him."

The young man, Langley, shook his head. "The chances are that she'll be picked up by a Sleer and killed."

Lania looked at Ed. His gaze fell to the floor of the globe, his expression unreadable.

She said, "Do you know why her father was taken?"

Langley said, "They take the brightest and best of the Fissure People from time to time, and have done for decades. We don't really know what they do with them, other than use them in some way to their own ends."

Villic went on. "Ten days ago, I mind-captured a Sleer from the edge of Fissure People territory. It had been sent out to gather wood to repair a hut. They're not that difficult to attract – the promise of food, planted in their heads, the promise of an easy life in the treetops. Anyway, in its simple mind I caught a hint of the collective excitement of the Weird, though perhaps *excitement* is the wrong word. Anticipation, let's say. They knew that a ship was coming from Expansion territory, a state-of-the-art vessel containing the latest Expansion void-technology."

Ed Carew closed his eyes.

Lania said, "Our ship?"

Villic nodded. "The *Hawk*."

Langley said, "The parasites can lie dormant for decades, biding their time. There cannot be many of them still extant in the Expansion, but it only takes a few, strategically placed, to bring about the desired results."

"Do you know who in the crew are infected?" Ed asked.

"Unfortunately not," Villic said. "Many Sleer patrol the clearing of late, and I could not get close. Which is why we sent our own Sleer instead, to bring back as many of the newcomers as possible."

Ed frowned. "And unfortunately you bagged us two."

Villic smiled. "Admittedly, it would have been more helpful to have captured those infected by mind-parasites – then we would have known who among the others were also carriers. As it is, I have learned much from having you here."

Lania looked up at the telepath. "Like what?"

"The fact that the Elder, Leah, is taking your people downriver to the lair of the Weird at full sunrise. This is important."

"It is?" Ed said.

"Those of the crew infected will be carrying information vital to the requirements of the Weird," Langley said. "Technical information about the *Hawk*, about the Void-space technology – even about the hierarchy of the Expansion authorities."

"Commander Gorley," Ed said out loud. He looked across at Lania. "I always thought there was something evil about the bastard."

She managed a smile. "You hate him because he was a fascist," she said.

He shrugged. "And now I have all the more reasons to dislike him."

"The chances are that there will be more than just one carrier," Langley said. "The Weird would take every opportunity to load the *Hawk* with its agents."

"Is there any way of telling who might be infected?" Ed said. "Some outward sign?"

"The only sure way to know is to establish mind-to-mind contact," Villic said. "There are certain signs, but they're not exclusively pointers to infection. Often the infected individual exhibits mood swings, general moodiness, tendencies towards uncharacteristically intemperate behaviour. But of course these are not always signs of infection."

Lania asked, "But does the infected person know what they're carrying?"

"Never in the early stages," Villic replied. "The parasite manipulates the subject subtly, subconsciously. Only in the later stages, when the Weird makes specific demands on its subject – for instance ordering a subject to defend himself against aggressors – does the subject realise that he or she is being manipulated, but obviously by then it's too late."

"And can an infected person be…" – Lania searched for the right word – "uninfected?"

"We have no evidence that they can," Villic replied, "but then you understand that our medical resources here are somewhat rudimentary."

Lania stared through the entrance, past the squatting hulk of the Sleer to the supergiant. It had risen so that half of its colossal globe spanned the treetop horizon, giving off its slow-motion display of spouts and geysers.

Ed said, "So if Leah is taking Gorley, Choudri and the others downriver to the lair of the Weird at full sunrise" – he looked across at Langley and Villic – "what do you intend to do?"

Villic hesitated, looked quickly at Langley. The young man said, "We will follow them downriver and with luck apprehend them before they reach the system of caves where the Weird have their portal."

Lania echoed, "The portal?"

"Deep underground, in a system of catacombs, is the interface between this realm and that of the Weird. We hope to apprehend them before they reach the opening to the caves. Their lair is swarming with Sleer and… other things."

"Are you armed?"

Villic said, "Not well. We have crossbows of our own devising, but little else. We'll take tame Sleer along with us."

Lania looked across at Ed. She could see that he was thinking through some strategy. He said, "Take us with you."

Langley looked at Villic. The latter said, "He has experience of combat, and the girl – she was once with the Expansion militia."

Lania stared at the telepath, with an odd feeling of violation. She looked at Ed, caught his glance and shook her head. A trip downriver to the lair of the Weird was madness; what might the two of them achieve that the Outcasts alone could not?

Villic said, "We are few in number. Your assistance would be invaluable. We would arm you, such as we can, and protect you as best we could."

"This is madness!" she began.

Ed looked at her. "Then remain here, Lania. But I'm going."

Villic smiled, even before she voiced her thoughts.

"I'm not leaving you, Ed. When I signed up with you, the agreement was that we stick together through thick and thin, good times and bad. I'm not walking out on you now, okay?"

He nodded. "Thank you, Lania. I'm not taking this decision lightly. It's something that needs doing."

Langley looked at her. "If the infected humans reach the portal with the information they're carrying, then there's no telling how that will empower the Weird."

She stared at him. "I'm not arguing, am I? I said I'm coming!"

Ed reached out and squeezed her hand – and that, she thought, was something he wouldn't have done just a week ago. She looked across at Villic, but he'd averted his gaze.

Ed said, "And the *Hawk*? They want the ship, right?"

Langley said, "Technically, they have it. All they need to do is to ensure that the humans who came in it are unable to leave aboard it."

"In other words, they want us dead?" Ed said.

Villic nodded. "Every one of you who isn't infected. Then the Weird can take the ship whenever they wish."

"There are two militia-men still aboard the *Hawk*," Lania said.

"The chances are that at least one of the two is infected," Villic said. "It would make sense to have their own aboard, once the rest of the crew are out of the way. My guess is that one of the remaining militia-men can also pilot the ship."

Ed looked at the two Outcasts. "What the hell can we do about that?"

Villic said, "If we make a slight detour, we can take in the *Hawk* before we reach the fissure. It won't take me long to scan the militia, and see if they are infected."

"And if they are?" Lania asked.

Langley nodded. "You get them to open the ship, and we will do the rest."

Ed nodded. "Very well. When do we set off?"

Langley glanced out at the rising sun. "We have an hour before full up, when Leah sets off downriver. That should leave us just enough time to get to the *Hawk* before we give chase."

Something flipped in Lania's gut. She'd thanked providence that Gina had not been left behind in the *Hawk*. But, of course, it was entirely possible that Gina was infected by the mind-parasite.

She felt sick.

Langley and Villic stood and made for the exit. "If you would care to follow us. We'll gather fruit and water for the journey, then set off."

The two men stepped onto the walkway; the Sleer rose before them and led the way.

Lania lay a hand on Ed's sleeve as he was about to step from the globe.

"I know why you want to follow the others, Ed. And it's more than just to kill the infected, isn't it?"

He smiled, grimly. "You've become a mind-reader, all of a sudden."

"Maatja, right?"

He hesitated. "You were honest with me, earlier. Remind me to be as honest with you when all this is over." He made to step onto the walkway, then stopped and turned to her. "There's also another reason, Lania, but this isn't really the right time."

She watched him duck through the exit and walk along the swaying timber bridge, then hurried after him.

THEY STOPPED ON a grey, pitted raft slung between the treetops, which looked like a growth of fungus. Men, women and children occupied the raft, watching curiously as Langley and Villic crammed fruit and gourds of water into backpacks fashioned from woven vines and leaves.

The two Sleer crouched nearby, staring at the dome of the rising sun.

Villic stood and shouldered his pack, then stared across at the Sleer. Instantly, both creatures rose and sloped off towards the centre of the fungal raft, to a where a deep dimple pocked the grey tegument. As Lania watched, the dimple dilated, became a dark hole, and first one Sleer and then the next stepped into it and disappeared.

Lania looked at Langley, who was doing his best to hide his amusement. "An elevator to the jungle floor," he said. "After you. It's perfectly safe."

She recalled the hovering trunks they had seen on first traversing the jungle floor. "It's alive?"

Langley nodded. "But you'll be happy to know it can't digest anything bigger than a naar fruit."

She stepped towards the opening and peered into it. The shaft angled down at perhaps forty-five degrees; she could see the domed head of the Sleer disappearing into the dimness. She stepped forward and instantly lost her footing. She fell feet first with a cry of alarm, then felt the flesh of the creature shrink around her.

She was carried down at speed in a peristaltic wave-front, aware only of the cloying heat in the confines of the creature's trunk and the loamy stench of its breath.

A minute later her descent slowed and her feet hit the jungle floor. She gained her balance and ducked and the trunk lifted up and over her head. The Sleer were nearby, waiting patiently, crouched like casual sprinters awaiting starter's orders. She stared upwards. The jungle canopy was two hundred metres overhead, with the thick column of the animal's trunk dropping through the dappled sunlight. As she watched, she made out three bulges working their way down the sinuous tube, and first Ed, then Langley and Villic were disgorged onto the jungle floor.

Langley took his bearings and pointed through the undergrowth. They set off, following the darting Sleer. Villic, with the privilege of age, rode upon the leading Sleer's back, a comical sight with his scrawny legs wrapped around the creature's varicose torso.

Lania and Ed kept pace at a jog. She considered what they had learned so far and what might lie ahead. It was perhaps best not to look too far into the future – certainly not to dwell on what might await them at the lair of the Weird – but she could not stop herself from considering the *Hawk* and the militia-men there.

"Remind me," she panted to Ed, "that if we get out of this alive, I want at least a month's arr-and-arr on a pleasure planet somewhere."

He looked across at her and smiled. "The slight problem of funding might put paid to that."

"The statuette, Ed. Don't forget that."

"I haven't. But the combined hundred thousand might, just might, buy us a clapped-out ex-Navy rust-bucket – with nothing left over to pay for a vacation, deserved or not."

She laughed. "Maybe the Expansion will pay us for our sterling service to the cause?"

"Dream on."

Up ahead, the two Sleer had slowed their loping run. They crouched, and Villic turned and signalled.

Lania ducked down beside Langley and peered through the vegetation.

The *Hawk* stood on its stanchions, a scintillating gold in the dappled sunlight. It was, she had to admit, a magnificent machine: she felt the sudden urge to board it, meld with the smartcore and get the hell out of this place.

She caught the telepath's glance and smiled at him. "Only kidding," she whispered.

Ed said, "Can you read them from this distance?"

Villic slipped from the back of the Sleer and stared across at the ship.

"Very faintly. They're both on the upper deck." He closed his eyes. "They're talking to each other, drinking something. But they're too far away to probe properly."

Langley said, "Can we approach without being seen?"

Villic nodded. "They're seated at a table, away from the viewscreen." He turned to Ed. "Is the ship set up to detect anything approaching?"

"Not that I'm aware –" Ed began, but Villic raised his hand.

Lania said, "So what do we do?" She looked up at the viewscreen, a lighted rectangle on the upper flank; there was no sign of the militia-men.

"We cross to the ship and hide under its belly," Villic said. "I should be well within range then."

Villic stared across at the ship, concentrating on the viewscreen. He looked around the group. "Okay, after three, follow me." He waited, then said, "One... two.... three. Let's go!"

Lania felt her heart pumping as they left the cover of the undergrowth and crunched through the incinerated vegetation surrounding the *Hawk*. Seconds later they passed into its shadow and crouched under its curving belly.

Villic closed his eyes, his ancient face a study in concentration.

Ten seconds later he opened his eyes and nodded. He said quietly, "They're both carrying. The damned thing is..."

For a second, his expression looked haunted. "The thing it, they don't know it. The infection is deep, deep in their subconscious, waiting to make its move. And you know something? They're decent people."

Langley gripped the oldster's arm. "That doesn't come into it! You know that. We've got to go through with this."

"I know, for chrissake. But it doesn't make it any easier. If you could read what I'm reading..."

"I know, and I realise it must be hell." Langley looked at Ed. "Can you contact the militia?"

Ed pointed along the ship's underbelly. "There's a com-console by the dorsal entrance. I can use that to get us aboard."

Villic was nodding impatiently, having already read the information and planned ahead. "So this is what we do. Ed gets the militia to open the hatch and I send in the Sleer. The militia will be armed, but with the element of surprise..."

"And if that doesn't work?" Ed asked.

Langley said, "You underestimate the Sleer, Ed. It will work."

Villic nodded towards the hatch. "Okay."

They crossed to the hatch. Lania watched Ed take a breath and reach out to the console. He tapped a code and waited.

Seconds later a suspicious voice said, "Director? Marshall?"

"It's me, Ed Carew." He licked his lips, went on, "I'm injured. I need a medi-kit."

He heard a hurried consultation between the militia-men, then, "Okay. Opening up. We'll get the medi-kit and meet you in the lounge."

The hatch sighed, eased itself back and swung open. The Sleer, primed by Villic, stepped onto the upchute plate. Between them, the creatures almost filled the narrow confines.

The hatch swung back into place and sealed itself.

Lania could not stop herself from watching Villic. The telepath crouched on the scorched jungle floor beneath the ship and gripped his head in his hands. He closed his eyes, his lips moving as he spoke to himself.

Thirty seconds later he grimaced, then cried out. His face contorted in horror and he wept. Langley was at his side, cradling the old man and murmuring something into his ear.

Villic opened his eyes, drawing a deep breath. "Okay. It's over. It was... swift, that's the best I can say. I'm relaying the exit code to the Sleer."

Langley helped him to his feet and a second later the hatch hissed open and the Sleer stepped out.

Lania looked away as they moved past her and fell into a crouch beneath the ship; they appeared, given the quick glimpse she'd taken, no bloodier than normal.

Ed led the way into the ship and she followed with Langley. Villic remained outside, unwilling, Lania supposed, to look at what his creatures had done.

They rode the upchute to the upper deck and stepped out.

They found the first militia-man sprawled in the corridor, the medi-kit still gripped in his right hand. His body armour was intact, but the place where his head should have been was now just a gory smear across the deck, a trail of blood, pulverised skull and gelatinous brain matter.

She recalled his name. Carlucci, a good-looking guy in his twenties from Nova Venice. The poor, poor bastard.

And he hadn't even had time to draw any of his side weapons. She knelt beside the dead man, unclipped his laser and tossed it to Ed, then withdrew the pulse-gun from its clip and passed it to Langley. The Outsider grasped it with an expression of delight.

She glanced along the length of the corridor to the lounge. She could see the boots of the second militia-man in the doorway, still twitching in the aftermath of his death.

She was about to stand when something gripped her arm. She screamed, more in surprised horror at what had happened than in pain. She stared down at her wrist, where the militia-man's gauntlet had her in its vice-like grip. It pulled her and she fell forward across the blood-spattered chest armour. From the corner of her eye she saw the right-hand gauntlet lift itself from the deck and approach her face. She screamed and attempted to pull away.

A second later she felt a great heat centimetres from her cheek, and she was momentarily blinded by a sudden, actinic flash.

The gauntlet released its grip instantly, and she rolled away, choking.

Ed was at her side, pulling her to him.

"What happened?" she asked, even though she knew. "I... I didn't think..."

Ed shook his head. "It's the latest body-armour, Lania. Programmed to fight on after the death of the wearer."

She stared down at the fused power-pack on the thigh of the suit, trying not to think about dying at the hands of a dead man.

Ed stepped carefully over the slick of blood and brains and approached the second militia-man in the entrance to the lounge. He took aim and fired, and the power-pack on the second suit went up like a miniature nova.

He relieved the suit of its laser and pulse-gun and rejoined the others.

"I've had a thought," Lania said as they were about to board the dropchute. "We could take the *Hawk* downriver, head off Leah and the others before they reach the opening to the caves."

Langley said, "And risk getting blown out of the sky by any Shufflers the Weird have patrolling? You'll need the *Hawk* to get back to the Expansion."

"The Shufflers are armed?"

The Outcast smiled. "The Shufflers project acid. One lucky strike and the *Hawk* might suffer. We'll do it our own way, okay?"

"And if the Shufflers are lying in wait for us?"

Langley fixed her with his penetrating blue eyes. "Oh, they will be, but with Villic along we should have prior warning." He lifted his laser. "And now that we have these..."

Lania considered the fight ahead. "In case we don't make it back to the *Hawk*, Ed, I think it'd be wise to instruct it to leave and return to the Expansion."

Langley said, "You can do that?"

She nodded. "And I'll leave a message in the core, recounting what's going on here."

She led the way to the flight-deck, marvelling. It had only been two standard days since they had left the *Hawk* and set off for the clearing.

She slipped into her sling and felt her smartsuit connect. She melded with the core and went through the complex routine of overriding all previous commands. Before programming the ship to leave the planet on auto-pilot and return through the void to the Expansion, she opened her eyes and looked at Langley. "How long should I tell it to wait before getting the hell out?"

Ed looked at the Outcast. "Will twenty-four hours standard give us enough time?"

Langley recalculated the duration into World time. He nodded. "More than enough."

Lania closed her eyes and instructed the *Hawk* to phase into the void twenty-four hours after they'd left the ship.

She withdrew from the meld and jumped from the sling.

"Okay. All set."

They left the ship and Villic, riding a Sleer, led the way through the jungle to the fissure.

CHAPTER SIXTEEN

MAATJA REMEMBERED THE fall, but she had no idea how long she'd been unconscious.

A day after setting out in her seed-boat, she had seen the timber jetty on the far bank and attempted to steer her boat towards it, but the current had proved too strong and had swept the boat past it. She'd been about to jump out and swim for it when the surface of the river was suddenly ripped by rocks, their jagged edges slicing through the surface like blades. She had waited out the rapids, by which time her boat was a kilometre past the jetty. Only then, when the river became calm again, did she dive over the side and swim to shore.

It was while climbing over the bare rocks, back towards the jetty and the upward path, that she slipped sickeningly, fell and cracked her head against a rock.

Now she dragged herself into the shadow of an overhanging ledge and sheltered from the heat of the sun directly overhead.

The journey downriver had taken more than a day. She had approached the jetty at around midday, so it must have been around mid-afternoon that she reached the shore and fell. She remembered coming awake from time to time, only to be pitched back into unconsciousness. She recalled at least two periods of night-time, perhaps three. All in all, she calculated that a couple of days had elapsed since she had left the clearing.

By now, she knew, her father would have been taken by the Weird.

But she had come so far, and she wanted to see their lair.

She ate a couple of handful of berries and, her strength regained, pushed herself to her feet and began climbing over the rocks towards the jetty. The terrain here was free from jungle; the growth began a little further up the hillside, only to peter out again as the incline became the almost sheer side of what looked like a cliff.

Hereabouts the land was different to the jungle where she came from: hills and small mountains erupted from the surface of the planet and it was among these mountains, according to what her father had once told her, that the Weird had their lair.

After two hours of scrabbling over jagged rocks, she came to the jetty and peered upwards. The sun was going down, and the peaks above her head were silhouetted against the last of the day's light. She could make out the wide, worn path snaking up the hillside, and in the side of the mountain, high above, the dark shape of a cave entrance.

She ate the last of her fruit and berries, then set off up the winding path.

As she climbed, she imagined the bearers carrying a Harvester up the hillside. The way was steep and the footing treacherous with loose rocks and scree – and she could only imagine the great weight of the alien creature. She wondered what she might find at the lair of the Weird, and for the first time she began to feel frightened at what she was doing.

She would go as far as the cave mouth, she thought, and see what she could see.

One hour later, the path levelled off and approached the high arch of the cave. She slowed and looked around. The cave was situated in a great saddle of land, a valley between two rocky outcrops. Beyond, the sun seemed to sit perfectly in the notch of the valley, a silent fiery ball, and the panorama was magnificent.

She approached the cave entrance and peered inside. Fungus grew on the walls, glowing dimly; it was like looking into one of the calm pools she had come across from time to time in the jungle.

She hesitated, then entered the cave. It looked artificial, but it had obviously been cut and widened here and there so that the Harvesters could get through. The floor of the cave was level for perhaps ten metres, then began to slope downwards. She wondered about continuing, but something pushed her onwards. She had come so far, after all; it would be foolish to return now without having seen anything.

She hurried downwards, her faint shadow her only companion. From time to time she thought she heard sounds, and stopped in panic to listen. But the only sound she could hear was the rush of her breath and her heartbeat loud in her ears.

She worked her way down into the heart of the mountain for what seemed like hours, wondering when she might arrive at the lair. Perhaps, she thought, she had come to the wrong place; perhaps the Weird had their lair elsewhere, approached by a concealed entrance so that curious humans like herself could not come snooping.

Then she heard voices.

They were faint and far away, carried in the still air of the cave. She looked around desperately for a place to hide. To her right, high up, was a ledge that seemed to go back a fair way. She scrambled up the sloping wall and rolled onto the natural shelf, cramming herself tightly into the gap. She lay face down, breathing hard and hoping whoever it was did not hear her panicky gasps.

The voices grew louder – a human voice, and a reply so low that she could hardly hear it.

Footsteps approached and passed by beneath her, and she chanced a glance down at whoever it might be.

In the dim fungus light she made out two figures. One was human and the other a stunted Weird manikin, trotting alongside the human as if in an effort to keep up.

She stifled a gasp. She recognised the human. It was an adult called Mattus, who many months ago had been taken by the Weird. They passed from sight, their voices fading.

She waited perhaps five minutes, her heartbeat returning to normal.

She was about to climb down and resume her descent when she heard more footsteps, this time coming from the direction in which Mattus and the Weird had gone. She peered out and seconds later saw Mattus retracing his steps, this time without the alien.

He passed beneath Maatja and continued downwards into the lair.

Without a second thought, she leapt down and followed.

She kept a healthy distance between herself and the Chosen, falling back when the corridor straightened out, then hurrying to catch up when it began zigzagging again.

She wondered if Mattus might lead her to her father, and if so... then how might her father react to finding that she had followed him?

Perhaps, she thought, it might not be a good idea to show herself, at least until she'd found out what was happening down here. She recalled how the Sleer had dealt with the Outcast the other day, and shuddered.

Up ahead, Mattus had come to a halt. Someone, or something, was with him. Maatja crouched behind a knuckle of rock and peered out. Mattus was speaking with a Shuffler in lowered tones, its mass dwarfing the human. It was facing him, and she wondered if it had been coming in the opposite direction. If so, when the Shuffler had finished its conversation with Mattus, it would continue on its way towards her...

She looked around for a better place to conceal herself. Around five metres away she made out a slit in the rock. She stood, hurried back along the corridor and slipped into the crevice. She was surprised to find that it was a second, narrower corridor, also lit by the spreading fungus. She backed further into the tunnel until a bend concealed her from the main corridor.

She waited a long time for the sound of the Shuffler to pass, and when it failed to do so she decided to investigate this second, smaller corridor.

She turned and crept along its length. After five minutes, she made out the first sounds from up ahead, and then saw that the walls of the corridor had turned from green to white as if illuminated by a bright light. She stopped and listened. She heard voices and a sound she had never heard before – a high-pitched buzzing like that of some kind of insect.

She crept cautiously forward, heart beating loudly, and the corridor brightened and the buzzing became louder.

The walls opened out, widening as they entered a vast cavern which was the source of the white light and the buzzing sound.

She crouched as she entered the cavern and looked for a place to hide. She saw a rock, a metre away to her right, and darted behind it.

Then she lifted her head and peered over the rock, as if to verify what her senses had taken in on entering the cavern.

In the middle of the chamber was a pool of light, the width of a long-house, shining white like the brightest moon. It flickered, the light shifting and swirling and giving off a high, insect buzz.

And all around the pool of light were the Weird. She saw the great bulk of a Harvester, and Sleer and Shufflers and the small, spindly manikins – three or four of each kind – and as she watched, a manikin approached the light and stepped into it as if it were a pool of water. The creature was white and as thin as a starving child, with a great bulbous head and vast staring eyes. It leaned forward, as if swimming, and was consumed by the light. No sooner had the manikin vanished than a Shuffler lumbered forward and immersed itself in the light and was taken. Each time a creature vanished into the light, she thought she saw strange, nightmarish images beyond, high buildings and monstrous beasts – but the images lasted only seconds before the white light intensified.

She looked around the cavern, but could not see her father. Then she chastised herself for even thinking that she might find him here. That would have been too much to hope for.

She thought of her return to the Outcasts, and what she would tell Kavan and the others.

As she watched, something *emerged* from the radiant light – a great bloody Sleer, wading from the pool and stepping onto the rock as casually as a bather.

She saw movement across the chamber and stared as Mattus entered through a wide corridor – evidently the same corridor down which she had started to follow him. She watched as he approached the pool of light and, without breaking his stride, walked straight into it and vanished.

She wondered, then, if this was where her father had gone.

She heard a sound, a loud, strangled cry, and when she looked in that direction she saw a Shuffler pointing a thick arm at her.

Beside it, a Sleer looked up, saw her and loped in her direction.

She lost a second to blind panic, before leaping to her feet and darting back into the corridor. She sprinted, knowing how fast the Sleer could move through the jungle and feeling despair. If she could make it to the main corridor without being caught, then secrete herself on the high ledge, perhaps she might succeed in getting out of here alive.

She heard a grunting behind her and gave a reflexive scream, too terrified to look over her shoulder. She sprinted, darting through the passage and hoping that, perhaps, it might just be too narrow a space for the Sleer to run through at full speed.

She had almost reached the main corridor when the grunts grew louder behind her and she could almost feel the Sleer's noxious breath on her bare back. Something fixed on her upper arm and lifted her off her feet, a sickening wet rubbery grip that had her screaming aloud and kicking out in fright.

The Sleer carried her into the main corridor and turned left, towards the surface. Dazed, she wondered if it was taking her back to the clearing to feed to the Harvester.

She saw movement up ahead and a group of people... humans, unbelievably... came into sight.

Her immediate reaction was one of relief, and then she saw that the party of humans was led by the Elder, Leah.

The Sleer lowered Maatja to her feet and she stood, knock-kneed, and paralysed with fear. Leah was with a group of strangers, people in strange clothing whom she had never seen before. Only when she saw the four giants in their midst and realised that they were not giants at all, but men in golden suits of armour, did she consider that these people could be from the starship.

Leah stared at her and smiled. The Elder reached out, touched her cheek and Maatja was surprised that so gentle a gesture could frighten her as it did.

Leah said, "I always thought you were *different*, Maatja. I don't know whether you're very brave, or supremely foolish."

Leah turned and spoke to one of the strangers, who nodded and addressed a golden man. "Take her to the surface," the thin-faced man ordered, "and leave her with Kaminski."

Maatja stared at Leah and the look in the Elder's eyes – something that was almost sadness – told Maatja that she was destined for the Harvester.

The golden man picked her up and slung her over his shoulder, and Maatja was powerless to resist.

CHAPTER SEVENTEEN

CAREW GRIPPED LANIA's hand as they raced through the jungle.

He could safely say that in all his years of star-faring through the Expansion, he had never experienced anything like the events – weird, grotesque and threatening – that had confronted him on the planet called World.

He had thought that his life of old, journeying among the stars of human space, interpreting the law as it suited him, had been about as thrilling as he could ever hope for. But he had to admit that he was now living through events that, as a star-struck child on far-away Temeredes, he could scarcely have dreamed about. And this time, the success of the mission would affect more people across the inhabited galaxy than any of his exploits to date. Only he and his small team had gained from his past ventures, even though he had liked to tell himself that the petty infringements in which he indulged were one in the eye for the Expansion authorities. The Weird were far more dangerous than the Expansion hierarchy, and he could not help but smile at the irony – as he leapt over a moss-furred tree trunk in pursuit of the galloping Sleer – that he was now fighting to protect his erstwhile enemies.

He gripped the laser tightly and told himself to concentrate.

Langley had warned them, before they set off from the *Hawk*, that the jungle would be hiding many Weird in their various forms. Leah would have alerted the Weird to their disappearance on the eve of the journey downriver, and they would suspect the Outcasts of being behind the snatch. What the Weird could not know was that now, thanks to the haul of arms from the *Hawk*, they were equipped with the latest Expansion weaponry. When Carew had asked the Outcast if this evened the odds of success in the imminent encounter, the young man had smiled and replied, laconically, "Not quite."

Well, it always helped to know where one stood.

After thirty minutes, they came to the fissure.

Its edge was not as well delineated here as it was back at the clearing. The pair of Sleer had come to an abrupt halt before them, and Carew and Lania almost crashed into their muscular thighs as the creatures stopped and peered down.

Lania said, "What's the problem?"

"Nothing," Villic said from his perch upon the leading Sleer. "We've come to the fissure."

Carew peered through the tangle before them, making out a dip in the land. He wondered whether the Outcasts had their own stair excavated down to the river, or if they would be forced to hack their way through the undergrowth.

The answer came very shortly.

The unencumbered Sleer set off again, barging its way through the vegetation, creating a tunnel through which the others followed. The land dipped precipitously beneath their feet, and Carew found that holding onto Lania only increased the likelihood of their both tumbling down the rapidly steepening incline. He let go and attempted to slow his descent by grasping hold of vines and whatever occasional handholds presented themselves.

Lania went before him, making it look easy. It was all very well, too, for the telepath, clinging to the back of the Sleer as it dropped with reckless abandon through the undergrowth. As Carew skinned his hands on whip-like vines armed with barbs, and slipped onto his backside for the tenth time, he wondered if he should suggest that, as the second oldest veteran of the party, he should have the privilege of riding the unburdened Sleer. On second thoughts, the idea of gripping the rubbery, blood-coloured creature around its bullish neck did not appeal. He'd had sufficient intimacy with the Sleer during his abduction the night before.

He looked up. Already the lip of the escarpment was a hundred metres above them. The ruddy face of the supergiant, swarming with sunspots, was free of the horizon and filling the sky. He wondered if Leah and the others had set off at the prescribed time, full sun up... in which case they would have the lead in the race to the lair of the Weird.

The pair of Sleer had stopped and were peering over a precipice. Langley conferred with Villic, and the Sleer carrying Villic leapt through the shrubbery on the lip of the drop and vanished from sight.

Langley looked from Carew to Lania. "I'm afraid this is the only way." He gestured for Lania to climb onto the back of the remaining Sleer, which she did after a short hesitation, and with evident distaste.

No sooner had she fastened her grip around the creature's neck than it leapt through the undergrowth. A minute later the first creature reappeared, then the second. Langley gestured for Carew to go first and he hitched himself onto the sickeningly warm, viscous back of the Sleer.

He closed his eyes as it dived forward and leapt through the air.

The fall seemed to last for ever, and he was wondering when the hell they might land when he felt the creature beneath him flex its legs and hit the ground. He slid from his perch and looked up.

Overhead, he saw the second Sleer appear, silhouetted against the fiery sun, and plummet towards him with Langley on its back.

He moved aside the creature landed with the grace of a gymnast, its massive thighs juddering with the impact. Langley climbed down and led the way to the shade of a tree growing almost at right angles from the steep embankment.

The Outcast suggested a break, and Carew sat on the mossy bank and took a welcome mouthful of water. "Where are we, in relation to the clearing of the Fissure People?"

"Downriver from it," Villic replied, before Carew had finished the question. "Perhaps ten kilometres. I'd hoped to intercept Leah and the rest before they set off, but I suspect they left before full sun up when they discovered you gone. I just hope that they don't reach the lair before we can stop them."

Lania asked, "How far are we from the lair?"

"It's around thirty kilometres to the underground opening."

Carew began to ask, incredulously, if they were going to walk all the way – but Villic cut him off.

"Of course not. It'll be far faster – even than riding the Sleer – if we take a boat. The current's pretty strong further downriver."

Lania asked, "And do you happen to have a –"

"– boat handy. Of course, though your definition of a boat, and mine, might vary a little."

Refreshed, Carew stoppered his water-gourd and replaced it in the improvised backpack. He looked at Langley. "When we find Leah and the others..."

Villic finished off for him. "...How are we going to go about stopping them reaching the Weird?" He nodded. "They'll be defended, that's for sure. Sleer, Shufflers, once they reach the caverns... I hope at some point we'll be able to get close enough, undetected, so that I can tell which of your colleagues – if you don't mind me calling them that – are infected."

Lania interrupted, laughing uneasily, "You don't think Jed is...?" She shook her head. "Jed's fine. Tell them, Ed."

She looked across at him expectantly. He held her gaze. At last he said, "That's another reason I wanted to come along, Lania. If Jed is one of the infected, I want to make sure he goes without knowing it, as painlessly as possible."

She looked aghast. "But this is insane. Jed's one of us. We'd have noticed something, wouldn't we?"

Villic said, "I'm sorry. Very likely you wouldn't have noticed anything." He stared at Lania, reading her thoughts. "Yes... his odd outburst aboard the *Hawk* when you said that you believed Choudri. Well, it might have been caused by the infection, or not. There's no way of telling until I get within range and probe him."

Lania appealed mutely to Carew and her looked pained him. She said, "But he's been with us over five years, Ed! We've been everywhere he's been! When could he have become infected?"

Carew looked away. "Remember what Jed told us about seeing that crashed Kurishen starship, Lania? Where was it – on Tamalkin? Well, if he is infected..."

Villic finished. "Then that's where he picked it up."

Carew thought of something that had troubled him way back, aboard the Expansion station. He said, in barely a whisper, "I wondered why they hired us, Lania. I wondered why Gorley went to all that trouble to make sure we were caught coming back from Hesperides, tried and found guilty, then reprieved and sent on this mission. It all begins to make sense if Jed is infected, doesn't it?"

He glanced at her. Tears made her eyes seem bigger than they normally were, and Carew reached out and took her hand.

"I'm sorry, Lania."

She looked up, smiled and dashed tears from her cheeks with the cuff of her smartsuit. "But we might be wrong, mightn't we? All that might just be coincidence, hm?"

He squeezed her fingers. "We'll see, Lania."

She sniffed and smiled bravely.

Villic stared down the incline. "Not far now. Another hour and we'll reach the river."

They set off again, and the incline proved less precipitous than on the first leg of the descent. The land levelled out as they travelled, parallel with the river far below, dropping gradually and making the hike less strenuous.

They passed in and out of cooling shadow, and this far into the fissure the temperature dropped significantly.

The terrain descended sharply again. The Sleer led the way through the undergrowth, snapping branches and uprooting shrubs as they went. Langley and Lania skidded along behind them and Carew brought up the rear, picking his way with care and occasionally shuffling along on his backside when the drop became almost sheer.

He'd slipped the laser into his belt, to free his right hand, when something shot past his left ear and slapped into a tree trunk directly before him. He saw the trunk dissolve before his eyes, the whole process taking perhaps two seconds. He fell onto his back and rolled. In an instant his laser was in his right hand and he was firing up the incline. Whatever was following them had vanished. He yelled to the others, glanced over his shoulder down the hillside. There was no sign of Lania, Langley, Villic or the Sleer. Then he caught a glimpse of Lania as she took cover behind a tree and drew her weapon.

He saw a boulder to his right and rolled into its shelter. He scanned the vegetation cloaking the incline above him. All was still, quiet. Only his heart sounded, deafening in his ears. He peered over the rock, willing whatever it was to show itself. A Sleer, he guessed. Armed with an acid weapon? He glanced at the unfortunate tree. It was stripped down to its inner rings, the wood steaming. An acid weapon of some kind, then. Which, in the hands of a Sleer, was a combination to be feared.

The Sleer knew the jungle, the terrain. It could easily move around him, silent in the undergrowth, and attack him from behind.

A noise interrupted his frightened thoughts. A hiss. Villic.

"Ed! See the red tree? Eleven o'clock? There's a Sleer behind it. It's... it's thinking to move to your right."

Trembling, knowing he had to make the shot count, Carew found the tree and sighted his weapon. He aimed two metres up from the gnarled root system. With luck he'd plant a charge right in the bastard's midriff.

"It's moving *now!*"

He saw a purple-red blur streak out from behind the trunk. He fired, missed. The Sleer was lightning fast, vanishing behind the foliage. He fired again, guessing where it might be. He heard a crashing through the undergrowth above him and fired again. The Sleer returned fire and the rock centimetres from his head bubbled and spat. He felt something molten pepper his right shoulder. He yelled out and fired again.

A ton of weight crashed from the jungle and fell across the rock. Carew rolled out from beneath a domed head, its slit mouth wide in screaming agony. The sound deafened him, something unearthly, like a cross between a siren's wail and an animal howl. He stood and found himself firing again and again into the torso of the creature, and chunks and gobbets of bloody flesh jumped from its body as if he were firing into a barrel of offal.

Lania was beside him, a hand on his arm. "Okay. It's okay, Ed. It's dead."

He stopped firing and stood there with his laser outstretched in both hands, as if the Sleer might miraculously come to life and resume its relentless onslaught. That was highly unlikely: he'd almost succeeded in slicing the thing in half.

In the creature's left hand he made out a bulky, organic-looking pistol – like an outgrowth of its bloody flesh.

"It's okay," Lania soothed.

He looked away, his heartbeat slowing.

The others had gathered around, staring at the carnage.

Villic peered over the hulking shoulder of his Sleer. "Well, now we know for sure that they're after us."

One Sleer, Carew thought... and there'll be more up ahead, as well as the Shufflers, whatever the hell they are.

What are our chances of getting out of this alive, he wondered.

Then Lania gripped his arm and led him away. They set off again. Together they hurried down the incline, away from the dead Sleer, towards the peacefully flowing river.

They came to the water's edge ten minutes later and stopped beside a tree overhanging the river. Villic slipped from the back of his Sleer and moved into the undergrowth along the riverbank.

Lania asked, "Where's he going?"

"We have a boat moored nearby," Langley said.

Carew looked down the river, taking in the steep bank. "Won't we be a sitting target, floating down the middle of the river?"

"We'll have two things going for us," Langley said. "First, the boat doesn't look like your conventional boat. Look." He pointed out across the water. Carew saw something floating swiftly in the current, turning as it went. It looked like some kind of giant seed pod; there were dozens of them, he saw now.

Langley went on, "The shyla trees drop their pods every late summer, and many fall into the river. Our vessel will be just one pod among many." He smiled from Carew to Lania. "And second, our Sleer won't be coming with us in the boat. They'll be tracking us along the riverbank. If they come across anything untoward, they know what to do."

Carew looked at the Outcast. "They don't mind attacking their own kind?"

"They're primitive beasts, Ed. Little more than wild animals at this stage. Villic has them safely in mind-thrall. They'll do his bidding and hopefully keep us safe while we journey downriver."

Lania was checking her pulse-beam rifle, stripping down its energy pack and cleaning the connections with the cuff of her smartsuit. "It's not the river part of the voyage that I'm worried about," she said, "but what might happen when we reach the caves."

Langley nodded. "That will be the hard part, yes," was all he said.

There was a commotion in the undergrowth and Carew raised his laser. He lowered it with relief when Villic stumbled into sight, pulling something attached to a length of rope. A hollowed-out seed pod, torpedo-shaped, with a slit opening in its top, bobbing at the water's edge.

Villic drew it closer to the bank and tethered the rope to an overhanging branch. Langley climbed in, followed by Lania. Carew went next, surprised at the room in the vessel. It was not unlike the scooped-out fruit the Outcasts used as dwellings in the treetops, the interior ribbed and padded with pith. Large stones were spaced evenly along its bottom. Langley said, "To make it ride a little lower in the water, so it doesn't capsize."

Villic was the last aboard. One of the Sleer set off along the riverbank at a loping run, while the second splashed into the water and swam across the river. Carew saw it emerge on the far bank, pull itself into the undergrowth and disappear from view.

Villic settled himself in the back of the seed-boat next to Carew and passed him what looked like a giant sycamore seed. Villic himself had a second. "Paddles?" Carew asked.

"Rudders. Slip them through here and hold them like this." Villic indicated slits cut through the flesh of the seed-pod, and Carew inserted his rudder through and into the water.

"It'll stop us swirling about," Villic said, "and make scanning the banks for our enemies a little easier. I'm still mind-linked to the Sleer. If we see anything untoward, I'll just steer the Sleer in the right direction. All set?"

He untied the rope from the overhanging branch they were immediately borne away on the current. Carew felt the pressure of the river on his makeshift rudder, pressing it into his ribs. He followed Villic's lead and leaned against the haft of the rudder, forcing it against the gunwale. The vessel straightened and careered downstream.

He looked up. The narrow strip of daylight far above seemed kilometres away. At one end, the ruddy disc of the supergiant took up the eastern portion of the sky. It was possible to stare at the surface of the sun with the naked eye, watching the pattern of sunspots and belching magma like something in a kaleidoscope.

He turned his attention to the steep banks of the river, his laser at the ready. The others were alert too. Langley and Lania sat facing him, watching the banks to either side. He looked at Lania, her long black hair tied back, her beautiful face smudged with jungle dirt and criss-crossed with small cuts and scratches. She saw him looking and smiled.

Langley broke out fruit from his pack and passed it round.

Carew thought about what Villic and Langley had told them about the Weird, and the threat they posed to humankind.

He said, "So the Weird want to break out from their realm, invade our space, enslave humans and Vetch alike. But why? Merely so that they can feed on us?"

"That's the obvious reason," Langley said. "The Harvester stage of their development requires... sustenance."

Carew shrugged. "So why don't they simply get it from animals? Why enslave sentient species and feed off these?"

Beside him, Villic grunted. "For the very reason that we *are* sentient, Ed. They crave our meat, yes – but they also want what's in here." He tapped the side of his head. "Our knowledge, our history, our culture. They're – or rather *it's* – a gestalt mind, remember, and it doesn't work like us individuals. The mind craves knowledge." He paused, then went on, "In a way, though we see the Weird as evil and cruel, it's merely following the rules of its evolution: it cannot see that what it's doing – enslaving and feeding off thousands of individuals – is wrong, for the simple reason that it cannot encompass the idea of sentient life as comprising so many individuals."

Lania said, "But can't it see that every human being is sentient and therefore like itself, an individual?"

Villic smiled sadly. "That's what I thought, once. I assumed that it must know that what it was doing was wrong, because as you say, it was aware of every human as an individual life like itself."

Carew looked at him. "You thought this once? But no longer?"

"I'd read the minds of the Sleer, but they were basic, embryonic. I wanted to know more. So I decided to approach a Harvester and make contact."

Lania looked at him wide-eyed. "And?"

"How to describe an alien mind?" Villic smiled and shook his head. "It was almost impossible. I went back again and again, attempting to come to some understanding, and I think in time I did." He paused, considering his words, then went on, "It was like looking into the mind of a megalomaniac, a monomaniac... someone who wanted only one thing and would stop at nothing to get it. It wanted knowledge; it wanted to know this new universe which it had discovered. It did not see us as sentient because our minds were so different from its own, and though our minds teemed with knowledge and experience, it could not conceive that this knowledge and experience was especial to the individual, because it was impossible for it to believe that the limited amount of knowledge and experience in each of us, in each unit, amounted to anything more than a part of some gestalt mind it could not locate. It was mystified by humans, these individuals that had no centre, and in lieu of finding our physical core or self, it assumed therefore that our *culture* was the central binding essence of humankind."

Carew smiled. "Which I suppose, in a way, it is."

Villic waved. "I'm simplifying, of course, and anthropomorphising. It took me a long time to come to some small understanding of the Weird, to come to see it not as evil, just *other*. And the horror – that's what I received from the contact. The sheer horror of its view of the universe, that does not admit things like love or hate, or anger or compassion, or the thousand other emotions in between. It was experiencing this horror that made me realise that the Weird, though not evil in the sense we understand the meaning of the word, is necessarily our enemy and needs eradicating." He stared at Carew and Lania in turn. "Because, please believe me, there is no enemy more inexorable, ruthless and fearsome than an enemy which cannot understand or feel compassion for its opponents."

Carew allowed his words to sink in. "And with knowledge gained from Gorley and the others, they'll be able to match us on our own terms?"

Villic nodded. "There's no knowing how many hundreds, possibly thousands, of humans are infected with the mind-parasite. For all I know the Expansion is teeming with them, each manipulating its host in order to bring the Weird to the Expansion."

Lania said, "But surely the military might of the Expansion, our weaponry... You said the Weird employ acid weapons, so how can they be any match for our pulse-beams and nucleonic charges?"

Villic held a hand up to stop her. "Lania, the Weird intend to defeat humanity in the very same way that it brought the Kurishen to its knees – by infecting, infiltrating. When it does this, it will in effect control the people who control our superior weaponry."

Lania closed her eyes at the thought, and Carew began to see the enormity of the fight that lay ahead. Nothing less than the future of humankind was at stake.

"So that's why we need to stop Gorley and his cohorts," Villic said, "and that's why you must return to the Expansion with word of what you've found here."

Carew saw a flash of something on the right-hand bank and sat up in alarm. Villic said, "Only a bek. Something like an antelope."

Carew smiled. "I'm seeing danger in every shadow."

"Can you imagine now our lives as Outcasts?" Langley said.

Lania was about to say something, but Villic forestalled her with, "The scene you saw in the treetops earlier, Lania, might have appeared at first sight idyllic, but it was not typical. We are forever on the move, alert for danger. The Weird send Sleer to hunt us down, and even humans posing as potential Outcasts. We find the treetops safer than the jungle floor, but even so we're vulnerable to the Flyers."

Carew said, "We saw them from orbit."

"They encircle the planet, searching for us and other renegades."

"There are others like you?"

"Scattered bands far to the south," Villic said, "though we haven't had contact with them for years. For all we know, the Weird might have succeeded in eradicating them entirely."

Lania looked across at Carew. "Ed, we could take the Outcasts back with us, or at least some of them. And then send back ships for more."

Villic said, "I know my people, Lania, and they would refuse your offer. We only know one way of life, that of the jungle; and one struggle, that against the Weird. It might be hopeless, futile, but this struggle is all we have." He smiled. "And anyway, I'm not sure that my people would find it easy to settle into the modern ways of the Expansion."

"But if you stay here..." Lania began.

"We have lost only a dozen souls in as many years to the Weird," Langley said. "Life might be hard, and we might have to be constantly on the move, but it has its own, small rewards. Sometimes we do make true converts of the Fissure People and sometimes we do manage to kill a Weird." He shrugged. "I know – an individual Flyer, Shuffler or Sleer is only a single unit of gestalt entity, so what can the merit be in killing one? But this is how we tell ourselves that the battle is not yet lost."

"To leave World," Villic said quietly, "would be to run away from danger."

Carew unstoppered his water-gourd and took a long drink. Langley squinted up at the sun. He said, "We have perhaps six hours before we reach the point where we must leave the boat and climb. If you would care to rest, we'll keep watch."

"I'm fine," Lania said.

Carew smiled. "The heat's getting to me," he said. "Or is it my age?"

He exchanged places with Langley, who took the rudder. Carew sat next to Lania and leaned back into the ribbed seat, cushioned by pith.

As the seed-boat drifted downriver, he dozed.

SOMEONE WAS SHAKING him awake.

"Stay down!" Lania hissed.

He blinked up at her. She fell on top of him, pressing him to the bottom of the boat. "One of the Sleer has seen a Shuffler."

He eased Lania from him and, still lying flat, peered towards the end of the boat. Langley and Villic were kneeling, using the erstwhile rudders as paddles.

"How long was I asleep?"

"A few hours." She smiled. "You were snoring like a pig."

The sun had advanced a little way along the length of the narrow strip high above. With an expanse of white daylight to either side of the orb, it resembled a bloodshot eye staring down at them.

The low branches of a riverside tree came into sight above the boat and Langley and Villic slowed their paddling. The boat bumped against the bank, gently, and Langley reached out to steady it.

"We're almost there," he said. "We'll make the rest of the journey by foot."

Lania helped him to his feet, and he stepped out of the boat. Villic tied it to a tree trunk and scanned the incline.

"The Shuffler?" Carew whispered.

Silently, Villic pointed uphill, slightly to their left. "About a hundred metres above us."

"It knows we're here?"

"I'm not sure, but I suspect so."

"And these critters spit acid?"

He nodded. "But the Sleer has it in its sights, which means I do too. So it can't move without me knowing exactly where it's going."

Lania said, "They shuffle, right? So they don't move that fast?"

Beside her, Langley laughed quietly. "They shuffle, but fast. And they can jump."

"Great," Lania said.

Carew heard a splash in the water at his back. He turned in time to see a Sleer rise from the river beside the boat. He raised his laser. Villic batted it back down.

"One of ours," he said.

The Sleer rose from the river, a cascade of water streaming from its great empurpled torso. "I'm getting jumpy," Carew admitted.

"That's okay," Langley said. "We all are."

Villic stared at the Sleer. The creature held the telepath's gaze for a second, then passed them silently and climbed the incline at speed, soon vanishing into the undergrowth.

"What now?" Lania asked.

"We follow," Langley said, "giving the Shuffler a wide berth."

Langley led the way along the riverbank, parallel with the river for perhaps a hundred metres, then heading up the incline. He stepped with pantomime care as he climbed through the undergrowth, stopping from time to time to assess the best course.

Perhaps thirty minutes later, they came to a bare ledge of rock high above the river. As they stepped onto it, Carew saw that the rock was the projecting lip of a recess into the hillside. They moved beneath the overhang and crouched down. Behind them, the Sleer almost filled the recess.

Villic was holding his head, his eyes closed. He murmured, "The Shuffler has seen the boat. It's going to investigate."

Lania asked. "You're probing the Shuffler?"

Villic opened his eyes. "I'm watching the Shuffler via the Sleer. Look, we can see the boat from here. The Shuffler should be coming into view in a matter of seconds."

Carew stared down the incline, a tightness in his throat. He saw the undergrowth move in front of the boat and then found himself staring down on the Shuffler.

He had been expecting something like a caterpillar, a green, hairy form, vaguely comical. But the reality was far from comical and not at all like a caterpillar.

He could see how it was the next evolutionary stage up from a Sleer; it retained that creature's humanoid mass and its skinned-carcass complexion, but there the resemblance finished. The Shuffler was larger, fatter, its legs splayed and its torso bloated, its head swollen and thrust forward. As it moved forward to inspect the boat, Carew could see how it had earned its sobriquet. It dragged its adipose legs in an ungainly shuffle – ungainly, he thought, but not at all slow. It moved with surprising speed for a creature of its size.

As they watched, the Shuffler bent over the seed-boat and spat something from its gross, shapeless head. At first Carew thought it was its tongue – in the manner of some insect-eating frog – but then he saw that the gob of matter had landed in the bottom of the boat and was smouldering.

"Acid," Villic said helpfully. "The bastards spit acid."

The acid burned a hole in the bottom of the boat and it began to sink. The Shuffler turned, its big black eyes scanning the incline. For a second, Carew thought the creature was looking directly at him.

Then it jumped.

One second it was on the riverbank – the next it had vanished.

Langley pointed. The Shuffler had come down noisily amid a stand of ferns halfway between the cave-mouth and the river. It squatted malevolently, turning its hemispherical head to scan the incline.

When the creature was staring directly at them, it opened its mouth and ejected a spinning bolus of acid. Carew saw it coming, dragged Lania to the floor with him and heard the acid hit the rock half a metre above his head. When he looked up, the rock was crumbling.

Lania knelt and aimed her weapon. Langley laid a hand on her arm. "We might need the ammunition later. Look."

As they stared, a Sleer emerged from the undergrowth before the Shuffler and attacked. Beside Carew, Villic squatted and screwed his eyes shut as he willed the creature to destroy the Shuffler.

The Sleer dodged a gob of acid, reached out and drove a vast hand into the creature's mouth. It pulled and emerged with something red and dripping. As the Shuffler roared in agony, the Sleer gripped the top and bottom of its wide mouth and prized it apart. The Shuffler's great domed head split, its pulsing brain revealed: for a second, the grey organ remained *in situ*, piled inside the braincase like the meat of an opened clam – then it slipped forward and dangled grotesquely on the end of its spinal cord.

The Shuffler collapsed, folding at the feet of the victorious Sleer, an inert mound of quivering, blood-coloured flesh.

The Sleer turned and sped away from the river.

"Deadly at a distance," Villic commented. "But lousy at close combat."

They stepped from the overhang. Villic pointed up the fissure to a knuckle of bare rock high above. "The cave entrance is up there," he said. "It will be guarded."

Lania looked at him. "By?"

"Sleer, most likely, and perhaps Shufflers."

Langley said, "We'll be able to get close without being observed, then assess the situation when we can see the cave entrance."

They left the overhang and continued up the hillside.

They climbed slowly, the pair of Sleer scouting ahead for potential danger. Langley led the way, assisting Villic. Lania strode on before Carew, on her toes and alert. For his part, Carew was exhausted and jumpy. Bringing up the rear, he felt exposed, vulnerable, and expected at any second some Weird horror to jump out and attack.

From time to time he turned at a sound, only to find that the culprit was an insect or bird. He gripped the laser to his chest, his finger on the firing stud. He wondered what Villic thought of his funk, but realised that he wasn't worried what the oldster thought: he liked the telepath, and knew that Villic was above sneering at an understandable fear.

He found himself wondering what it must be like to be a telepath, to be constantly privy to the most secret thoughts of one's fellow man. Were there times when Villic felt cursed, and wished nothing more than to be away from the pollution of human thought?

They came to a tree growing at an angle from the hillside. Bright yellow blooms spangled the boughs, and a spread of blue flowers carpeted the ground in its shade. A miasma of overwhelming scent met them as they paused and drank water.

Villic sat on an exposed root, panting, and looked at Carew. "To answer your question, Ed. There are times when I feel cursed and wished I'd never had the cut." He shrugged. "Those times, I just up and leave the commune. After about three or four days, I feel sane again and return."

Lania looked at him. "It must be hard to... to sustain a relationship?"

The old man smiled with what Carew thought was bitter humour. "Almost impossible, to tell the truth. A normal relationship, yes. Or what's accepted as normal. But then that's relative, isn't it?" He paused. "There was someone, once."

Carew wondered what had become of the relationship, decided not to ask, then realised the futility of that decision.

Villic smiled. "She died, Ed. A Sleer got her. Is it any wonder I take great delight in controlling the bastards?"

A thought occurred to Carew, and the telepath said, "Is that right?"

Carew said, "The psi-science has come a long way since your day. These days telepaths can turn off their ability at will, controlled by some kind of damping device."

"Well, isn't that something?" Villic laughed. "Pity I'm so far from home."

Five minutes later, they set off again. The climb became steep, almost precipitous in places. Villic chose the route that was hidden from the cave entrance high above and that meant crossing rough terrain until they reached the high ground.

After an hour, Carew's limbs shaking with exhaustion, Langley called a halt. Carew thought he'd never heard such welcome words. They were on a high, bare ledge, cupped by surrounding peaks. Carew sank to his haunches and gulped deep breaths.

Langley passed around segments of a sickly sweet fruit and exhorted them to eat. "Energy," he said.

Lania said, "The cave entrance is somewhere across there?" She pointed beyond the bastion of rock that hid them from view.

Villic nodded. "But I'm too far away to probe here," he said. "I've sent a Sleer to scan the entrance. We'll find out what kind of reception committee is awaiting us."

Carew drank his water and watched the telepath as he closed his eyes in concentration. A minute later Villic opened them and looked at Langley. "The Sleer saw Leah and the others about five minutes ago. They've left just a single militia-man to guard the entrance."

Lania looked at him quickly. "You sure it's a man?"

Villic stared at her, reading her concern. "Sorry. Loose terminology." He shook his head. "The Sleer can't tell, and although I can see the figure via the Sleer, I can't make out if it's a man or a woman. Anyway, there's just one, and he or she is concentrating on the river down there."

"Mind if I take a look?" Lania asked, indicating the fanged rocks at her back.

"Be my guest, but keep your head down."

Carew joined her as she crept to the spur of rock and peered over. Across the valley cleft was a dark, arched opening in the opposite rock face. Before it, a golden-suited human stood guard, laser rifle braced on its hip. He or she was perhaps three hundred metres away, and it was impossible to identify the soldier.

He looked at Lania, who was biting her bottom lip. "Do you who it is?"

She shook her head. "No, dammit."

Langley and Villic joined them. Villic said quietly, "I'm sorry, but it's the only way. I'm sending in a Sleer."

Lania turned to him. "No! You can't."

"Look at the damned terrain," Villic said. "I can't get close enough to probe the identity, so I have to send a Sleer."

Lania said in almost a whisper, "But it might be Gina... and for chrissake, she might not even be infected!"

Villic winced at the pain he read in her mind. "I'm sorry. We've got to stop them. And we can't sit around debating this – we know the others are making their way down to the lair, so we have to act fast."

Carew found Lania's hand.

Villic hesitated, then said, "Look, I'll get the Sleer to attempt to disable the guard without killing, okay? But, if we get over there and find out he or she is infected... no matter who it is, they're dead. Agreed?"

She nodded at Villic with obvious reluctance, then walked off and sat down with her back to them.

Before he could join her, Carew saw movement on the far side of the valley. His vision was drawn to the drama about to be enacted and he found himself unable to look away.

He watched as a Sleer emerged from a rock and, using boulders as cover, made its rapid zigzag across up the scree-covered incline towards the unsuspecting guard.

The creature came to a halt five metres from the guard, taking cover behind a boulder. The guard sat down on a rock, weapon laid across armoured thighs. Carew glanced at Villic. The telepath's eyes were closed in concentration.

Across the valley, the Sleer made its move.

It leapt, the suddenness of its spring startling. The guard was caught totally unawares. The Sleer barrelled into the armoured human, dashed the laser from its grip and wrapped its long, muscled arms around the torso with one hand covering the face. The Sleer stood up, the soldier dangling in its grip like some kind of oversized plaything.

"Let's go!" Langley said, and Carew and Lania ran from their hiding place and crossed the scree-covered slope to where the Sleer was standing with its prisoner.

As they drew closer, Carew saw that the guard was not Gina Alleghri but Thomas, the militia-technician. His eyes, above the blue-veined meat of the Sleer's hand, bulged with terror.

Carew glanced at Lania, who said, "It isn't Gina. Christ, that means she's somewhere down there."

They reached the Sleer and the militia-man, and as they drew close, the expression in Thomas's eyes became pleading.

Carew glanced at Villic. The telepath scanned Thomas, then shook his head. To Carew he murmured, "Infected..."

Lania gave a shocked, indrawn breath and looked away quickly, and Carew followed suit as the Sleer tightened its grip on the militia-man's face. He heard a soft, osseous crunch as the human's skull caved in, then a squelch, followed by the loud rattle of armour on rock as the Sleer discarded its victim. Carew lasered the suit's power-pack, turning it to slag.

Villic sent the first Sleer into the cave, then he and Langley followed. Carew glanced at Lania, who smiled bravely in return.

"We've got to be strong," he said. "We don't know what we're going to find down there."

"I think I do," she murmured.

"And that is?"

"Gina's infected. I know it. And I know what that means, and part of me agrees with what we must do because of that, but another part..."

"We don't know that, yet," Carew said. "Let's wait and see, okay?"

She swore. "And Jed... how can he be infected? I mean, we've lived with him for so long."

He took her hand and pulled her into the entrance to the cave, followed by the second Sleer.

Lania activated a twin beam inset into the shoulders of her smartsuit in order to light their way, and they left the dazzle of the sunlight behind them. It soon became obvious that no artificial illumination would be needed.

Langley whispered, "Turn it off."

She did so and Carew's eyes adjusted to the aqueous twilight. A green fungus mantled the walls, shedding a low jade light.

Carew said to Villic, "Are you picking anything up?"

The old man turned to him, the fungal bioluminescence giving the telepath a deathly pallor. "Faintly, but not well enough to scan individual minds. They're in the gallery a couple of hundred metres below us, about a kilometre from the chamber."

Lania said, "The chamber?"

Langley explained. "Where the Weird have their interface to their home realm."

"And that's where they're heading, right?"

Villic said, "The infected will pass through and join the Weird. The ultimate goal of their mission."

"But not if we can help it," Langley said.

"I've sent a Sleer on ahead," Villic told them. "It should have them in sight within minutes. I'll have a better idea of how to proceed then. Let's go."

He led the way, followed by Langley. Lania went next, then Carew. Behind him, the second Sleer loped, its ogre-ish presence giving Carew the shivers.

He gripped his laser and peered ahead through the verdant half-light, expecting opposition to show itself at any second.

The rocky path sloped down at a gentle angle, working its way around great bulges in the wall.

Ahead, Villic raised a hand and came to a halt. "They've stopped, for some reason. They're in a wide open chamber."

"Are you close enough to...?" Carew asked.

The telepath shook his head. "Still just beyond range. I'm seeing this through the Sleer's vision. There are plenty of rocks and boulders about, should they wish to take cover. It's not the best place to attack them. Okay, there's nothing for it but to wait until they move off again." He sat down against the wall and closed his eyes.

Carew found himself too jumpy to rest. He stood with his laser at the ready, looking back and forth, up and down the corridor. The temperature this far underground had dropped appreciably, chilling him to the bone.

He said, "How did the Weird get here? I mean, did they... manufacture the interface, or...?"

Langley glanced at him in the half-light. "We hope to hell they didn't manufacture the interface," he said. "Because that'd mean they could do it anywhere. The very fact that they haven't... well, it suggests that they can't. We think this interface here is a natural phenomenon, a weakness in the fabric of space which they've utilised. We just hope it's a one-off."

Lania said, "If they could manufacture the things, open them at will across the Expansion..."

"Let's not even think about it," Carew said.

Villic started. He sat upright, eyes staring ahead. At last he said, "They've found someone, a girl. One of the Fissure People. They've detailed a guard to take her back to the surface, presumably to hand her over to the other guard. They're on their way now. I've instructed my Sleer to conceal itself."

Maatja, Carew thought.

Lania stared at Villic. "The guard...?"

"It's a militia-*man*," the telepath said.

She slumped against the rock, relieved.

Carew asked Villic, "What do we do?"

Langley was on his feet, peering down the corridor in search of cover. He moved off a few metres, then returned hurriedly. "The corridor widens, further down, and there are rocks a couple of us could hide behind. When the guard comes past..."

"I'll come with you," Carew said.

"Ed –" Lania began, but he silenced here with a glance.

Langley turned and dashed down the corridor. Heart hammering, Carew set off in pursuit.

The corridor widened, and here the air was brighter. They took cover behind projecting slabs of rock, Carew fractionally further down the corridor.

He set his rifle to stun and forced himself further into the narrow gap. The freezing rock pressed against his back and he became aware of a salty mineral smell. He glanced across the corridor; Langley crouched a little further up, his weapon at the ready.

He soon heard voices, echoing up the corridor, and made out the child's piping question. "Where are you taking me?"

A grunted, masculine reply. "Back outside."

"But are you taking me to the Harvester?" the girl cried.

"Just shut up."

"No, you can't!"

He heard the sound of footsteps, running.

The guard yelled, "Stop, or I'll fire!"

The girl flashed past where Carew crouched, a blur of tanned flesh and sun-bleached hair. He heard the heavy boots of the guard in pursuit, closing in – and before he could think about what he was doing, he rose from his hiding place, levelled his rifle and fired.

The attack caught the guard by surprise; Carew's shot glanced off the militia-man's chest armour, stunning him. He gave an abbreviated grunt and fell on his back.

Langley rushed past him, knelt and examined the groaning militia-man. Carew turned. The girl was pressed against the wall further up the corridor, staring at him with terror in her eyes.

He smiled and held out a hand, as if coaxing a frightened animal. "It's okay, Maatja. You're safe now."

He came towards her, the sight of her evoking painful memories. He buried them, approached her and knelt. "I've come for you. You're safe now."

She stared at him, not sure whether to place her trust in this stranger. "You know my name."

"I spoke with Hahta. She wanted me to come after you."

She burst into tears. "They took my daddy! He went into the light. They took him!"

The others emerged along the corridor. Carew drew the girl towards him and held her as she sobbed.

Villic said, "The light. She means the interface."

The telepath moved to the sprawled guard, knelt and stared at the man. He looked up. "Another infected one," he said.

He glanced at the Sleer and the monster stepped forward. Carew pressed Maatja's head to his shoulder, ensuring she didn't witness the messy execution.

Langley stood over the militia-man and fried the suit's power-pack, ensuring its destruction. He looked up. "Come on, we need to be moving."

Maatja opened her eyes wide and stared at Carew. "Where are you going?"

"It's okay. We won't leave you. We need to... we need to stop Leah and the others, before they reach the light."

She shook her head. "But you can't," she began.

Then Villic was beside her, staring. "She knows something."

She went on. "They have Sleer and Shufflers in the big chamber."

Villic interrupted. "When she came down here earlier, looking for her father... she found the way blocked by Weird. But she found a narrow corridor, a detour that took her to the white light."

Carew gripped her shoulders. "Can you lead the way, Maatja?"

She nodded, mutely.

"Let's go," Langley said.

Maatja gripped Carew's hand and led the way. They stepped around the headless remains of the guard and ran along the corridor.

Villic said, "I reckon we have around ten minutes before the others reach the interface."

The corridor opened out again and kept expanding. They emerged into a vast cavern, the floor of which dropped away dramatically to their right. They slowed as Villic signalled silently and hissed, "They're down there."

Carew came to the edge of the drop and peered down; a long, shallow ramp had been hewn from the rock, and at the foot of it, perhaps a hundred metres away, he saw a troupe of humans disappearing into a darkened tunnel entrance: two militia, Jed, Choudri, and Gorley bringing up the rear. Leah, presumably, was leading the way.

He held Maatja's hand, feeling her shiver with cold and fear.

As he watched, Gorley vanished into the shadows, and Carew was taken by the sudden disappointment that he hadn't had time to reset his laser and shoot the bastard dead.

Villic was beside him, eyes closed as he probed.

He swore. "They've passed out of range. I managed to probe the last in line, Gorley." He shook his head and smiled at Carew. "Despite your assumptions, Ed, he isn't infected."

"What?" Carew asked, incredulous.

Villic said, "He might have been instrumental in organising the mission, but he was only doing it on the orders of others, higher up."

He stared at the telepath. "Choudri," he whispered.

Villic shrugged. "I didn't have the chance to probe him, but it certainly looks that way."

"Choudri?" Lania said, crouching beside Carew and staring down the natural ramp. "But... but I trusted him. Of all the Expansion peoplé, he was the one we trusted."

Carew thought of the mild-mannered, amicable Indian, in all likelihood infected and oblivious of the fact. Then he thought of Jed and felt sick.

The girl pointed and said, "The smaller tunnel's down there. It leads around the main corridor and comes out in the big chamber where the white light is."

Carew said, "Good girl."

Below, the dark shape of a Sleer slipped from behind a covering spur of rock. Maatja jerked in fright, but Villic said, "It's okay, Maatja. It's friendly." The telepath instructed the creature to enter the tunnel entrance Maatja had pointed out.

They followed and slipped into the narrow confines of the tunnel. Up ahead, in the half-light, the leading Sleer squeezed its bulk between the rocky walls, moving quickly despite the restriction. The tunnel took a long parabolic curve, then twisted and dropped as it followed the fractures in the rock formation.

As they walked, the tunnel widened and the sickness in the pit of Carew's stomach intensified. Up ahead, around the bulky outline of the Sleer, a bright white light shone, growing even brighter as the space around the creature increased.

The Sleer continued its lope into the chamber, and Villic turned and whispered, "I've sent it ahead to reconnoitre. With luck, the others haven't arrived yet."

Carew dropped to his knees and pulled Maatja to him. "Listen to me. This is important. You must stay here, do you understand? Stay here, and I promise I'll come back for you in five minutes." He looked around and found what he was looking for. A rill in the rock formed a perfect niche for a small child. He backed her into it and stroked her cheek. "Don't move, Maatja and I'll be back."

Wide-eyed, she said, "But the chamber is full of Weird!"

Villic hissed, "Leah's entered the chamber!"

"I have to go, Maatja," Carew said.

The telepath took off, Langley in pursuit. Lania followed, and with a glance at Maatja to ensure she was obeying his instructions, Carew gripped his laser and went after them.

The light in the chamber was blinding, and it took a few seconds for his eyes to adjust. He was standing with the others on a projecting shelf of rock, a couple of metres above the surface of the chamber. It was, he gathered, shaped like an amphitheatre – whether natural or constructed, he was unable to tell – and lying at its centre, where the arena should have been, was the source of the brilliant white light.

It was roughly circular and perhaps fifty metres across, looking like a shimmering layer of opal, backlit by a million searchlights. He thought he saw threads and streamers twisting and turning in the light, reminiscent of the patterns he discerned when staring into void-space.

The interface between the universes...

Occasionally figures entered the light or emerged from it – manikins, Shufflers and Sleers – and each time they did so, the light diminished in intensity and Carew made out what looked like a phantasmagorical city beyond. The odd thing was that the universe through the interface intersected with this one at right angles, so that it seemed to Carew that he was looking *down* the vertiginous length of a vast boulevard with monstrous buildings ranked on either side. He stared, sickened, and made out a thousand pullulating creatures in that nightmare realm, Sleers and Shufflers and other monstrous shapes slithering and crawling between what might have been eldritch mausoleums and cenotaphs. Then the light returned, dazzling him, and when next a creature emerged from the interface and the light dimmed, he briefly beheld a stomach-turning sight. It lasted only a few seconds, but what he saw was a crowd of ghastly Weird gathering around the dripping end of an ovipositor which, as he stared, spasmed and ejected the slime-smeared forms of a dozen tiny, squirming manikins.

Then the light brightened, thankfully banishing the grotesque scene, and he looked up, dazed.

Only then did he become aware of the figures entering the chamber from an opening to his right. They were led by Leah and the two remaining militia – Gina and the captain, he realised – with Jed, Choudri and Gorley bringing up the rear.

And all around the chamber, he saw Sleer and Shufflers, positioned like a guard of honour to welcome the visitors, and to one side of the interface, the slumped mass of a Harvester.

Langley pulled Villic to him, and together they jumped from the shelf and landed in the chamber, rolling and fetching up behind a rock. Lania took his arm and they followed, scrambling across to the Outcasts.

Villic crouched, eyes screwed shut as he concentrated. He said, "The two militia..."

Lania gripped his arm. "What?" she said desperately.

"One is infected, the other..."

"But which one!" Lania almost screamed.

"The woman, Gina – she's... she's not infected. It's the captain – he's host to the parasite."

Langley raised himself above the cover of the rocks. "I'll take him first."

Carew said, "And the others?"

"I can't quite make out..."

Carew stared across the shimmering lake of light. The two militia were closest, staring in wonder at the interface, while the remaining three had moved around the circumference of the light so that, now, they stood directly opposite where Carew and the others were hiding.

Langley fired, and an intense beam of blue light vectored from his weapon, lanced across the chamber and instantly beheaded the militia captain. His armour remained upright for perhaps five seconds, a puppet unable to credit the cutting of its strings, then fell to its knees and pitched forward into the lake of white light.

The response was immediate. Alleghri dropped, took aim and fired. The laser beam zizzed above Langley's head, missing him by a centimetre.

Lania yelled, "Gina! Don't fire!"

Carew saw Shufflers and Sleer move around the interface, heading their way.

Carew screamed at Villic, "What about Choudri? Is he infected? Tell me!" He knelt and drew a bead on the Indian as Leah led him across the rocky shore towards the shining interface. "And what about Jed?"

The engineer was behind the Indian, crouching in fear but fully exposed on the rocky shelf that sloped down to the light. Carew told himself that Jed didn't have the body language of a man possessed by an alien parasite, but knew full well that he couldn't possibly know.

"I'm not close enough," Villic said, and in desperation, rose and sprinted around the interface towards a boulder.

He never made it.

Whether it was one of his own Sleer – freed from the telepath's mind-thrall by its proximity to the mother-mind – or one of the creatures stationed in the chamber, Carew would never know. As Villic reached the cover of the boulder, a Sleer leapt and landed beside him. Villic just had time to register surprise, then terror, before the Sleer thrust out its arm and crushed the telepath's skull.

Beside him, Langley grimaced and fired at the Sleer.

Carew knew what he had to do, and fired. The beam clipped Choudri in the shoulder, knocking him off balance. He fell in a heap a metre from the white light. Carew took aim, and was about to fire again, when the Indian launched himself.

The interface accepted the human with scarcely a ripple, and Carew was rocked by his failure.

To his right, Lania broke cover and sprinted across the chamber. Alleghri was on her knees, a Shuffler coming up behind her. Lania screamed aloud and fired, and the Shuffler slithered into two distinct halves. Lania launched herself at the militia-woman and dragged her behind a rock, firing at and beheading an approaching Sleer as she did so.

To his left, Langley took aim and shot Leah through the head. She fell to her knees, then onto her face, reaching out for the white light as she did so.

Langley swung his rifle and aimed at Jed.

"No!" Carew hissed.

Jed had recovered from his funk and rolled from the light, and Carew felt a welling of relief as he watched the engineer take up the fallen militia captain's pulse-gun. Jed knelt and swept the laser across the chamber, discharging a wide beam of blue light and incinerating three Shufflers and a pair of Sleer that were bearing down on Lania and Alleghri.

And he'd always thought his engineer a pusillanimous, lily-livered chicken.

Jed saw Carew and he pushed himself to his feet, sprinting around the white light. Lania and Alleghri took the opportunity to run, bent double, towards the rock behind which Carew and Langley crouched.

Jed arrived, panting, and Carew gripped him, "Good to have you back, Jed."

"Where the hell have you been, boss? I thought you were dead!"

"It's a long story. Once we're safely aboard the *Hawk*, okay?"

Lania arrived with Alleghri in tow. Lania grinned at Jed. "I think I owe you one, runt."

Jed stared down at the weapon in his hand, appearing surprised at his sudden courage.

Carew searched the chamber. "Where the hell is Gorley?" he said to himself. Then he saw the Expansion man, cowering in the cover of a rock ten metres away.

He said to Langley, "Cover me while I fetch the Marshall."

He left the upright rock and sprinted across the chamber, aware of a Sleer to his right. He heard a hiss, and the creature fell to the ground under Langley's laser beam.

Carew reached Gorley and gripped the man's arm. The Commander looked up, his dark eyes petrified. Carew hauled him to his feet and half-carried him back across the chamber.

They rejoined the others. "Right," Langley said. "All we have to do now is get out of here. This way."

Lania and Alleghri laid down covering fire as the others sprinted from the chamber. Langley took Gorley's arm and half-dragged him towards the tunnel where they'd entered, Jed in pursuit.

Carew dropped to his knees before the niche where he'd left Maatja. The girl was squeezed even further into the recess, eyes tight shut and hands pressed over her ears.

She jumped when Carew reached out and touched her arm. "I said I'd be back."

She opened her eyes and the sudden look of joy on her pinched face brought tears to his eyes. "On my back," he said. She jumped onto him and he rose, staggering under her weight, and ran after the others.

Behind him, Lania fired back into the chamber, yelling "Run! Run! Run!" as she covered their retreat.

They left the lair of the Weird and made their way to the surface of World.

LANGLEY LED THE party through the jungle on a route parallel with the fissure.

At one point Carew asked Lania, "How long before the *Hawk* lifts off..?"

She consulted with her smartsuit and said, "Four hours, give or take a few minutes."

He looked across at Langley and raised his eyebrows. The Outcast replied, "It'll be touch and go, Ed. If we keep on without stopping, we might just make it."

Seeing how Carew was flagging, Lania said, "Here, I'll take the girl."

Maatja clambered from his back and settled on Lania's like a monkey.

They set off again, alert for Sleer and Shufflers. How tragic it would be now, Carew thought, if they were to be stopped so close to gaining the safety of the *Hawk*.

"Do you think," Gorley said as they ran through the jungle, "that once we reach the *Hawk*, you might find the time to explain to me just what the hell is going on?"

Carew glanced at the Expansion man. He would have an apology to make, after all the explanations were out of the way.

Enemy mine, he thought.

"We'll have plenty of time for that on the flight back," he promised.

When they'd been jogging through the undergrowth for what seemed like hours, Carew looked across at Lania. "How long before the *Hawk*...?" he panted.

"Three hours, Ed," she replied. "Maybe a little over."

"I'm beat."

"Keep on, Ed. You can do it. Think of all those cold beers back on the *Hawk*."

"Cold beers..."

"Ice cold beers, Ed. And plenty of them."

They ran on, Carew hallucinating condensation-dewed beer flasks in a bid to take his mind off the pain in his legs.

The sun was directly overhead, periodically penetrating the jungle canopy and sending down searing rays of heat. Up ahead, Lania jogged along at an even place, seemingly unperturbed by the weight of the girl on her back.

Jed ran after her, clutching the pulse-gun protectively to his chest – the symbol, Carew thought, of his new-found bravery.

A while later he called out, "Lania... how long now?"

She shouted over her shoulder, "The *Hawk* lifts-off in around eleven minutes."

"Langley," Carew panted, "Please tell me we're nearly there."

The Outcast nodded. "Five minutes, ten at the most."

Up ahead, Lania accelerated, Gina Alleghri beside her.

TEN MINUTES LATER the streamlined shape of the *Hawk* came into sight, and Carew almost wept with relief.

They stumbled through the last few metres of undergrowth, then crunched through the cindered vegetation. Lania entered the code and slapped the entry panel, and the hatch sighed open. She dived aboard, followed by Alleghri, Gorley and Jed.

Carew paused and turned to Langley. "The offer's still open, Langley. We could take you with us, along with –"

"My place is with my people, Ed. Especially now... now that Villic is dead." He smiled. "My people need a leader."

Carew passed Langley his laser. "We'll be back. I promise you now, we'll be back."

Langley looked at Maatja. "And the girl?"

Carew stared at the thin child, something tugging his heart. Briefly, he considered taking her with him, back to the Expansion – then dismissed the idea. Her home, for all its hardships, was here on World.

"She won't be safe with her people, now," he said.

Langley nodded. "She has a friend among my people, Ed. We'll make her welcome."

Carew said, "Her sister, Hahta, was fed to the Harvester. Maatja will have to be told."

"I'll see to it, Ed." He moved across to the girl and spoke to her. She clutched the Outcast's hand, and Carew stepped into upchute. Before the hatch sealed behind him, Maatja raised a hand and smiled in farewell.

He returned the gesture.

He rose to the flight-deck to find Lania in her sling. "I've stopped the pre-set command, Ed. I'm running through take-off diagnostics. We should be out of here in about ten minutes." She smiled across at Gina Alleghri, who was sitting on Carew's couch. Gina had already broken out the beers, and passed one across to him.

He looked at the engineer's sling. "Where's Jed?"

"He said he'd be right with me," Lania said.

Carew looked through the viewscreen at the jungle, expecting at any second to see Flyers bearing down. "I'm getting jumpy, Lania. I want to get out of here."

A minute later Jed appeared in the doorway, swaying. He still clutched his pulse-gun, like a kid with a teddy bear.

Carew stared at him. "Jed, you okay?"

A strange expression passed across the engineer's face and something turned in Carew's stomach.

"Oh, Christ, Jed."

The engineer said, "I don't know what's happening, boss. A voice in my head... it's telling me to do things. Wants me to kill you all, wants the ship." His face contorted as he spoke, and tears streamed down his cheeks.

"Jed," Carew said, "give me the gun."

"It wants all our knowledge, boss. Wants the *Hawk*... And I have to kill you, kill the only family I've ever known."

Jed raised the pulse-gun, and Carew tried to stand, but it was as if his legs had frozen solid.

Jed lifted the gun and fired. His head dissolved in an atomised spray of blood, bone and brain. Carew looked away, crying out, and heard the body slump to the deck.

Carew slipped into the engineer's sling and Lania yelled, "I'm getting us out of here, Ed."

The *Hawk* phased into the void.

CHAPTER EIGHTEEN

As THE *HAWK* sped through void-space, Carew recounted to Commander Gorley what, in essence, Langley and Villic had told him about the Weird. He stressed the danger of the aliens and their parasites, and the fact that untold thousands of humans all across the Expansion were already infected. The only solution, as far as Carew could see, would be to declare the Devil's Nebula off-limits to all but Expansion warships, and to combat the hordes of infected humans by using telepaths to probe the minds of those suspected of harbouring the alien parasites.

Gorley heard him out, here and there interjecting a question or requesting clarification on some point.

When Carew had finished, the rat-faced Expansion man regarded him impassively. "From an enemy of the state," he said, "you have become its... benefactor."

Carew smiled. "Who would have thought it?" he said.

"I'll convene an extraordinary meeting of the Council on our return," Gorley said, "and furnish them with the facts."

Later Carew ejected the bodies of Jed, and the two militia-men killed earlier, into void-space, murmuring a helpless farewell to the engineer. He returned to the flight-deck.

"Would you like a beer?" Lania said.

"That'd be great."

She fetched two ice-cold flasks and joined him on the couch. They drank in silence for a while, then Lania said, "You said, back on World... you said you'd tell me something. You said you'd be honest with me, but that then wasn't the right time."

He looked at Lania. They had, he reflected, been through a lot together over the past few days. She had told him about her father, her escape from Macarthur's Landfall.

He nodded.

"I had a sister called Maria. She was just ten when the Vetch invaded Temeredes."

"What happened?" Lania asked.

"My parents were killed in the first strike. They were working in the capital city – but we lived in the country. Maria and me... we were at school when the strike happened. We saw the city wiped out in the neutron strike. There were no survivors."

Lania tipped back her beer. Carew took a long drink, recalling what happened next.

"Apparently, the Vetch had given the authorities two days to evacuate the planet, or else. But the authorities vacillated, called the Vetch's bluff... and suffered the consequences. The second wave consisted of a Vetch invasion force, to mop up the survivors. They weren't especially barbaric. They rounded up most of the men, women and children left alive and herded them to the spaceport for evacuation. But..." He stopped, took a mouthful of beer and stared through the viewscreen at the swirling grey void.

"Maria and me, we hid in the ruins for days, lying low. I can't remember what we thought might happen – that the Vetch would just go away. Anyway, they didn't. They stayed and combed the ruins and found us. I can see now that we should have simply given ourselves up, but..." He felt a terrible pain and guilt as he recalled the incident. "but I was twelve, and resentful of the aliens who had killed my parents, so I attacked a Vetch soldier with the only thing I had to hand, a stone – and he turned when it hit him and fired instinctively. The blast should have hit me. I deserved to die, not Maria."

He paused, then went on, "But she was just behind me and she didn't stand a chance. The Vetch could have killed me, I suppose – and for years afterwards I wished it had – but he just scooped me up and threw me kicking and screaming into a flyer and ferried me to the spaceport."

He shrugged and looked down at Maatja. "So when Hahta begged me to find her sister," he said, "how could I refuse?"

Lania reached out and touched his cheek. "You saved her life, Ed."

She fetched another beer from the cooler, and they sat in silence, drank and stared through the viewscreen at the void.

* * *

A DAY LATER they phased into normal space, and Lania joined him before the viewscreen.

They stared out at the majestic expanse of the station, scintillating against the velvet backdrop of deep space. A dozen starships came and went, and Carew was surprised at how relieved he was to look upon an Expansion station.

Lania said, "Quite a sight, isn't it, Ed?"

"Do you know something?" he said. "It feels like coming home."

Lania returned to her sling and eased the *Hawk* into one of the many hangars that pocked the underside of the station. She cut the drives and silence settled over the ship.

They left the flight-desk, joined by Gina Alleghri, and cycled themselves through the air-lock.

A reception committee of six bulky guards awaited them. Gorley advanced, spoke in lowered tones to the guards, then marched off down the corridor without a further word.

Carew looked at Lania, frowning, and the leading guard gestured with his rifle for them to move.

They were taken to the very same room in which, before the mission, they had been held – and the significance was not lost on Carew.

Lania crossed to the bar and examined the cooler. "Hey, more beer. Remember how Jed drank himself senseless, Ed?"

Carew smiled at her.

Lania tossed a beer to Alleghri. The militia-woman said, "But what gives? I thought we were heroes?"

Carew moved to the screen and stared out. He thought through the events of the last day on

World, the pitched battle in the interface chamber, and wondered if he'd got it wrong.

Later he said to Lania and Alleghri, "I've got an awful feeling about this."

Lania looked up at him. "How come?"

He took a breath. "Okay, so what if Villic was wrong about Gorley? What if he is infected, but Villic didn't detect the parasite?"

Lania shook her head. "But surely...?"

"I don't know. What if the parasite hadn't manifested itself, was lying low just like Jed's? He brought us back here and now he'll have us executed so word of the infection won't get out."

He told himself he was being paranoid, that surely Gorley would have disposed of them on World. But his fear would not go away.

A minute later the door at the far end of the room hissed open and a guard gestured for them to exit.

He followed Lania and Alleghri from the holding suite. He recalled the first time they'd been escorted down this corridor, and how he'd attempted to maintain the upper hand by chatting with Lania and Jed, but he had never felt less like speaking now.

They entered an elevator and descended. He wondered if they were being taken to the place in the nether regions of the station where they would be summarily shot and ejected into space.

The guards escorted them from the lift and along a succession of grey corridors, and paused outside a sliding door. When it opened, Carew saw that he'd been here before.

He led the others into the amphitheatre with the long viewscreen set into the far wall.

A tall, thin man was standing before the viewscreen,

his back to them. He turned and stared across the room at the new arrivals.

Commander Gorley... Carew hadn't expected to see him again.

"Please," Gorley said, "won't you join me?"

Circumspectly, Carew led the way across the room. The Commander nodded at Carew, then at Lania and Alleghri, as they joined him before the viewscreen.

Gorley stood aside and gestured for them to look through the screen.

Carew stepped forward and stopped in his tracks.

He stared down into the hangar, then turned to Gorley. "Is this some kind of joke?"

Gorley smiled. "No joke, Carew. Your eyes do not deceive you."

He heard Lania's indrawn gasp beside him; she imagined the incredulous look on her face must mirror his own.

He turned again and stared down at his ship, *The Paradoxical Poet*, standing proudly in the middle of the hangar. Behind it, through the transparent hangar membrane, the stars of the Expansion shone.

"But," Lania managed at last, "but we saw it destroyed."

Gorley said, "What you saw was a computer-generated mock-up of the *Poet's* destruction. Even the Expansion is not so profligate as to wreck a functioning starship."

Carew gestured. "But I thought... when you left us in the holding suite –"

"I'm sorry for the delay," Gorley said. "I had to meet with my fellow Councillors, to appraise them of the situation and discuss tactics. I apologise if any distress was occasioned."

Lania looked down on the *Poet*. "But why?"

"Well, it is, after all, your property. If you would care to go down and inspect it."

They left the room, climbed down a set of iron steps, and crossed to the battered, upstanding starship. Carew felt emotion constrict his throat. He never thought he'd feel like this about an ugly chunk of machinery.

Then he saw the bulky boosters at the rear end of the ship. Gorley nodded. "We thought we'd better upgrade the drives," he said. "The previous one were rather old, wouldn't you agree?"

Carew shook his head. "Would you mind explaining?"

Gorley cleared his throat. "We're giving you the *Poet*," he said.

Carew looked at him. "I sense a 'but' coming..."

"But, we would like to hire your services."

Lania laughed. "Our services?"

"As interplanetary chauffeurs, between your... salvage work, let's say."

"Chauffeurs?" Carew echoed.

He heard a door open and footsteps rattle down an iron staircase. He turned to see a tall, tanned man being escorted across the hangar by a guard.

Gorley said, "Allow me to introduce Mr Daniel Lampeter, telepath."

Carew's reaction must have been evident in his expression, as Gorley said, "Fear not, Daniel is not in probe-mode at the moment. Mr Lampeter, meet your new team, Captain Ed Carew, Pilot Lania Takiomar and Security Chief Gina Alleghri – your team, that is, if they agree to my proposal."

In a daze, Carew found himself shaking hands with the smiling Lampeter. He looked at Gorley. "Proposal?"

"The Expansion faces a threat greater than any it has ever faced before," Gorley said. "You know the nature of that threat, and you yourself proposed one way of combating it. I have mobilised every telepath in the Expansion to track down and eliminate every last infected human in our midst. It will be a long, arduous and dangerous job, and the telepaths will need the support of reliable, efficient people, such as yourselves." Gorley allowed himself a rare smile as he took in their reaction.

Lania spoke for Carew, "Do we really have any choice?"

Gorley had a ready reply, "Would you really want a choice, Lania?"

She laughed, found Alleghri's hand and held it tight.

Carew turned and stared at the *Poet*, and he thought of the years that stretched ahead and smiled.

He looked at Lania and said, "I might even rename the ship."

"Rename it?" She sounded surprised.

"In honour of Jed," Carew said. "I think he'd like that."

She smiled. "I think he would," she said.

Who would have credited it, he thought? Ed Carew, in the pay of the Expansion...

But, he admitted, Gorley was right. There really was no choice.

Yet again.

He stared past the *Poet*, and through the hangar membrane, to where the massed stars of the Expansion were waiting.

ACKNOWLEDGEMENTS

I'd like to thank Patrick Mahon, Finn Sinclair, and Philip Vine, whose comments of early drafts of this novel were invaluable.

Also, I'd like to thank Jon Oliver and everyone on the team at Abaddon for giving me the opportunity to develop the *Weird Space* universe.

ERIC BROWN

Eric Brown's first short story was published in *Interzone* in 1987, and he sold his first novel, *Meridian Days*, in 1992. He has won the British Science Fiction Award twice for his short stories and has published forty books: SF novels, collections, books for teenagers and younger children, and he writes a monthly SF review column for the *Guardian*. His latest books include the novels *Guardians of the Phoenix*, *Engineman* and *The Kings of Eternity*, for Solaris Books.

He is married to the writer and mediaevalist Finn Sinclair, and they have a daughter, Freya.

His website can be found at
www.ericbrown.co.uk